D0009898

Titles by Eileen Rendahl

DON'T KILL THE MESSENGER
DEAD ON DELIVERY
DEAD LETTER DAY

DEAD
LETTER
DAY

EILEEN RENDAHL

ACE BOOKS, NEW YORK

THE BERKLEY PUBLISHING GROUP
Published by the Penguin Group
Penguin Group (USA) Inc.
375 Hudson Street, New York, New York 10014, USA
Penguin Group (Canada), 90 Eglinton Avenue East, Suite 700, Toronto, Ontario M4P 2Y3, Canada
(a division of Pearson Penguin Canada Inc.) • Penguin Books Ltd., 80 Strand, London WC2R 0RL,
England • Penguin Ireland, 25 St. Stephen's Green, Dublin 2, Ireland (a division of Penguin
Books Ltd.) • Penguin Group (Australia), 707 Collins Street, Melbourne, Victoria 3008, Australia
(a division of Pearson Australia Group Pty. Ltd.) • Penguin Books India Pvt. Ltd., 11 Community
Centre, Panchsheel Park, New Delhi—110 017, India • Penguin Group (NZ), 67 Apollo Drive,
Rosedale, Auckland 0632, New Zealand (a division of Pearson New Zealand Ltd.) • Penguin Books
(South Africa), Rosebank Office Park, 181 Jan Smuts Avenue, Parktown North 2193, South Africa •
Penguin China, B7 Jiaming Center, 27 East Third Ring Road North, Chaoyang District,
Beijing 100020, China

Penguin Books Ltd., Registered Offices: 80 Strand, London WC2R 0RL, England

This is a work of fiction. Names, characters, places, and incidents either are the product of the author's
imagination or are used fictitiously, and any resemblance to actual persons, living or dead, business
establishments, events, or locales is entirely coincidental. The publisher does not have any control over
and does not assume any responsibility for author or third-party websites or their content.

DEAD LETTER DAY

An Ace Book / published by arrangement with the author

PUBLISHING HISTORY
Ace mass-market edition / March 2013

Copyright © 2013 by Eileen Rendahl.
Cover art by Tony Mauro.
Cover design by Diana Kolsky.

ISBN: 978-0-425-25801-9

ACE
Ace Books are published by The Berkley Publishing Group,
a division of Penguin Group (USA) Inc.,
375 Hudson Street, New York, New York 10014.
ACE and the "A" design are trademarks of Penguin Group (USA) Inc.

PRINTED IN THE UNITED STATES OF AMERICA

10 9 8 7 6 5 4 3 2 1

ALWAYS LEARNING   **PEARSON**

*To Jeff and Teresa
and the Tuesday-night spin class*

ACKNOWLEDGMENTS

Much of this book was written during a time of emotional turmoil for me. The fact that I was able to get through it at all is a testament to the support of my family. A huge thank-you to Debbie, Diane and Marian Ullman and to Andy Wallace for the love and encouragement and ridiculously naïve belief that I could do it. I hope never to disappoint any of you.

Many thanks to Jeff and Teresa Olson for the knife-throwing demonstration and for telling me about Ulfhednar in the first place. Who knew that spin class would be as good for my writing as it is for my legs?

The Jewel Tones are always there to support me uphill and down, but I must single out Kelly Judd Safford for her help with the end of the book. Thank goodness I didn't get a flat that day! Thank you also to Anna Stewart for a lightning bolt of a good idea that she tossed off without ever breaking stride.

Very special thanks to Catriona MacPherson and Spring Warren for a fantastic and productive weekend in Petaluma as well as help with the demonic cows.

1

"I WANT TO TALK TO PAUL." I KEPT MY EYES AVERTED, BUT
my tone firm and commanding. It's important with werewolves to know where you stand and make sure they know
where you stand. I needed to show deference to Chuck. He
was the Alpha of this pack, after all. It was also important
to make sure he knew that I meant business. Because I did.
It was a fine line to walk, but I was doing it.

Chuck clenched his fists for a second and then released
them. His stance relaxed, too. Then he lowered himself into
the desk chair opposite me, ready to talk.

Seriously. I'm like the Werewolf Whisperer.

"Get in line." Chuck had kept me waiting in his office
for fifteen minutes. Just enough time for me to get a little
antsy. Not enough time for me to get pissed off. Or any more
pissed off than I already was. He was walking a line, too.
Ah, the games we play.

It would be nice, for once, to get a straight and clear

answer. Niceties observed, I decided to cut to the chase. "What the hell is that supposed to mean?"

Chuck smiled at me. I took a good long hard look at his teeth. They looked totally human. They also looked like he flossed regularly. My mother would approve. "It means that I'd like to talk to him, too. As would a few other members of the Pack."

"So you don't know where he is?" That news surprised me enough that I slipped and looked directly into Chuck's eyes. Mistake. His eyes narrowed a bit and I heard a little growl in his throat. I looked away. Fast.

"Let's go for a walk, shall we?" Chuck said.

I stood and followed him out of his office. It hadn't really been a question. It had been a command. Chuck was being polite by pretending to ask if I wanted to walk. I figured I could at least try to follow suit.

I followed him out into the hall, past the stairway to the upper floor, past the dining room and the living room and out the door. It was a big house. Somewhere near the back was a kitchen. I could smell the food cooking and hear voices, although I couldn't make out what they were saying and my hearing is damn good.

Chuck had built the place himself. Well, not by himself. He had help. An Alpha pretty much always has help. Besides, it was his business. Chuck was a contractor, which is in some ways kind of a perfect job for a werewolf. Who is surprised when their contractor disappears for a few days every month? Hell, most people are so thrilled to get one that shows up most days that they wouldn't think to question a little flakiness around the full moon. Who notices a few extra flashes of temper or a bloodstain or two on a ripped pair of jeans on their contractor? I'll tell you who. No one in northern California.

A vampire couldn't do it. First of all, day work is not a vampire's strong suit. Group loyalty? Also not totally their thing. Which isn't to say they don't band together, but there's not a lot of trust and camaraderie there. Their politics are much more Borgia-like. But werewolves? They're strong. They're loyal. They work well together in groups. They love to be outdoors, no matter what the weather is like. Construction work? It's like the universe invented it for werewolves.

As a contractor, Chuck can provide employment for a whole range of men and women who are trying to find where they belong. Sometimes it takes a while to find a pack. There are always lone wolves wandering around. Chuck offers employment for a few days, a few weeks, a few months. Whatever's needed. Some wolves stay with him. Some move on. It's a good system. At least, it looks good from the outside. Paul always thought it was a good thing, too. Of course, Paul never said anything bad about the Pack. Never. Not in all the years I'd known him.

I was seventeen when I first met Paul. It had been hard enough to figure out how to park in Old Sacramento, but then to walk into a bar? Especially a big old trendy bar like McClannigan's? I'd been intimidated before I'd placed a hand on the big brass doorknob.

Watching Paul become aware of me being there hadn't helped. He'd known what I was within seconds of me walking into the bar. It was the first time I saw him lift his head and scent the air in recognition of something Arcane entering the bar, but it sure wasn't the last. Then he'd taken one look at me and muttered, "They make 'em younger every year."

After that, he'd started calling for more and more deliveries. It took me a while to realize that most of them were messages and items he could easily have delivered himself. It took me a little while beyond that to figure out that he was

keeping an eye on me. After a first flare of teenage resent-
ment, I'd learned to appreciate knowing a werewolf who
had my back.

He'd been protective of me then. He'd wanted me to
understand who I was and what I was, but he wanted me
to survive learning the lessons. Mae had been my mentor at
the dojo and she taught me so much that I am still processing
it all, but Paul was like that cool young uncle who would tell
me how it really was. He's never stopped either.

Which brings me right back around to where I started.
Where the heck was Paul? I had needs, damn it, and he wasn't
around to meet them.

I turned to say something to Chuck, but he shook his head
and gestured to a path ahead of me and to the right. I can
take a hint. I walked. I wasn't totally happy about him walking behind me like that. It made the little hairs on the back
of my neck stand up like steel filings under a strong magnet.
I wasn't sure if he was watching my back or thinking about
snapping my neck.

It's bad form to hurt a Messenger. That doesn't mean it
doesn't happen. I deal nearly every day with beings that
often consider humans prey when they bother to consider
us at all. Even those that don't consider us a food source,
don't always have good impulse control. Granted, I'm not
your average human. I'm stronger. I'm faster. I'm meaner.
Hurting me comes with consequences. Sometimes I think
that just makes me a challenge. I was pretty sure that Chuck
was smarter than that. I was gambling quite a bit on that
assumption as I traipsed up into the woods with him.

It didn't help that Chuck was most definitely not the only
werewolf around. The place was swarming with them. One
had answered the door when I'd rung a while ago. She was
the only one I'd seen but I could feel the others nearby. It

wasn't exactly threatening. I didn't feel a huge amount of aggression directed toward me. There was no imminent attack.

It wasn't exactly peaceful for me, either, though. In addition to all that strong, loyal, outdoorsy stuff that I actually kind of like about werewolves, they're also territorial, protective and, frankly, a bunch of hotheads. A lot of intense feelings were swirling through the air. Walking through the area around Chuck's house was like walking through the emotional equivalent of a hot humid day in the middle of July.

Being in the presence of that many 'Canes had all my Messenger senses tingling at such a high frequency that it was actually a little difficult to listen to anything else.

I reached the top of a hill. A valley spread out below me. The sky was blue with big fluffy clouds creating patterns over the hills in front of me, like moving shadows. Patches broke through in brilliant almost fluorescent greens and yellows while other areas fell into velvety shadow. It would have made a beautiful painting. It was even more spectacular spread out before me as a reality.

"Nice spread, Chuck," I commented.

He sighed. "It sure is."

I turned back toward him. "That generally isn't something to sound depressed about."

"I'm thinking it's about time I moved on." He took another step so he stood next to me. "I've been here long enough. Maybe even a little too long."

The downside of being nearly immortal and not aging very much is that people eventually notice that kind of thing. For a decade or so, you might be able to get away with everyone thinking you had good genes. Let twenty years go by? People start to wonder out loud. The next step after that is people talking and the last thing any group of 'Canes out there wants is to have the 'Danes talking about them. It's trouble for people with supernatural powers when the regular folk start to gossip about them. And by trouble, I mean the pitchfork-and-torch kind of trouble.

"That's too bad," I said and I meant it. "You've built a nice place up here. A lot of people count on you." I paused a little on the word "people." It's bad form to talk out loud about werewolves and vampires. You never know who might be listening. Still, they weren't actually people. At least, not anymore. I'm guessing Chuck hadn't been a "person" for several hundred years.

"True that." Chuck shoved his hands into the back pockets of his jeans and rocked back on his heels. "Still, it is what it is."

He had a point. As much as I ranted and railed about what I was, plenty of folks, 'Cane and 'Dane, had it worse. Or, at least, not better. Sometimes you had to do what the Boss said and learn to live with what you can't rise above. I really should have been born in New Jersey. It would have suited me so much better than California. Well, maybe not the big hair, but definitely the attitude. "Where will you go?"

He propped one leg up on a rock. "Not sure. Used to be you didn't have to go far. My last place isn't even fifty miles from here. Nowadays, though, with the Internet, well, I'm not sure if any distance will be far enough." Then he just stared out over the valley spread below us.

"So did you come up here to show me the view and let me know what you're planning to give up?" I finally said.

Chuck shook his head. "No. I was hoping for a few moments of privacy." He turned away from me now and scanned the trees behind us. "Beat it," he growled, although I couldn't see anyone or anything to growl at. Sure enough, though, I heard a faint rustling noise and then a slight lowering of the supernatural temperature around us a few seconds later.

He waited another minute and then said, in a low voice, "You, too." That was followed by more rustling.

"Is that it?" I asked. I had only recently begun to be able to distinguish between the different kinds of 'Canes that I could sense, and while I could sense intensity, I wasn't exactly certain of numbers. Yet. I felt like my senses had been becoming even more acute and not just my Messenger senses. Food tasted more savory. Smells were stronger. Noises were louder. It was like everything was on high alert, and yet it didn't come with a feeling of anxiety. Which was surprising since I wasn't sure that anything ever in my life came without a sense of anxiety. That said, with all those wolves around I was feeling jittery.

"For the moment," he said. "Now about Paul. He's been gone for about two weeks now."

"How uncommon is that?"

Chuck shrugged. "It's not totally out of the usual."

"Did he tell you where he was going? What he was going to be doing?" Paul hadn't said anything to me—or to Meredith—about going anywhere.

Chuck shook his head. "I'm his Alpha, not his mother. If he needs to be gone for a while, then that's what he needs. I trust him."

That surprised me again. "That's not what I've been hearing." What I'd been hearing was that the Pack was uneasy about Paul's relationship with Meredith. That there was something about a strong and virile werewolf playing fetch and tickle with a seductive and powerful witch that made the Pack nervous. And by "the Pack," I'd figured everyone pretty much meant Chuck.

"What have you been hearing?" Chuck asked with a surprising lack of edge to his voice.

"That Paul was a threat to you. That there had been words, at the very least. That his present relationships weren't to the Pack's liking."

Chuck's eyes narrowed the slightest bit. "You aren't entirely misinformed."

"So what's the deal then? Where is he?" Paul wasn't exactly the most predictable being I knew, but he had his favorite places and he hadn't been seen at any of them. Meredith was half out of her mind, and the last thing I needed was a half-crazed lovesick witch wandering around Sacramento looking for trouble. Ted was acting stern and concerned. It wasn't like I hadn't seen my boyfriend like that before, but it didn't mean I had to like it. Even Alex seemed anxious. No one likes an anxious vampire. They're already so damn narcissistic, anxiety makes it ten times worse. Plus, if Alex was anxious, my roommate Norah was anxious. None of that made my life any easier. Besides, I missed him. Paul was my buddy. He patently refused to pour me a decent drink down at McClannigan's, but he was my bro.

Chuck rocked back on his heels a bit. He was a big man. Not as big as Paul, but easily as powerfully built. His biceps bulged under the black T-shirt he was wearing and his shoulders were broad and powerful. Right now, they were also creeping up toward his ears. Talking about Paul was clearly making the tension build in him. I'd never seen him fidgety like this. "I honestly don't know. We had words a few weeks ago. I told him he needed to examine his priorities. No one has seen him since."

"So what were those words you had about?"

Chuck made a noise of disgust in the back of his throat. "That woman, for one thing."

By "that woman," I assumed he meant Meredith. I sort of got that. A werewolf and a witch together? It did sound like a power play. It wasn't like that, though. "Anything else?"

"Yeah. Frankly, his involvement with you."

I took a step back. "Me?" What did I have to do with Pack politics? If there was something I was truly uninterested in, it was definitely who got the biggest bone at dinner up in the Sierra pack.

"Yes, Melina. You. His involvement in all your little schemes and battles. He ran the risk of exposing himself when he was swooping in to save your ass, and if he's exposed, guess what? The whole Pack is exposed. Paul was getting to be a problem. At least, that's how quite a few of us up here perceived it. We talked to him and he didn't seem to want to change his behavior. Not with that woman and not with you."

I felt ill. Literally. My stomach lurched with a sudden bout of nausea. "I . . . I didn't know."

"Well, now you do." Chuck's jaw clenched. He took a moment to calm himself. "I'm hoping that he's off somewhere taking a good hard look at his priorities."

"And if he's not? You said yourself, no one's heard from him around here. I haven't heard from him either. Neither has Meredith or anyone else I've talked to. What if something's happened to him?" I hated to be a Debbie Downer, but someone needed to do something.

Chuck turned and stared at me again, his muscles flexing. "What exactly do you think is big and bad enough around here to take down one of us? And Paul is far from our weakest link, Melina. Don't you think I would have heard of something that powerful if it was in my territory?"

I chewed on my lower lip. He had a point. It's not like someone could come in and casually take down a werewolf. There's a reason everybody knows about the Big Bad Wolf.

On the other hand, those three little piggies came out on top in that story and they weren't exactly big and powerful. "So what are you going to do?"

"About what?"

"About Paul being missing?" I knew he was being deliberately obtuse, but I hadn't driven up here to come away with no answers whatsoever.

"You're assuming that being out of touch with you is the same as being missing. Give Paul a break. Give him some space." Chuck turned away from the vista in front of us, then stopped for a second and turn around again. "Let me be clear, though, Melina. If I had wanted to get rid of him, it wouldn't have been like this."

"Like what?"

"Sneaky and underhanded. Paul wouldn't have mysteriously disappeared. I wouldn't have slunk around and done something behind the Pack's back. If I'd wanted Paul out, I would have challenged him directly. If an Alpha can't do that, well, it's time to step down." He sounded almost sad, in a growly tough-guy kind of way.

I believed him. It made a kind of werewolfy sense and everything in his tone and posture spoke to his frustration and his concern. So this was a dead end. Chuck didn't have anything to do with Paul's disappearance and he didn't know anything about it either.

In fact, it sounded suspiciously as if it wasn't a disappearance. Maybe Paul really had taken some time to think about his priorities. It wasn't like he and I sat down each month and compared our calendars. If I took a little vacay, I wouldn't necessarily tell him.

Still, it seemed weird that he hadn't at least told Meredith he was going, even if he didn't say where.

Chuck gestured for me to walk back down the hill toward the house. "Oh, and congratulations, by the way," Chuck said from behind me.

"What for?" I asked, turning to look at him.

He paused mid-step and then said, "You know, for, uh, how well things are going at Mae's studio. Congratulations on keeping that going."

"Oh. Thank you." I turned and resumed walking down the hill.

Werewolves are good at lots of things. Lying isn't one of them, and that sounded like a lie to me. The hairs on the back of my neck stood up even taller.

"WHERE ARE YOU? I CAN'T HEAR ANYTHING YOU'RE saying," Ted yelled through my phone.

I was in my car with the windows rolled up and the radio cranking. "I'm trying not to be overheard." I wasn't sure who might be listening in or why, but I didn't like the lengths that Chuck had felt he'd had to go to to keep from being eavesdropped on. It made me even more uneasy. If Chuck didn't trust the members of his own Pack to know what was going on and why, how could I? I also knew that there were wolves all around me. I could feel them, but I couldn't see them. I didn't know why I was being spied on. It might have been standard operating procedure for when someone who was not pack was in the area. I didn't have to like it, though.

"Great job. I can't even overhear you and you called me." Was that an edge of annoyance I heard in the usually solicitous tones of my sweetheart? It had taken quite a bit for me to finally annoy him, but apparently I had managed. I am nothing if not persistent.

I'm not one to gloat over my victories, though. "I talked to Chuck. He claims not to know where Paul is. He thinks Paul's off somewhere straightening out their failure to communicate."

"Do you believe him?"

"Maybe." I didn't know what to believe. The idea that I was causing Paul problems with the Pack wasn't exactly pleasant. I certainly didn't want to cause him more by poking around where I wasn't wanted or needed. On the other hand, I didn't want to not check things out, in case he was in trouble. And what the hell had Chuck really been congratulating me about? That made me uneasy, too.

"So what's your plan?" Ted asked.

"What makes you think I have one?"

"The fact that I don't think I've ever seen you without one, even if it's just a way to get whatever it is you want for dinner." Okay. So the Pack may not be the only ones with control issues. Ted said it without rancor. I have to grant him that. Still, it seemed like I was no longer quite a woman of mystery to my boyfriend and I wasn't sure how I felt about that. On the other hand, it did seem like he had me pretty well figured out and had yet to run screaming for the hills.

"I'm going to head into town. Chuck's second has a hardware store there. Maybe he's heard something that Chuck hasn't."

"See you tonight?"

"Not until later. I promised my mother I'd meet her at the gym."

"The gym?"

"Yep. She thinks her spin instructor might be demonic. She wants me to check him out." Ever since I'd told my mother what and who I was, she'd been dragging me from place to place like a supernatural Geiger counter trying to figure who in her life was a problem and who was a Problem.

It wasn't all bad. We were having mother/daughter bonding we'd never really experienced before. She also paid for me to get my hair done at her salon because she wanted to see if there was something magical about her hairdresser. She was right about that one. Teri totally had a touch of fairy blood. It probably explained why everyone loved the haircuts she gave them so much. They all came with a soupçon of glamour. On the other hand, the receptionist at my mother's office? No troll blood at all. She was just mean.

Plus it was better than her first reaction, which had been stunned silence and then several attempts to get me psychiatric help. It had taken Alex and Norah together to help me convince her that I hadn't lost my mind. Alex had had to show her his fangs and Norah had had to help me explain. Even then there had been several extended days of pure hysteria. I still think she must have bought it at least a little bit because even as convinced as she was that I'd lost my mind, she never told my dad. He was still bumbling along quite happily thinking that his daughter was a little eccentric and not either bat-shit crazy or some kind of evil denizen of the dark.

"I could come by late," Ted suggested, without even a little of the irritation I'd heard in his voice earlier. In fact, he was using a tone that made a blush creep up my neck and gave me a bit of a tingle.

"That would be nice. Around eight?"

"See you then, babe."

We hung up. I turned off the radio and rolled down the Buick's window. "I'm going now," I said out in the open air.

It might have been my imagination, but it felt like the whole forest let out a sigh of relief.

―――――――

IT OCCURRED TO ME THAT CHUCK BEING A CONTRACTOR and his second owning a hardware store was a pretty cozy setup. I wondered if anyone in the Pack ever worried about antitrust law. Of course, people in the town would have to figure out all the connections first.

My guess is that if they did, that would be the least of the Pack's problems.

I pulled into town and my first impression was that a troll had thrown up everywhere. There didn't appear to be a single storefront without rosemaling somewhere on it and there were a lot of store names with *O*s with slashes through them and little dots above *U*s. I pulled into a parking space in front of the hardware store. Everyone was certainly into their Norwegian heritage here. I'd had no idea. It probably started out as a tourist thing, but a lot of people seemed to be taking it pretty seriously.

Seriously enough to make me a little nervous. As a girl who has spent most of her life feeling different, too much same same-iness makes me uneasy. I don't even like to buy matching towel sets. I thought about lighting out before someone pounced on me and forced me to eat lutefisk, but it seemed like too good of an opportunity to get a look at Kevin.

The inside of the Spivey's Hardware was like some place I thought existed only on TV or maybe in books. The air was scented with sawdust, and motes of dust swam in the filtered sunlight that came through the shop windows. Shelves filled the big open room like a maze. I pretty much expected someone in a leather apron to hand me a butterscotch candy at any moment.

The place was far from crowded, but it wasn't empty either.

Two older men leaned against the counter, and toward the back, a woman was looking at a display of shelving supplies.

I took a few seconds in the doorway to let my eyes adjust to the relative gloom and to let my other senses catalog what they could find as well. Werewolf, duh. I'd expected that. Possibly a soupçon of brownie. Also not surprising. Even 'Canes needed the occasional tool to get the job done and brownies are all about making sure chores are completed.

I relaxed a little more and that's when it hit me. The wave of emotion was so intense it nearly knocked me to my knees. I had never experienced anything like it and I staggered backward a step, nearly tripping over the threshold. A nearly unbearable sadness clutched at my chest, weakening me at the knees and making it almost impossible to draw a deep breath. It was a melancholy so deep and black, I felt for a moment as if it was going to rob me of my eyesight.

I slammed my senses shut as hard as I could. It was some protection, although it wasn't complete. Whatever hit me had been powerful, but it hadn't been a weapon. Or, at least, it hadn't been meant as one. Someone here walked around feeling like that all the time. I couldn't imagine. How could someone get out of bed in the morning feeling like that? I felt like curling up in the fetal position under the counter with only traces of it seeping through my defenses.

I shook my head to clear it from this new sensation. It's not that I don't sense any emotions. I am a person, after all, but I wasn't any more sensitive to them than anyone else. Or I hadn't been until now.

It was another something new. A few weeks before, I'd managed to send some kind of otherworldly zaps out of my fingertips and taken down a *bruja* in a cemetery. I had no idea how I'd done that and hadn't been able to reproduce it. It had been a brand-new thing.

Let me be clear. I'm not fond of new. I like old and familiar. I drive my grandmother's Buick. My roommate is my best friend from second grade. I've owned the jeans I was wearing today for three years and the shoes for four. Newness brings surprises and adjustments and compromises, and all those things make me nervous. With Paul missing, I was already a little on edge. I didn't want any more new. I wanted something like my jeans, a little worn at the cuffs but utterly predictable and expected.

I took a deep breath and blew it out and walked back into the store with my walls up a little higher and a little stronger than usual. This time, nothing smacked me back. The sadness was still there, but the tsunami-like quality of it had subsided.

The two old guys leaning against the counter hadn't moved. The man behind the counter, however, had straightened up. He wasn't exactly sniffing the air, but it was pretty close. I was pretty sure I'd found Kevin. I walked over and stuck out my hand.

"Hi. I'm Melina Markowitz. I'm—"

"I know what—who—you are," he said, interrupting me. He did not take my hand.

I left it there, hovering in the air for a second, and then dropped it. Can you say awkward? "Okay, then. Back atcha, I guess." I wasn't guessing, though. I knew exactly what and who he was, too. He wasn't, however, exactly what I'd expected.

Most of the werewolves I know are big men with a lot of muscle packed on them. I've met a couple of female werewolves over the years and even they were pretty toned and strong in human form, with Michelle Obama arms and shoulders. The toll on a body of becoming a werewolf is pretty extreme. Not everyone can withstand it. It helps to already be big and strong to start with. Once you become a werewolf, that strength builds on itself. They tend to be pretty solid.

Kevin, on the other hand, looked a lot like a distance runner, whippet thin, not all that tall and way more stringy than solid. Still, there was no mistaking what he was, at least not by me. If he'd been wholly human, I would have guessed his age to be in his mid-forties. His hairline had started to creep back away from his forehead and what hair was still there was thin and dark. I wondered what his wolf looked like. Would it be skinny and little like him?

Regardless of size, he had to be formidable in a fight. There was no other way to rise to be second in a pack, especially not a pack as large as the Sierra Pack. I guess what they say about it being more about the size of the fight in the dog than the dog in the fight was true.

The two old guys at the counter excused themselves to let Kevin and me talk.

"How can I help you, Messenger?" Kevin asked. His tone didn't make me think he really wanted to be helpful.

"I'm looking for Paul," I said, watching his reaction. Unfortunately, there wasn't one. Not a twitch. Not a grimace. Not a winking eye tic. Nothing.

"He's not here," he said, finally. He leaned back against the counter behind him and crossed his arms over his chest.

"Really? Thanks so much. That's helpful. I can cross this place off my list. Any suggestions on where else I might look?" I smiled. I didn't mean it. I hoped it showed.

Another werewolf came out of the back. This one was younger than Kevin. He looked like he was barely into his twenties. He was easily five or six inches taller than Kevin, though, and most of that seemed to be leg. "Everything okay out here, boss?" he asked.

"It's fine, Sam." Kevin didn't take his eyes off me as he spoke. "Have you tried the bar?"

I nodded.

"His . . . lady friend's?"

I didn't care for the way he said lady friend. He made it sound dirty and not in a good way. I nodded anyway.

"You got me," he said and turned away to the woman who had been at the back of the store. She'd come to the counter while we'd been talking. "Anything I can help you with, Inge?"

"Just these, Kevin. Thank you." She set some brackets on the counter and smiled. Or tried to. It was one of the saddest smiles I'd ever seen. Her lips moved, but her eyes stayed the same. She was definitely the source of that tidal wave of sadness that had hit me as I first tried to walk into the store. I tried not to stare at her, but it was impossible not to steal a glance or two at her. How could one person carry that much melancholy around and not be completely crushed by the weight of it?

She didn't looked crushed. She looked thin, but she had that kind of naturally thin willowy frame. Purple smudges under her eyes marred the otherwise alabaster perfection of her skin, but a lot of people look tired.

Kevin rang up her purchase and told her the total.

Inge frowned.

"Is there a problem?" he asked.

"It's less than I expected, Kevin. I'm pretty sure those brackets were five dollars apiece. The total should be closer to forty dollars."

"Didn't I put a sign up?" he asked. "They're on sale this week."

Inge sighed. "Kevin, that is not necessary."

"I don't know what you're talking about," he said. Man,

if I thought Chuck sucked as a liar, it was because I hadn't seen Kevin give it a stab. Those brackets were so not on sale. He wasn't fooling anyone.

"It's the least I can do, Inge."

Her head dipped a little. "Thank you, then."

He smiled and this time it was a real one. Inge took her change and brackets and left. It felt like the room actually brightened when she left it. That's how intense the little black cloud she was trailing around was. Although based on the look on Kevin's face as he watched her walk out of the store, his world had gotten a little colder and darker with her leaving.

Ah, werewolves in love. It was kind of sweet.

Even in human form, werewolves are closer to their inner beasts than most of us. Their emotions are powerful and hard to control and way too close to the surface. Inge totally rocked Kevin's world and it would be hard for even the most obtuse person not to see it.

After the jingle of the bell on the door fell silent, signaling that Inge had left, I waited a few seconds to make sure we were alone. "Does she know what you are?"

Kevin turned to face me again. It did not look like he loved me. I'm pretty sure he didn't even like me. I was also fairly certain that he didn't really want me in the store, and if I went and bought brackets, they would shockingly no longer be on sale.

"None of your business, Messenger. In fact, nothing up here is your business."

Wow. So much for the soft voice he used with Inge. "Paul's my friend," I said, keeping my own voice pleasant although it was getting to be an effort. There's only so much rejection a girl can take in one afternoon.

"Then be an actual friend and let him be. Your presence in his life hasn't exactly been positive."

Chuck had said the same thing and it stung. I deserved it, though. I had dragged Paul into a few situations recently that had been dicey, to say the least.

"I'd like a chance to change that," I said.

Kevin snorted and leaned forward on his elbows on the counter so we were basically eye to eye. I stood my ground, but it was a near thing. In werewolf circles, this was a challenge and damn near an act of aggression. I willed my feet to stay planted on the floor although my soles were itching to take off.

"You've had plenty of chances. You've done enough harm. Stop meddling where you're not wanted or needed. If we need a delivery, we'll call. Otherwise, get out and stay out."

"I'd like to hear that he's okay from him." In the end, nothing else would really satisfy me.

"Can't you take a hint? He left. He's not calling. He didn't leave a note. Maybe he's not that into you."

That hurt. Not only because I hated that movie. I mean, really, why is it so hard to make a decent romantic comedy these days? But also the idea that Paul might not want to see me anymore. Honestly, of all the scenarios that had occurred to me, that one hadn't.

He straightened and turned away. I took that as my cue to exit, preferably with my hide still intact.

I went back to my car and climbed inside. The solid thunk of the Buick's door as I shut it made me feel a little more secure. I didn't want to leave. Paul was somewhere near here and I wasn't 100 percent sure he was okay despite Chuck's and Kevin's thoughts on the matter. Plus I didn't like Kevin's defensiveness. I mean, really, what had I ever done to him?

On the other hand, taking on the second in command in a werewolf pack on my own was just plain foolhardy, and one thing Paul had tried very hard to teach me not to be was a fool. Plus, there wasn't any proof that Kevin had anything to do with Paul's disappearance, if it even was a disappearance. All I had were my bad feelings and now a general dislike of him, which, let's face it, were pretty much based on his dislike of me.

Whatever. I had a schedule to keep. I put the Buick in gear and pulled out of my parking place. As I coasted down the street, that rolling wave of melancholy hit me again. I looked over to see what was nearby and saw the flush of Inge's blonde hair behind the window of a yarn shop.

2

"ADD A GEAR," THE MADMAN AT THE FRONT OF THE ROOM growled at us over the pounding bass of Led Zeppelin.

I glanced over at my mother who dutifully turned the knob on her spin bike a third of a rotation to the right, then raised her eyebrows at me.

I shook my head and sweat dripped into my eyes. There was nothing supernatural about the instructor. He might well be evil, but not in an Arcane kind of way.

He'd seemed so pleasant when we first walked in, laughing and joking with what were clearly his regular students, all of whom were about my mother's age, a phenomenon explained in many ways by his playlist. It was the music of my mother's youth. He'd shaken my hand and called me by name, which creeped me out for a second. Then someone else had chimed in with "Oh, you must be Melina. Your mother talks about you all the time."

I'd turned to look at my mother on the bike next to me

and she'd given me a big smile, as if this was totally normal. My mother talked about me? To her buddies in spin class? I'd pretty much assumed that my mother spent most of her time pretending she only had one child, my brother. The one who did things like stay in school and play soccer. Not the moody one who was always running strange errands that she refused to discuss.

"Pick up the pace," the instructor growled from the front of the room. I glanced down at the rpm on the bike display. Could I stand to bump them up a few? It'd only be for a minute, but it did seem like a lot of effort for someone who could not curse me, kill me or zap me. I decided to do it for my mother, who talked about me.

Just because the instructor was 100 percent Mundane, didn't mean that everyone in the room was, though. There was something in the room or, more to the point, someone in the room with a little magic to them. I would have liked to have taken a moment to cast around and figure out who it was and what it was, but I was too busy trying to breathe. My mother seriously did two of these classes a week? On purpose?

When the torture, I mean the exercise class, was finally over, the good mood returned to the room. Everyone went back to laughing and smiling even though they were now drenched with sweat. The instructor took us through a series of stretches, ending with a toe touch. I straightened up, and as everyone gave him a round of applause—applause, I tell you, and after he damn near killed us—the room swam around me and the edges of it turned gray.

I grabbed a bike to steady myself. The room righted itself and I realized that everyone was staring. "I'm okay. Just a little dehydrated."

"Make sure to finish that bottle up," the instructor said,

pointing at the water bottle my mother had brought me. "Then follow it up with another."

"Sure," I said.

"You're sure you're all right?" my mother asked as we left the room.

"Yeah. I'm a little tired, I think." That had to be it, right? I didn't like it, though.

My mother stopped on the stairs. "You're never tired."

"That's not true." Well, it was mainly not true. I don't need a lot of sleep, not anywhere near what other people need. Three or four hours a night and I'm full of piss and vinegar, as my grandma Rosie would say.

"It is, too," my mother said, starting to descend the stairs again. "You're bored, sometimes. Distracted. Uninterested. But not tired."

"Well, I am now. Maybe it's part of growing up."

"You're sure you're not coming down with something?"

I also don't come down with things. I've got an immune system that's locked down tighter than Fort Knox. No sniffles. No sore throats. My mother has always been more than willing to take credit for that as proof of her good parenting. Apparently she was letting go of lots of things these days.

I shrugged. "Maybe. I don't know. I gotta go, Mom."

She sighed one of those mom sighs that communicates how much sharper than a serpent's tooth it was to have a thankless child, and offered to walk with me to the parking lot.

"So nothing?" she asked once we'd left the club. "He's . . . a regular person?"

I appreciated her not asking if he was normal this time since that would make me the opposite. Mom was still stumbling over words and concepts with me. "Sorry. Not that I could sense. I think he just wants to make sure everyone has a good workout."

"I can't decide if that's a relief or a disappointment." She pushed her sweat-dampened hair off her forehead.

I smiled. "I know what you mean. Sometimes it's a relief to realize something is supernatural. 'Canes' motivations are often a lot clearer than 'Danes'."

Mom shook her head. "I'm still not used to all your fancy lingo."

I wasn't used to the fact that I was using my "fancy lingo" around my mother at all, so I could relate. After twenty-five years of trying to keep her from knowing anything about this part of my life, it was weird to have even some of it out on the table and open for discussion. "People are complicated. Supernatural beasties often aren't. Generally speaking, vampires want blood, dwarves want gold, and zombies want brains. People want all kinds of crazy stuff for completely unpredictable reasons."

Mom tends to nod her head when she's thinking things over. She was nodding now. "I can see that."

I paused. She'd asked me specifically about the instructor. She hadn't asked about anybody else. Still   "Somebody else in the room had a little tingle to them, though."

Mom raised her eyebrows. "Who?"

"I'm not one hundred percent certain. I think maybe the redhead in the corner. The tall slender one who looks like a dancer?"

"You mean the instructor's wife?" Mom's eyebrows climbed even higher up her forehead.

That would explain a few things. There was something a little elvish about her. Maybe not a lot of it, but definitely a little. Something that would keep her young and vital for her age. She could easily be spreading a little of that effect to her husband who was way too gleeful about telling us to add a little burst of speed.

"Is she . . . dangerous?" Mom asked, her eyes wide now.

I shook my head. "No. I doubt she even knows what she is. And if she has some inkling, she doesn't seem to be using it. At least, not for anything malicious."

"I won't worry, then. Thanks, hon." She gave me a quick hug. "I hope you feel better. I'll see you this weekend, right?"

"You bet."

NORAH, TED AND ALEX WERE ALL AT THE APARTMENT BY the time I arrived. "Finally," Norah said when I walked in. "I'm starving."

It was so weird to hear her say things like that. She'd never been much of an eater. Instead she'd been one of those obnoxious girls with seemingly no appetite at all who stayed thin without even trying, which was only slightly less obnoxious than the skinny girls who ate like horses.

There had, however, been a period of months where she'd barely eaten at all. She'd gotten so thin she'd been practically translucent. Now she was glowing. She'd put on a few pounds and, even as another girl, I knew they'd landed in all the right places. Who knew that taking a vampire as a lover would make someone look so damn healthy? Maybe those medieval medics with their leeches and their bleeding had been onto something.

Ted, however, was frowning. "Are you okay?"

I waved away his concern. I knew I looked like hell. "I went to spin class with my mother. The instructor was brutal."

"But was he demonic?" Norah asked.

"No. His wife's got a little elf blood and he's a little enthusiastic. Mom is seeing demons under every bushel these days." And behind every desk and at the other end of every phone line. "Sometimes it's not demons. Sometimes it's elves."

Norah shuddered. "I know how she feels."

Part of Norah's not-eating thing had been figuring out how much there was out there that she didn't know about. It had made her damn paranoid. I'd ended up loaning her the *grimoire* that Mae had given to me years ago. I never read it. Someone might as well use it.

I'd worried that it might freak her out even more. Instead of suspecting that there were nasty things around every corner, she'd know there were. Somehow, though, knowing what might be there and what definitely wouldn't seemed to help her. I was mainly relieved she'd stopped trying to cast protection spells. There wasn't an ounce of magic in the girl and she'd made some awful messes, although I supposed a little salt across a windowsill never hurt anyone.

I couldn't quite imagine my mother reading the grimoire, though. First of all, I wasn't sure how she'd hide it from my dad. He was charmingly clueless a lot of the time, but even he might have some questions about a giant old book sitting on my mother's bedside table. Second, she didn't seem to want to know too many details. Mainly she wanted a thumbs-up or a thumbs-down on whether something was supernatural or just weird.

I headed off to shower. I stripped down and stepped into the hot spray. Why did I feel so logy? I needed to pull it together.

Afterward, I wrapped myself in a big towel and padded down the hallway to my bedroom. Ted was stretched out on my bed, waiting. Sadly he was fully dressed. I took a second to admire him anyway. He truly was a beautiful man, all golden blond and tawny skinned, muscled shoulders and long powerful legs. His parents might have been crazier than june bugs, but other than that, he'd totally hit the genetic jackpot.

"Where are Norah and Alex?" I started pulling clean clothes out of my drawers.

"You looked tired. I sent them out for takeout." He didn't move off the bed.

I sank down next to him. "Thanks. I don't know what's wrong with me. I'm beat, though."

He reached behind his head and under the pillow and tossed me a pair of yoga pants and a tank top. I clutched them to my chest. Oh, yes. Stretchy pants on my couch. Life was good.

"Have I mentioned lately that you're the best boyfriend ever?" I leaned over and gave him a kiss.

He caught my wrist and pulled me closer. "Care to show your appreciation?"

I smiled and kissed him again. "I might. After dinner."

He loosened his grip on my arm. "I can wait. You sure you're feeling all right?"

I shrugged. I wasn't feeling all right, but I couldn't really quite put my finger on it besides feeling tired and a little dizzy here and there. "It's been a long week. A bunch of long weeks, actually."

"So what else is new?"

I knew that was right. I'd been burning the candle at every end imaginable for a while. Between the dojo and training my protégée, Sophie, and my job at the hospital and whatever this new relationship with my mom was, I'd been running nonstop for days on end. I might not need much rest, but I do need some.

"I'll take a break soon. I'm going to close the dojo for Thanksgiving week."

"Mmhmm," he murmured.

I could hear Alex and Norah coming up the stairs. I pulled on my comfy clothes and shook out my wet hair. "We can talk about this later. Right now, we need to talk about Paul."

Norah and Alex set the pizza out on the coffee table and I pretty much descended on it like a vulture.

I reached for Ted's beer to take a sip to wash down my pizza, but Alex took the beer from my hand before I could even lift it to my lips. "You need to hydrate." He handed me a bottle of water instead.

"You're starting to sound like Paul," I grumbled. Paul was forever micromanaging my drinking, or absence thereof. No one liked a drunk Messenger, not even me. It had been years since I'd even contemplated letting my guard down enough to actually get drunk, but that didn't mean I didn't appreciate something relaxing to drink in a place, and with people with whom, I felt safe.

I looked around the room. It was strange, but I did feel safe. These people knew what and who I was and they had my back. They'd proved it in a lot of ways. We'd forged a family, but now one of our members might be in trouble and we needed to do something.

"So what did you learn?" Norah asked, leaning back in the papasan chair, curled up like a knot.

What I'd learned was that I was way more trouble for my friends than I should be. "Chuck doesn't think Paul is missing. They had . . . an argument. He sent Paul off to do some thinking."

"How long ago?" Alex asked, his dark eyes narrowed.

"Two weeks." Which was about right as far as I was concerned. It had been about three since I'd last seen Paul.

"No one's heard anything from him?" Ted asked.

I shook my head.

"They're not worried?" Norah chimed in.

I shook my head again. "Nope. And they don't want any help from me either. That's for sure."

"So what's our plan?" Norah asked.

I blinked. I didn't think we really needed one. It didn't make much sense to try to track down a non-missing werewolf. Especially if he was avoiding you.

"I'll check police logs," Ted said.

"I'll see if I can find out any good gossip," Alex said. "You, however, are going to have to talk to Meredith."

I winced. Someone needed to tell her what was going on, though. She'd been frantic. She wouldn't be any happier about the idea that we were the cause of Paul's sudden departure than I was.

"But before that, you need to get some rest." Alex grabbed my wrist, his fingers cold against my pulse point. "Do you take vitamins?"

I stared at him. "Really?"

He shrugged. "It wouldn't hurt. I'll drop some by tomorrow night."

Whatever.

"COME ON, SLEEPYHEAD. TIME TO GET MOVING." TED WAS prodding me with the toe of his running shoe. The only reason he didn't pull back a bloody stump was that he also had a cup of coffee in his hand that he was holding just out of my reach. It wouldn't do to spill it.

Ted loves to run. He bounces along with a high-stepping stride like a Lipizzaner stallion. I am not such a happy camper out on the road. Mae spent years turning me into a runner. She begged, threatened, bribed and cajoled me through the years until it got to be a habit. Now the problem is that as much as I dislike doing it, I know I'll feel like crap if I don't. I'm totally stuck. Damned if I do and damned if I don't, which is a pretty distinct pattern in the warp and weave of my life. Lately, though, Ted and I have been going together in the mornings before he has to go to work. As much as I hate to admit it, it does take some of the drudgery out of it. Not that I want him to know that.

I rolled myself upright and took the mug of coffee from him. "Fine, but I'm not going to be happy about it."

"I'd probably have a heart attack from shock if you were. Now get your shoes on."

Fifteen minutes later, I'd slammed down my coffee, wrestled myself into my running bra and double knotted my shoelaces. The sun was up, but just barely as we left my apartment. We turned left and headed up Sixteenth Street.

"Race you to the bike bridge," Ted said, his breath even and deep.

"I am not racing anyone anywhere. You promised I didn't have to go far and I didn't have to go fast. I just had to go." He'd also made some promises regarding cardiovascular fitness, but I mainly focused on the not far, not fast part.

He grinned down at me. "Fine. Just trying to make it interesting."

I caught a glimpse of movement from the corner of my eye and felt a faint buzz in my skin. Crap. He might well be about to get his wish to make the run interesting, but not in a good way.

"Did you see anything over there?" I asked.

"Where?" he asked, not breaking stride. I could tell the nonchalance was a little studied, though. Ted was always watchful. I'm not sure if it's being the overly wary kid of a

Class A nut job, or the cop thing, but wariness is ingrained in him. The watchfulness just stepped up a notch, though.

"Over to your right. In the bushes." I kept my eyes on the sidewalk in front of me and focused my other senses over in the bushes on the right. "Keeping pace with us for the moment."

"Is it . . . human?" he asked. Ted gets a little delicate about how to ask if what we're encountering is of the Arcane world or the Mundane world.

"Nope." That much I was sure of. I was also sure we were bigger than it. Unfortunately, size does not always matter.

"What do you want to do?"

"I don't know. It's not attacking us. It's going to have to come out in the open sooner or later. It's going to run out of shrubs." We would be turning up Sixteenth Street in a block to head to the American River Parkway. It wouldn't have a place to hide after that.

Maybe we were too focused on it. Or maybe it was too damn early in the morning and the light was no good, but as we stepped off the curb onto McCormack Avenue, a car seemed to come out of nowhere. Ted was half a step ahead of me—damn those long legs of his—and right in the path of a baby-shit brown Ford Fiesta. I grabbed him by the back of his T-shirt and hauled him back onto the sidewalk just as it whooshed past us.

Another second's hesitation and it would have definitely clipped Ted, if not creamed him.

"Are you okay?" I gasped.

"No. Let go of my shirt." He twisted away. "You're burning me."

"I'm what?" I dropped his shirt and looked down at my hands. A glow surrounded them. As I held them out in front of me, some kind of lightning-bolt thing shot out of the ends of my fingers. I turned and hurled into the bushes, and two of the biggest crows I had ever seen in my life burst out of them and scattered into the clouds.

"I THINK YOU SHOULD GO SEE A DOCTOR," TED SAID AS he laced up his shoes. We hadn't finished our run. We'd come back to my apartment and I'd crawled directly back into bed. I felt like crap. Apparently I sort of looked like it, too.

Ted, on the other hand, had showered and was putting on his uniform to head to work. He looked as shiny and bright as a new penny.

"You have no idea how difficult that is for me." Consulting with doctors was about as high on my list as hanging out with cops, although look where I was now. I was compromising my principles left, right and upside down.

"You work in a hospital. You see doctors every day," he said as he tucked in his shirt.

"There's seeing and then there's seeing." I made a point as often as possible of people seeing what they expected to see when they looked at me. At the hospital, they expected to see a slightly sullen file clerk and I did my level best to live up to that expectation. I like to set the bar high for myself.

"I know that, but you haven't felt well for a few weeks. I totally honor the stiff-upper-lip thing, but it's gone on long enough." He wasn't smiling.

"Seriously, it's tricky when I go to the doctor's office. Not everything about me reads right." I explained. My resting heart rate is crazy low. So is my blood pressure. My temperature runs a bit low, too. Then there's the matter of my reflexes. Hit my knee with one of those little rubber hammers and you're likely to lose a tooth.

"Then ask Alex to take a look at you." He strapped on his belt.

No, no, no. I had avoided coming into physical contact with Alex as much as possible for years. The fact that he was presently in a big R relationship with my roommate made that an even better idea. "Alex is an emergency room doctor. This isn't an emergency. That's like going to a butcher shop and asking for a doughnut."

He started loading up his hardware. "Ask him or I will ask him for you." His tone was mild, but there was steel beneath it.

I pulled the blankets up around my shoulders. I felt like each one of my limbs weighed about a bazillion pounds. "Fine. I'll ask."

"And see if you can find out what was with those ginormous crows while you're at it, okay?" He shoved his hair back and put on his cap.

I shuddered. I hate crows. I've never been a fan, but after I'd been attacked by a flock of them at the behest of an evil *bruja* a few weeks ago, they were pretty darn low on my list of favorite species. "Yes, boss. Anything else?"

"Yeah." He leaned down and kissed my forehead. "Feel better."

I glared at him. How dare he use sweetness on me like that?

AS MUCH AS I WANTED TO STAY IN BED FOR THE ENTIRE day, it simply wasn't going to happen. First and foremost, Paul was out there somewhere.

It was entirely possible he needed some werewolf "me time," and it wasn't like he could check into a spa to do that. I was going to feel like a total fool if after rattling everyone's cages, he showed up in a few days all refreshed and at one with his wolfiness. On the other hand, I'd feel a hell of a lot worse if he was in trouble and I'd done nothing. It was damn sure his precious pack wasn't going to do anything and what was up with that anyway?

I knew I needed to check in with Meredith. She'd started out acting nonchalant about not having seen Paul and then progressed pretty quickly through the phases of witchy worriedness. Denial. Secret scrying. Charm and amulet manufacture and, finally, random spellcasting. I didn't really want to find out what stages might come next. I was equally sure that the rest of Sacramento didn't want to find out either.

I picked up my cell and punched the speed dial for her number.

"Did you find him?" she asked, her voice breathless.

My heart clenched a bit. What the hell was up with that? Normally I'd get irritated about the lack of greeting or any niceties or at least give her a hard time about it. Instead I was feeling a little *verklempt* about how worried she was. "Sorry. No. I didn't. No one I spoke to in the Pack has seen him for a while either, though."

"What are they doing about it?"

"Nothing that I know of. The general consensus is that he's spending a little alone time." I decided to leave out the bit about Chuck wanting Paul to get his priorities straight. It sounded a little too much like they might have a failure to communicate and I'm a big enough fan of old Paul Newman movies to know how that can turn out.

"I'm coming over."

I sighed. It wasn't like she was waiting for an invitation. She was coming whether I wanted her to or not. "I'll start the tea."

I THOUGHT ABOUT HOW TO HANDLE THE MEREDITH situation while I took my shower. The farther she kept away from all this, the better, as far as I was concerned. She wasn't reasonable when it came to Paul, anymore than he was reasonable when it came to her. We needed to approach this with clear heads. After all, I still wasn't entirely certain there was any situation to do anything about.

It wouldn't hurt to come up with an assignment for Meredith that might keep her busy and not sticking her nose, or foot or wand for that matter, into places where those things didn't belong.

Meredith arrived right as I dropped two tea bags into mugs of water that I'd microwaved. She looked in horror at what I set on the breakfast bar of Norah's and my tiny kitchen, shook her head, got up and dumped both mugs down the sink. Then she proceeded to pull bags of things out of her purse and start a complicated process in the kitchen.

Fine by me. My ego is not even loosely tied to my cooking or tea-making abilities. Good thing. I'd have even lower self-esteem than I already had.

"I can't decide which is worse," Meredith said as she carefully measured something that looked way too much like weed into a teapot. "Thinking that he's hurt or in trouble, or thinking that he's blowing me off."

"Has he ever been out of touch for this long?" I asked. I sniffed. The aroma coming off her tea was amazing, sort of flowery and sweet, but with a spicy note to it. Maybe there was more to tea than putting a dried-out packet of Lipton's into a mug of hot water.

"Not recently. Back in the beginning . . . Well, you remember how he was." Meredith grinned.

I did. It had actually been kind of fun to see Paul all discombobulated and tongue-tied whenever Meredith waltzed into McClannigan's. In all fairness, she didn't really waltz. She more strode in like a tiger looking for prey. Anyway, then he'd get all cranky because he was all flustered and stomp off. It had been terrifically entertaining. "I do, indeed. When exactly did that change?"

"It was a process." Her attention was back on the tea now, which she was pouring through something. "I don't think I could put an exact date on it, but even if we didn't talk every day of the past few months, I always knew where he was. And vice versa."

"And it's been how long since you heard from him?"

Meredith bit her lip and thought for a second. "I think I talked to him twice after . . . well, you know, what happened down in Oakdale."

Oh, she meant after I suddenly started shooting lightning bolts from my fingertips. "So it really hasn't been that long. Maybe he did go off to think for a while."

"I really think he would have told me first, if for no other reason than to avoid exactly this situation. If he's really off being wolfy, can you imagine how pissed he's going to be when he comes back and realizes we've been poking around like this?"

Reasonably pissed, in my own approximation. "I can see it upsetting him somewhat."

Meredith started adding honey and lemon to my cup. "I think that's an understatement."

I did, too.

"I think he would have taken the time to send me some kind of message to avoid that. It's not like he doesn't know us. He knows we'll worry. Or, at least, that I will." She set the mug down in front of me.

I took a sip. It was heaven. "I worry, too."

Meredith made a face. "If pushed. That mother hen instinct isn't exactly your thing, though."

True enough. I was more than happy for people to take care of themselves. Most of the time, I felt barely able to take care of myself, much less anybody else. Plus, my plate was more than full with my own problems. I didn't have the time or the energy to go out seeking other people's problems to solve.

"Speaking of which, have you had any more episodes?" She held fingers out in front of her like she was zapping someone.

I was about to say no, but then remembered the weird glow around my hands when I'd pulled Ted away from that car this morning. "Sort of."

"How can you sort of shoot electricity from your fingers? That seems like an all-or-nothing proposition." She wrapped her hangs around her mug.

"I more sort of glowed." I paused. "Right after I shot the lightning bolts."

Meredith set her mug down and cocked her head to one side. "You were glowing?"

That didn't sound right. "Just my hands."

Meredith frowned. "For how long?"

"Just until I barfed." There. That was so much more me than glowing.

Meredith sighed. "I think I need more information."

I filled her in as best as I could, leaving out the crows. Everyone thinks I'm paranoid about them. They might be right, although just because I'm paranoid doesn't mean they aren't actually out to get me.

"So what did you feel when your hands were glowing?" she asked after I explained the sequence of events.

I put my head down on the counter. "Please, no. Not feelings. I'm so bad with those."

Meredith smiled. "Try."

I blew out a breath and tried to remember what I'd been feeling. "I guess concerned. I thought that car was going to hit Ted."

Meredith nodded her head. "So a car is about to run over your lover and you experienced concern." She rubbed at a crease in her forehead with her thumb. "Try not to be such a drama queen, Melina."

"It surprised me, too," I offered.

"Concerned and surprised, then."

"That sounds about right."

"And how about in the cemetery in Oakdale. How were you feeling then?"

I swallowed. I didn't like to think too hard about that night in the cemetery. I didn't want to call up the sensations of panic and devastation that had howled through me like a very, very ill wind. "I'd say concerned and surprised then, too." That should cover it, right?

"Melina." Meredith sounded disappointed in me.

I looked up from my tea. "What?"

Her face didn't look disappointed. It looked sad. "Didn't you learn anything that night?"

"Of course I did. I learned that I can sometimes shoot lightning bolts from my fingertips. It was very handy." Silly witch.

Meredith shook her head. "Dig a little deeper. It won't kill you."

I wasn't so sure about that. "Fine. I was terrified. I thought she might kill Ted right in front of me and I wouldn't be able to do anything to stop it." I was surprised at the way my throat clogged up as I said it.

Meredith went very still as if she was trying not to frighten a wild animal. "And this morning?"

"We already went over this morning. I think we settled

on concerned and surprised." How much did she expect from me?

"Because you thought Ted was in danger." She gathered up her thick hair and started twisting it into a bun.

Ohhh. I saw what she was going for. "So you think love has given me new abilities?" I laughed. "I don't think it works that way."

She shrugged. "You don't really know how it works, do you?"

True that. I hadn't exactly been issued a manual at any point along my path of Messengerdom and my main source of information, Mae, had died months earlier. I didn't even have anyone to ask. Still, it didn't sound possible to me. "I don't think an emotional state can do that. It doesn't make sense."

"Can you think of another explanation? In both cases, you were worried about Ted, and let's face it, you love him." She smiled a little, then the smile faded and she looked sad again.

Oh. We were talking about love. Her love was missing, possibly in danger or possibly simply staying away from her. I put my hand over hers. "I'm sorry. I know this is hard." Damn. Were those tears pricking at the back of my eyelids?

Meredith stared at me and snatched her hand away as if I had burnt it. Oh, no. Had I? Had I zapped her without knowing? I held my hands up in front of my face. Nope. No glow.

"What is it? What happened?" I asked.

Meredith's eyes were wide. "I've never seen you do that before."

"Do what?" If I hadn't zapped her, had I done something else? Did I have even more new abilities that I didn't know about yet?

"Express . . . empathy, I guess." She still looked shocked.

"Oh, come on. I'm a better friend than that." At least, I thought I was. Of course, I was also pretty convinced I was a badass and lately I'd been getting dizzy after attending my mother's spin class and getting weepy because my friend was lovesick.

"I didn't say you weren't a good friend. You're an excellent friend. You're usually not very touchy-feely. At all." Now she was peering at me like I was some sort of interesting specimen under a glass.

This was the problem with letting people into your life. They figured too much out about you. I wasn't sure I liked Meredith having my number this completely.

She was right. I'm not touchy-feely. I'm not a hugger. Along with the senses I gained when I became a Messenger, my regular ones became even more acute. I see, smell, taste, hear and feel things with a lot more intensity than most people. It's easy to get overwhelmed by something as simple as the smell of someone else's shampoo or the heat of their hand on my arm. It made it easier to keep a little bit of a moat around me. I was way better now at handling those senses, but the moat thing had become a habit that I'd never seen any real reason to break. I mean, why let people in too close when they might be able to hurt you so easily?

"Sorry," I said.

"It's okay, but what the hell is going on with you?" I wished she would stop staring at me like that.

I would have liked to know the answer to that myself, but it was going to having to wait. "I'm fine. I've been too busy. I need a vacation."

Meredith stared some more. "Have you ever taken a vacation?"

"Of course I've taken vacations. I wasn't raised in the

wilds of Siberia." Besides my family lives in northern California. We're driving distance from easily a dozen places that the rest of the country spends hundreds of dollars flying to for their vacations. Lake Tahoe. Napa. San Francisco. Lassen. Yosemite. Monterey Bay.

"When did you take a vacation?"

"Last summer?"

"This past one? I don't remember you taking any vacation. There was the whole *kiang shi* thing, then the whole deal with the *bruja* started."

"So maybe it was the summer before that." I scanned my memory. It must have been.

"Where'd you go?"

"I'm thinking." I must have taken a vacation. Everyone took vacations. But no, I couldn't muster up a memory of me getting on a plane or into my car and heading off to someplace to do anything besides work or deliver a message or a package or letter. "Fine. I don't vacation. What's your point?"

"My point is that there's something going on with you." She looked at me through narrowed eyes.

I had been thinking the same thing, but didn't really want to deal with it. "And whatever's going on with me is more important than what might be going on with Paul?"

She sucked a breath in through her teeth. "No. You're right. Let's stay on the topic."

That was more like it. "Ted is going to check out any odd reports that have crossed the police blotter around were the Pack is most active. Alex and I are both checking our sources for gossip." Working at one of the busier emergency rooms in Sacramento meant that both Alex and I heard about a lot of what was going on in the area before anyone else did. Add to that Alex's fairly extensive network of supernatural buddies and we knew about most of what was up and what was way way down.

"And me? What am I supposed to do?" she asked.

"Have you looked for him with . . . you know, other methods?" I asked.

Meredith bit her lip and then nodded. "I have, but I'm getting nothing but static."

I thought about that for a second. "Maybe you're too close to it. It's making static for you, like my feelings for Ted are making static for me, apparently."

"Interesting," she said. "I could ask someone else to do a little scrying for him, I suppose."

I blew out a breath. That hadn't been so bad. Meredith had a job to do and she wouldn't get in our way or get herself into any trouble. I walked her to the door a few minutes later.

I opened the door and found a package sitting on our welcome mat. It looked like it had been wrapped in an inside-out paper grocery bag and had an address written in neat block printing in Sharpie. Meredith froze and looked from the package to me. "What is it?"

"It's a package." I have a very firm grasp of the obvious that I am nearly always willing to share with others.

"I can see that. Who left it here?"

"I don't know. I didn't hear anyone. Did you?"

She shook her head. "What about with your other senses? Did you feel anything?"

"Nope. Not the least little tingle." I looked down at my hands. They weren't glowing, but that didn't mean anything. I crouched down next to the package. I was getting nothing from it. Literally, nothing. Not a shiver, not a tremble, not a frisson on an ant's ass. Nada. I picked it up.

Meredith gasped. I shot her a look. "It's a package. Not a bomb."

"Well, pardon me for me being concerned, but I've had some experience with a few of your packages and no way would I pick one up with my bare hands." She crossed her arms over her ample chest.

It wasn't like she didn't have cause for concern, but not with this one. "Don't worry your pretty little head about it. This finally looks like a simple one. I might even have Sophie do it."

Sophie is, for lack of a better word, my protégée. She's my Messenger in training. She came to Mae and me just a few weeks before Mae was killed. In retrospect, I should have realized what it meant, having her appear like that. I sometimes think that Mae did.

Sophie's an amazing kid. Smart, funny and kind. She'd been doing a great job and I'd started letting her do more and more deliveries on her own.

Sort of like Mae had done with me. I looked at the address again. It was out near the Sacramento Slough, not exactly close by, but it shouldn't be a big problem for her to find.

Meredith nodded. "That's good. You need to delegate more. You've been swamped for too long."

True that.

3

IT WAS NEARLY NOON WHEN I GOT TO THE RIVER CITY
Karate and Judo. The message light was blinking on the
phone and there was a pile of mail inside the door. I sighed,
scooped up the mail and listened to the messages. There
were two hang ups, one robo call telling me about a fabulous
opportunity to refinance my home and one call from a guy
wanting to know more about the studio's children's classes
and if they would be appropriate for his five-year-old.

I jotted down the number of the actual phone call and
deleted all the messages. The mail was the same time-
consuming waste. Ads. Flyers. Circulars. Offers for credit
cards. Catalogs. Oh, and the electric bill. On the best of
days, this administrative stuff made my head hurt. This
wasn't the best of days. I put my head down on my desk and
closed my eyes.

I woke up with a start, fifteen minutes later, drool crust-
ing the side of my face. I had fallen asleep at Mae's desk.

I am not a napper. Meredith was right. I needed to start delegating more and I needed to take a vacation, even if the only place I traveled to was my own bed.

I went to the bathroom, splashed some water on my face and returned to the desk. I kept my head up and my eyes open and slogged through all the annoying and irritating stuff that makes a small business like a karate studio run. I even returned the phone call from the concerned dad who wanted his five-year-old to channel some of his wild energy into something more productive. I have to admit, I have a soft spot for the rambunctious five-year-olds and I happen to think our Little Dragon classes are the perfect place for them, so that call was at least a pleasant one.

By the time I was done with all that, Sophie showed up. She hadn't even sat down when I presented her with the package I'd found on my doorstep and said, "This one is all yours."

She stared at it then looked up at me. "It's got no buzz."

"Not that I could sense either." I liked that she had used her Messenger senses before she ever reached out to touch the thing. It made me feel like a good teacher and it was all about me, wasn't it?

"What do you think it is?" she asked, now taking it in her hands and turning it over.

"I have no idea. Nor do I much care." Caring about these things invariably got me into the kind of trouble I couldn't seem to get out of by myself. Caring had ended up with me in a cemetery shooting lightning bolts from my fingers while the man I loved lay trussed up and helpless at the feet of an evil *bruja*. It also apparently got one of my best friends in trouble, enough trouble that he was told to go and get his thinking straight, which in turn had set me on a path of sticking my nose where it wasn't wanted in the first place. Can you say downward spiral? I know I can.

"Okay. Have you looked up the address at all?" She set the package back down on my desk.

Sophie was asking all the right questions. I felt so proud of her. "Yep. It's the middle of nowhere."

"Okeydokey, then. I'll put it in my car for now." She grabbed it and headed out the door.

It wasn't uncommon for our deliveries to be made to places that didn't appear to be places at all. Supernatural beings called things home that didn't look like homes to most 'Danes. While I preferred to know where I was going and who I was looking for, it certainly wasn't a requirement. I was glad that Sophie seemed to be adjusting to that as well.

After she came back from her car, we set up the studio for the afternoon and evening. Classes started pretty much right after school let out most afternoons and ran into the early evening. For a while, I'd been teaching most of them, but now Sophie was to the point where she could teach the Little Dragons classes. I'd even let my former nemesis, T.J. Hamilton, teach some of the upper-level classes.

To be honest, if I'd known how much T.J.'s attitude toward me would change, given a little responsibility and a whole lot of extra work, I'd have done it hella faster. He'd gone from constantly trying to knock me down—often quite literally—to being one of the people I relied on most to keep me standing, on a metaphorical level.

The first time I'd asked him to teach had been a fluke. I'd been desperate. I'd had a delivery to a leprechaun that really could not wait. He was only passing through the area and I had a very tight window when he would be here. Sophie had been busy with finals and Mae was, of course, gone. T.J. had been the most experienced person in the room. I asked him to take over during warm-ups and he'd done a terrific job.

He really was a natural teacher. He had a good sense of where everyone was ability-wise and where their strengths and weaknesses were. It's also what made him a formidable sparring partner. He had everyone sized up. When he was teaching, though, he used that knowledge to help them work on deficiencies while making sure they knew their skills were valued. I should probably be taking a few teaching lessons from him.

For now, I was content to use him, which remarkably seemed to make him like me. We'd always had an adversarial relationship. I always thought he'd resented my relationship with Mae, and even after Mae was gone he resented my position at the dojo.

Now it seemed like we were on the same side. He was respectful without being too deferential, which was good because brownnosers irritate the hell out of me. He'd had some suggestions about scheduling that had been really helpful and his rapport with the teenage boys was awesome. I counted myself lucky.

The afternoon whirled by with one class flowing into another until T.J. came in to oversee the green belt sparring session. Sophie and I retreated into my little office.

"So I guess I'll get going," Sophie said, gathering up her jacket and keys.

"Does your mom know you'll be late?" I asked.

Sophie's mom didn't interfere much with Sophie's work at the dojo or as a Messenger, not that she realized the latter was going on. I figured the best way to keep it that way was not to upset her much.

"Yep. She thinks I'm studying for my statistics test with Ben."

I blinked. Math was not my thing. "Do you need to go study?"

She dismissed me with a wave of her hand. "All covered, Melina. Not to worry."

"Great. Text me later and let me know how it went."

"You bet." She headed out.

And came right back in. She tossed the package back on my desk. "I've got a flat."

I sighed. I can change a flat. My father felt strongly that no girl should leave home without knowing how to swim, drive a stick shift and change a flat tire. "Come on, then," I said. "We'd best get to it." Too bad it was already dark out. Tire changing was significantly easier in daylight.

"Don't worry about it. My dad is coming to pick me up. He said he'll come by tomorrow and fix the flat while I'm at school. I couldn't figure out how to tell him that I needed the car tonight. Can you make the delivery?" She flung herself down in the chair, clearly disgusted.

"No problem. I'd rather make the delivery than change your tire in the dark, to be honest. T.J. has things handled here."

Sophie swept her blonde ponytail around and twirled it with her index finger. "So you're not mad?"

"Of course not. In fact, call your dad and tell him I'll drop you off on my way out. Save him a trip." Mad? At a flat tire? What kind of monster was I?

"I could go with you on the delivery. Keep you company." Sophie tilted her head and smiled.

I turned the idea over in my head. Normally company wasn't actually high on the list of things that I wanted. I spent a lot of time alone. I always had. I was used to it and was about to tell Sophie that.

Then I saw her face. Really saw it. She was the one who wanted the company.

Being a Messenger isn't the easiest thing in the world.

It's made a bit harder by the fact that you don't really have anyone to talk to about it. If you told most people that you spent a big chunk of your time delivering items to mermaids or goblins or even elves and fairies, they formed opinions of you that were not uniformly positive. I knew it had been hard for Sophie to maintain the friendships she'd had before she'd had her accident and become a Messenger. Let's face it. Friendships are pretty darn important when you're a teenager. I'm not sure there's anything more important to most adolescents. It had been easier for me as a teenager. I'd been weird since I was three. I didn't have many friends. Pretty much just Norah and Mae. I hadn't had to keep any secrets from Mae, and as it turned out, I had pretty much sucked at keeping them from Norah.

"Sure," I said. "Come with me. It'll make it more fun."

If I'd been Pinocchio, I would have poked the other side of the office with my nose.

"WHY DO YOU THINK IT HAPPENED TO US?" SOPHIE ASKED after we'd gotten onto I-5 headed toward Woodland.

"I have no idea, Sophie. A flat tire can happen to anyone at anytime. It's just one of those things." I glanced at the GPS, not that I really needed it. It was nice to have confirmation, though. It was so rare that anything told me I was headed in the right direction, I'd take what I could get. Yep. Exiting on County Road 102. I felt totally validated.

"I'm talking about us being Messengers, not the tire," she said. A little bit of teenage disgust tinged her voice.

"Oh." It wasn't like I'd never thought about it, but I had taken a lot longer to get around to it than Sophie had. Then again, I don't think most people ponder existential thoughts about the nature of their beings when they're still in pre-school.

I'd actually probably been around Sophie's age when I'd asked Mae about it. Maybe it was a teenage thing to ponder. Why am I so different? Mae had not enlightened me. Until pretty recently, I'd thought Mae had been deliberately obtuse, that she chose not to tell me things. I used to get pretty frustrated with her, too.

It hadn't occurred to me until recently that she might not have known the answers herself. If she ended up in charge of me the same way I ended up in charge of Sophie, there was a darn good chance she had no idea. I certainly didn't.

The next question was, why not just tell me that? Why not admit that she wasn't the all-knowing all-seeing Oz that I thought she was?

I looked over at Sophie and figured I might know the answers to that question, because there was more than one. Sophie trusted me to guide her. If I admitted I was as lost as she was, would it panic her? Would it make her feel even more insecure than she already did?

Would she still trust me if she knew I didn't have all the answers?

Poor Sophie. I hadn't thought to put on a show for her until it was way too late. She already knew I didn't know the answers to a lot of her questions.

Then there was the pride thing. It's not much fun admitting how much I don't know. Mae probably didn't relish the feeling either.

To be honest, and this isn't entirely easy for me since I've spent a lot of time trying to skirt the truth with a lot of people, it kind of pissed me off in retrospect. I'd trusted Mae. When she said that I wasn't ready to learn something or that I'd understand later, I believed her. To figure out at this late date that she was blowing smoke up my ass left me doubting everything she ever taught me, which is a lot.

My mother, on the other hand, has always been a big believer in telling the truth as well as she can. If the trip to the dentist was going to be unpleasant, I knew about it beforehand. If a visit to Great Aunt Anna was going to be boring, she didn't try to shine me on and tell me it would be fun. I was prepared.

Weird. I never thought there'd be a day where I compared my mother and Mae and found Mae to be the one wanting. I'd adored Mae. Worshipped her, even. My mother? I tolerated her. I treated her with respect because that was what was expected of me. It was starting to be reality, though.

I stole another glance over at Sophie, who was chewing her bottom lip as we drove along. "I honestly don't know," I told her. "I think there has to be something about us, though."

She flung her hands in the air. "I think so, too. I mean, I wasn't the only girl to get resuscitated around then. There had to have been some near drownings or something like that, right?"

I nodded. I'd thought the same thing. We cruised past the Costco and the Target in Woodland and headed back out into open farmland.

"So why did we become Messengers and those other people had to stay normal?" She paused and thought for a second. "Or die."

Whoa. Totally not how I would have phrased it. "I'm not sure. I figure we must have some sort of hardwiring in our brains or something that made us more . . . sympathetic to the change."

"That's what I thought, too! I thought maybe it might be

something genetic so I've been asking my mom and dad about my relatives, especially the old dead ones." She twisted in the seat belt to face me.

I winced. I knew what she meant, but there had to be a better way to say it. "And?"

She sunk back in the seat of the Buick. "And not much. I had a great, great aunt that I thought might be a possibility, but it turns out she might just have been crazy. At least, they put her away in a mental institution and then they did one of those lobotomy things on her."

"Ouch." There were all kinds of reasons to keep ourselves to ourselves, weren't there? I merged onto 113 North and into Knights Landing.

"No kidding." She twisted back again to face forward. "Think about it, though. Back then, if a woman acted like we do and disappeared a lot and got a lot of weird visitors and things, maybe they would label her crazy."

"And what do they call us now?" I was pretty sure "crazy" had been applied by more than one person and more than one time, too.

She shrugged. "Quirky. Eccentric. Unique."

Not necessarily what I'd choose for myself given my druthers, but a whole lot better than crazy and next in line for the ice-pick lobotomy. "Can we back up a second?" I asked.

"Conversationally, right? Because I don't think you should back up on this road." Sophie glanced behind us.

"Yes. Conversationally. What you said about other people having to stay normal. Is that really how you feel about this? Like it's some kind of reward?" I kept my eyes steadfastly forward.

"Of course. Don't you?" She sounded surprised.

"It doesn't bother you that we have to hide so much? That

we have to lie? That we never know what's coming around the corner?" I didn't want to lead the witness, but surely she experienced a few of the frustrations that I did.

"I don't see it like that. I see that every day is an adventure. That each day I might find out about a creature that I never knew existed or an object that someone created that's unlike anything else. My life will never be boring."

Or predictable or easy to plan or stable or calm. I turned onto Knights Road.

"Arriving at destination," the GPS lady said, a few minutes later.

I pulled the Buick over to the side of the road and got out. Sophie got out on her side and looked around. "There's not a lot of destination to our destination."

She was right. There wasn't much of anything. Most notably, any light. It was black as pitch and without a moon, too. I waited a moment or two for my eyes to adjust. I don't need much light to see, but this was difficult even for me. "Do you see anything?" I asked.

Sophie shook her head. I sensed the motion more than saw it. "No. You?"

My deliveries often take me to places that don't feel safe and comfy. It's in the nature of the beings that I fetch and tote for to live in the shadows and lurk in the dark corners. This place, however, felt especially creepy right now. I turned in a slow circle, squinting into the murk, but didn't see anything. Nothing to hear or smell either. I reached out with my other senses. For a second, I got something. It was fast and it flickered.

Nothing I could nail down and examine, but someone or something was out there.

A darker shadow emerged onto the road ahead of us maybe twenty-five yards away. I turned toward it, trying to get a sense of its shape and size. It seemed big and blocky. I peered harder into the darkness. Nope. I wasn't mistaken. It had four legs. "Is that a cow?"

Sophie stared, too. "I think it is."

I turned around. It was hard to see much in the darkness, but I couldn't make out any barns or houses. "Where did it come from?"

"I don't know. The fields over there, I guess." She gestured off to our right.

Another shape appeared next to the first one. "There's two of them now."

"No," Sophie said. "Three. Look behind you."

She was right. Another cow had appeared about twenty-five yards behind us.

"They're just cows, right?" Sophie asked, her voice getting a little higher than normal.

"I'm not sure. They seem sort of . . . big." Actually they seemed huge, but it was dark and it was hard to calculate distances.

"Four, now," Sophie said.

Great. "Do you have the package?"

"It's in the car."

"Go get it. Let's leave it right here and go." It seemed ridiculous, but those cows didn't seem normal to me. I didn't like the way they'd appeared out of nowhere or how big they were or, frankly, how they seemed to be blocking the road in both directions. Or the weird prickly feeling I was getting.

Sophie started for the car and that's when they charged. Not only were they big, but they seemed darn fast for cows. "Run!" I shouted at Sophie and we both dashed for the car.

I jumped into the driver's seat, gunned the engine and fishtailed out of the dirt onto the road.

"What about the package?" Sophie gasped, trying to get her seat belt fastened.

"Toss it out the window."

She did as told. Good girl.

Now the question was which way to go, and I didn't have long to answer it. The cattle were bearing down on us damn fast, fully blocking the road in both directions. I had only the vaguest sense in the dark of what the shoulder looked like. Would the Buick be able to make it? Or would we get mired down in something? Or worse yet, hit something and flip?

My hands jolted on the steering wheel as if I'd gotten an electric shock.

"What the hell was that?" Sophie asked, pointing at my hands.

Crap. How was I supposed to explain that? I didn't understand it myself. "I don't know."

"Do we have any weapons?" That's my girl. Ever pragmatic.

"There's some knives in the glove box." What a knife would do against four enormous charging cows, I had no idea, but it was all I had. I'd almost forgotten they were there.

She flipped open the box. "Got 'em. Now drive." She rolled down her window.

I looked over at her. "What are you going to do?"

"You'll see."

I wrenched the wheel of the Buick to the left to skirt the cows coming toward us. As we pulled closer and they began to veer toward us, Sophie took one of the knives and flung it. I was too busy watching the road and the weird glow that was forming around my hands to see where it went, but I couldn't miss the bellow of pain that came from one of the animals.

"Again," Sophie commanded.

I darted back onto the road and over to the other side, coming up. As I passed the cow, Sophie flung another knife and we were rewarded by another bellow.

"You didn't want those knives back, did you?" Sophie asked, glancing at me.

"I'm willing to give them up for a good cause." I am such a giver.

Sophie snorted. "Good, because I'm not going to try to fetch them."

"You ready for the other set?" The other two cows were getting closer.

She paused. "Sort of."

Great. Now she was doubting herself? "What does that mean?"

"It means I only have one knife left."

Oh, right. It was a set of three.

"Make it count." I wrenched the wheel of the Buick to get us in position once again.

Sophie threw and hit again. The cow veered off into the darkness leaving only one left on the road. Easy breezy. I swerved around it and headed back toward Sacramento.

"It's still after us," Sophie informed me, looking out the back window.

I pressed the accelerator toward the floor. The Buick's engine is huge. We gained speed fast.

"It's staying with us," she informed me.

"You're kidding." What was top speed for a bovine? What would it be for a demonic cow?

"Nope. Not kidding."

The road was narrow and dark. Even with my reflexes, the idea of going much faster than I was now was unappealing.

"It's gaining on us," Sophie reported.

Okay. This was not an ordinary cow. I supposed I knew that already, but the fact that it was now gaining on us when we were doing over sixty miles per hour pretty much sealed the deal. I looked down at my hands. They still glowed.

"Fine." I slowed and spun the wheel of the Buick, spinning us around to face the charging bovine. I came to a full stop.

"What are you doing?" Sophie screamed.

"What I have to." I got out of the car and walked to the front of the car. The cow—or whatever it was—got closer and closer.

I wasn't sure what my range was or how fast my fingers could reload, for lack of a better term. So I waited.

"Melina," Sophie screamed.

I held up my hands, pointed my finger at the cow and let loose a lightning bolt.

I hit the cow in the forehead and it stopped instantly. For a few seconds, it stood there, frozen, then slowly it toppled to the side. A smell remarkably like barbecue wafted toward me.

I got back in the car and headed back to Sacramento.

"SO HOW LONG HAVE YOU BEEN ABLE TO ZAP THINGS LIKE that?" Sophie asked after we'd observed a decent amount of silence.

"How long have you been able to throw knives like that?" I countered.

"That was my first time."

"Pretty good aim to hit your target like that from a moving vehicle the first time," I observed.

She smiled her big sunshiny smile. "It was, wasn't it?"

"How did you know you could do it?" I glanced over at her. She was still smiling.

"I just . . . knew. It was the weirdest thing. It was like my body just knew." She spread her hands in front of her and stared at them.

I could see that. I'd had that happen a few times. Not with knives. I was a little jealous. That was a skill that could come in handy.

"And now it's like my brain knows, too." The expression on Sophie's face made it seem like her mind was totally blown.

"What does it know?"

"It knew how many rotations the knife would have to make to stick into those cows and what distance I would have to be from them to have enough space to make them." Her smile faded. "So what do you think that was all about? The cows and that package."

I hadn't had time to process much about that. "I'm not sure."

"It felt like a trap, Melina. Someone lured us out there and sicced those cows on us." Now she sounded angry.

I nodded. I'd come pretty much to the same conclusion, but who did things like that? First of all, there was that rule that no one was supposed to mess with the Messengers. Second of all, who used cow assassins to do their dirty business? Third of all, just plain why? Near as I knew, I hadn't pissed anyone off lately, certainly not enough for them to send cow assassins after me in the dark of night.

"So tell me more about the knives," I requested, reverting to our earlier conversation.

"I honestly don't know. The second I had them in my hand, I knew it, though. I knew how to hold them. I knew when to release." She leaned back in her seat. "It felt pretty awesome."

I understood what she meant. There's something about an action feeling automatically good instantly that is incredibly satisfying. I'd felt that way the first time I'd done a spin kick. It was still one of my best moves. "We should probably capitalize on that. Get you some lessons or a practice board or something. I bet we could set something up in the studio."

"I'd like that. You're a good teacher, Melina. Thank you."

I was shocked by how good that felt, too.

I DROPPED SOPHIE OFF AT HER HOUSE, WATCHING UNTIL she was inside and had flashed the lights at me to know she was safe, and then went back to my own apartment. I dragged myself up the stairs. The apartment was dark and quiet. Norah had either already gone to bed or was staying at Alex's. I didn't know or really care which. All I wanted was my own bed. I texted Ted that I was home but was headed straight to dreamland.

I slept in the next morning, not even bothering to pretend that I might go for a run without Ted there to drag me along. Besides, I wasn't feeling completely safe. The cow attack was still creeping me out and it seemed better to err on the side of caution. Besides I'd have a long night tonight. It was one of the few shifts I was still taking, over at the hospital, and my shift went from eleven at night to seven in the morning.

I puttered around the apartment until it was time to go into the dojo. I peeked out the peephole and spent a minute or two letting my other senses feel their way around the area before I opened the door. The routine was going to get pretty old if I had to do that every time I left the apartment, but

I was having a big case of better safe than sorry at the moment.

There was nothing there. There were no packages on my doorstep and no mad cows lurking in the street. I took the Buick through the car wash—she had treated me well the night before and I felt I should return the favor—and went to the studio.

Again, I was cautious as I opened the door, casting about with everything open. Again, I felt nothing. Maybe I was being paranoid. Maybe the cow thing was a one-off. I couldn't imagine who or why, but maybe the danger had passed. I certainly hoped so.

The different classes filed in and out over the afternoon and early evening. Everything seemed totally normal. After the last students left, I locked up the studio, changed into my work clothes for the hospital, slipped out the back door and headed out. No one seemed to be following me. I finally started to relax.

Maybe the cows had been a fluke. They'd attacked on their own. That could happen, couldn't it? I mean, it wasn't something you read about in the papers on a regular basis, but certainly stranger things had happened. Spontaneous human combustion, for example. That was totally stranger than demonic attack cows.

I parked the Buick on the top floor of the hospital parking garage and took a few seconds to appreciate the night. It was desperately dark, but the air was crisp and clean in that way that only happens in the fall. I allowed myself a few moments of peace before I waded into the barely controlled chaos that was our inner-city emergency room.

I hit the doors and did an immediate detour. Suddenly I wanted grapefruit juice. No. I didn't want it. I needed it. I'd make a quick run through the cafeteria, pick myself up a glass and then I'd get to work. Even with the detour, I still ended up at my desk on time. I got a nod from my boss for that. I favored her with a smile.

Then the humanity began to drag itself past me in all its glory. I had two pretty obvious drug seekers first, not that it was any of my business. They were most definitely the doctors' problem and not mine. Still, I'd been working here long enough to recognize all the signs. Non-specific pains and lots of drug allergies to anything non-narcotic.

Then I had one niece admitting her elderly aunt who she'd come to visit for the first time in months and found the poor dear a little more confused than the last visit.

After that came a woman in her late twenties who was clearly in agony. Every few minutes she would literally double over in pain, groaning. The pain had started that morning and had gotten progressively worse throughout the day. It wasn't easy to get her information, since with each wave of pain, she'd be unable to talk or even really hear my questions.

Then after one particularly intense-looking spasm, she gasped, "Oh, no. I'm so sorry. I think I peed all over your floor."

I stood up and looked over the counter that separated us. Yep. Body fluid all over my floor. Fantastic. Still, it was hard to get angry with her. She looked like hell. I hit the buzzer to ask for an orderly to come help her back into the emergency room in a wheelchair and to bring a mop. I couldn't believe the triage nurse had sent her over here rather than straight back into a bed.

By this time, most of the other file clerks were starting to watch what was happening. What can I say? We don't get out much.

Everyone was quiet until she was wheeled out, doubled over again in the grips of some terrible cramp.

"That chick is having a baby," Letitia said.

Okay. The woman was a little plump, but she did not look like she was nine months pregnant. Besides, it's kind of a salient point when one is seeking medical care. "She didn't say she was pregnant. In fact, I'm pretty sure she said she wasn't." I sat down to look at the part of the form we'd actually managed to fill out.

Letitia crossed her arms over her chest. "I don't care what she said. She's pregnant and she's having that baby now."

A loud scream came from behind the doors as if to punctuate her point.

"How is that possible?" I asked. "How can you not notice that you're pregnant?"

"Haven't you seen that TV show? The one about all the women having babies who didn't know they were pregnant and then having them in toilet stalls?" Veronica, another clerk, asked, sitting down and wheeling her office chair over next to mine.

I don't watch a lot of TV. It doesn't exactly fit into my schedule. "There's a whole show about this?"

Letitia nodded. "With reenactments. Personally, I think all those women are idiots." She peered over my shoulder to look at the half-filled-out registration form. "I mean, how can you not notice that you haven't had your period? How can you not notice the morning sickness or how tired you get."

"Or how emotional you get," Veronica chimed in from behind her partition. "I cried over everything the first three months I was pregnant. And I was barfing when I wasn't busy crying."

"I used to get so dizzy, I could barely unload the dish-washer," Araceli threw in from two cubes down.

I started to get a very uncomfortable feeling. Some of those symptoms sounded a little too familiar to me. Dizziness. Throwing up. Fatigue. When had my last period been? I wasn't in the habit of keeping track.

"There's no excuse for not knowing your pregnant," Letitia said. "You can buy a pregnancy test at the dollar store."

"Can you trust a dollar store pregnancy test?" That sounded way dicey to me. "I mean, you get what you pay for, right?"

"Chemicals are chemicals. I'm pretty sure they work just fine." Veronica shrugged.

We all stopped as a howl emanated from behind the door. Then there was the distinct sound of a baby crying.

"Told you so," Veronica said.

Letitia crossed her arms over her chest. "Eeshh. I hate that noise. It makes me feel like my milk is going to come down again."

I excused myself and went to the bathroom to throw up.

4

NORAH WAS HOME WHEN I GOT IN, MAKING ME VERY glad that I'd jammed the box with the pregnancy test in it into my purse. No way was peeing on this stick going to be a group project. I knew that Norah would make it into one if she got even the slightest whiff of my concern.

It really could be nothing. It could totally be what I'd been thinking it was. Fatigue. A bug of some kind. Over-work. There might be no little pink plus sign about to form on the end of that stick.

Please. Let there be no pink plus sign about to form on the end of that stick. Let it be a big fat blue minus.

Whatever was going to be there, I did not need an audi-ence or a cheering section or a Greek chorus, all of which Norah was capable of being all at one time. I needed—wanted—solitude. It was going to require thought. Plus I had a little bit of a shy bladder.

So I smiled and made small talk as Norah drank tea and

ate oatmeal, although, quite honestly, I wasn't paying a whole lot of attention to what she was saying. The spoon made the rest of the journey to her mouth. My stomach rolled. Had she always chewed and swallowed that loudly?

It took forever for her to leave. At least, it seemed that way. It probably wasn't any longer than she ever took, but today with that pregnancy test weighing my purse down as if it were fifteen pounds, it seemed like an eternity. I practiced my deep breathing and sipped coffee and tried to smile.

"Are you okay?" she asked, one hand finally blessedly on the doorknob.

I startled. "Why? Do I not seem all right?"

"No. You don't. You seem a little tense." She paused. "A little tenser than normal, I guess."

So much for my deep breathing. "I'm a little tired."

"You've been tired a lot lately." Dear Lord, would she never turn the doorknob and leave?

"Meredith thinks I need a vacation."

"She's a smart woman."

"Got it. I need to slow down a little bit. I'm all over it." Now go so I can figure out exactly how much I have to slow down.

Finally finally finally Norah left with a little wave. I waited a few minutes. She's been known to forget things. When a decent amount of time had passed, I fished the package out of my purse and headed to the bathroom.

THE TIMER WENT OFF AND I LOOKED OVER TO WHERE I'D set the stick, covered by a washcloth. I knew if I didn't cover it, I'd sit there and watch it change. So instead I watched the washcloth over it. Big improvement.

I stood, took a deep breath and lifted the cloth.

Plus. It was a plus. A pink plus. I was pregnant. Suddenly it felt like there was no air in the room. None. It even started to whirl a little. I sat down again.

Maybe I'd gotten confused. Maybe plus meant I wasn't pregnant. I pulled the box back out of the trash and fumbled the instructions open. Nope. Plus meant preggers. As in I was now plus one, soon to be closer to plus sized, myself plus another.

I put my hand on my stomach, but I felt nothing. It was still flat, taut even, because of how much I worked out. There was no bump, no bulging, no nothing. There was nothing to give me away.

How long would it stay that way? I had no idea. I'd have to figure out how far I was along before I could even begin to answer that question. Surely I had a few weeks, though. A few weeks to think. There were options. I could make a decision that no one had to know about except me. It could be my secret.

That's when I felt it. My hand was still pressed against the lower part of my stomach. Right where it was pressed, maybe a half inch below my belly button, I felt a flutter like butterfly wings.

I gasped and snatched my hand away. Had I really felt that? Had it really happened? Or was that flutter a product of my overactive imagination?

With equal amounts of hope and dread, I placed my hand against my stomach again. Nothing. I took a deep breath and blew it out. Okay then. I'd imagined it.

Nope. Not my imagination. There it was again. A fluttering, deep inside me. I gripped the edge of the sink and looked at myself hard in the mirror. How could I look so much the same as I always did when everything had changed completely?

———

TED BUZZED ME IN THE LATE AFTERNOON. "HOW'S IT going?"

"Fine. Great." Actually, panicked and confused, but I wasn't quite ready to tell Ted about that yet. I wasn't ready to tell him anything. I wasn't sure I had even completely absorbed the news. How was I supposed to break it to him?

"Wow. That was . . . upbeat."

Crap. I was overcompensating. Upbeat definitely didn't describe how I felt. "Any reason I shouldn't be upbeat?"

"Oh, that you've been exhausted lately and threw up in the bushes on our morning run the other day comes to mind, but otherwise, no." He paused for a second. "Hey, have you looked into those crows at all?"

"No. I haven't had a chance." Crows and cows. Weird. I wondered if they were going to be related in any way. I had to look into them. I had been a little distracted by the fact that my life had just taken a turn that would alter its course forever. A baby. How was I going to cope with a baby?

"Do you want to do some sparring tonight?"

That didn't sound like a good idea, but maybe I was being overcautious. It's not like anyone ever kicked me in the stomach when sparring, although weird things did happen on occasion. Not with Ted, though. With Ted, sparring was more like a dance. Weird as it might sound, it was often kind of a mating dance with the two of us. Moving together with him, clashing, feinting, twirling. It was hot.

I hadn't thought about that either. Was that okay for the baby? Surely people didn't stop making whoopee for the whole nine months, did they? I was going to have to get a book or something. But if I did get a book and accidentally left it lying around, there would be questions. I wasn't ready for questions. Mainly because I didn't have any answers.

The Internet. That was where I needed to go. Nobody ever looked at my browsing history.

"Melina? Are you still there?"

Oh, yeah. Ted had asked me a question. "Would it be okay if we passed on that tonight? I want to get a little more rest."

"No problem. Should I meet you at your place? I could bring a pizza," he offered in his best wheedling voice.

Pizza. I love pizza. I practically live on pizza. That was probably not appropriate nutrition for a baby, though. "I thought maybe a salad might be nice."

"Just a salad?" Ted sounded horrified.

It did sound kind of horrible. "How about pizza and salad?"

He sighed. "I think I could live with that."

We hung up, but I sat there for a while staring at the phone. I was going to have to tell Ted. If there was anyone who deserved to know, it was Ted.

But not yet. I knew my man. I knew exactly what he would do. That boy would be down on one knee proposing before I finished stammering out the word pregnant. It was simply the kind of man he was.

How on earth did I end up with such a Boy Scout as my baby daddy? The universe certainly had a sense of humor.

THE SALAD WASN'T ANYWHERE NEAR AS BAD AS I'D thought it might be although I was glad it wasn't the only thing on my plate. Ted apparently felt the same.

"I like this," he said. "We could eat more healthy. It wouldn't take much."

I hoped he was right. It was everything I could do to keep my hand from straying to my stomach to see how the baby was enjoying the influx of green leafy vegetables. "That's exactly what I was thinking. I don't think we have to go full Norah, but we could slide closer to her on the continuum."

Ted took a bite of pizza and chewed it, a thoughtful look on his face. "I'm not giving up coffee."

Damn. Coffee. I was going to have to look that up, too. Could I have it at all? Of course, just because I was pregnant didn't mean that Ted couldn't have whatever he wanted. Being a man is a total racket. They get away with everything. "I wouldn't dream of asking you to give up your beloved caffeine," I said.

He arched a brow at me. "You're thinking about giving it up?"

"We'll see." I shrugged.

"And the crows? You find out anything about them?" Ted took another bite of his pizza.

I hadn't. I'd been too busy trying to figure out what I was supposed to eat or not eat and what other restrictions I might have. "I'll look tomorrow. I promise. Why are you so keen on finding out about them anyway?" Crows were totally my phobia, not his.

He shrugged. "I keep seeing them around."

"It is the fall. It's kind of that time of year."

"I know, but I keep seeing two of them and those two are freaking huge. It's probably nothing. Oh, I did find some interesting bits and pieces in the police blotters," he said.

My head shot up. "What does that mean?" I was usually the one firing off the cryptic replies.

"It means there are a few things that jumped out at me, but nothing definitive." He leaned back on the couch, clearly enjoying his moment in the sun.

"Care to elaborate?"

He sighed and sat back in his chair, stretching those long legs in front of him. "I'm not sure there's anything to elaborate on. Some woman surprised two burglars in her garage and one growled at her."

"That's it?" I suppose growling isn't typical among burglars, but it didn't amount to much.

"Well, on that one. There's another report about an officer chasing someone down an alley."

"Another vicious growling incident?"

"No. This time someone got bit." Ted sat back up and took another piece of pizza.

"The cop bit the guy?" Now that surprised me. They have clubs and Tasers and guns, for Pete's sake. Why bite a guy?

"Other way around." He shot me a look.

Ohhh. "And?"

He took another piece of pizza. There were still two left in the box. I hoped that would be enough. I was suddenly really hungry. "And I don't know. I tried to call the cop who got bitten and he's off duty. They put him on leave."

"For a bite?" It sure didn't take much to draw a disability check, did it?

"I'm looking into it, Melina, but it makes me uneasy."

I thought about it for a minute. "Well, it wasn't Paul, right?" Could Paul be going rogue? It seemed so unlikely that I hadn't really considered it before. He had to be at least a little angry at how the Pack was treating him. After years and years of dutiful service, he gets a girlfriend they don't like and suddenly they're demanding he rethink his priorities. I could see where that could cheese a guy off. But was it enough to have him turn his back on them completely? And even if he did, why bite a cop? It didn't seem like anything but trouble could come from munching on the local constabulary.

"I doubt it, but I can't be sure. The guy got away. The cop seemed certain that he at least winged him, but nobody has turned up in the emergency rooms with any kind of bullet wound."

"A regular old bullet wouldn't make a wound bad enough for a werewolf to end up in the emergency room, not unless it was made of silver. Especially not if he only winged him."

"I know. Still we've got a missing werewolf and somebody running around biting cops and growling at citizens." Ted ran his hands through his hair.

When he put it like that, it didn't sound good.

"Anything else?" I asked.

"No, but there are a lot of holes in the report. I was thinking of making a little trip to visit the cop who was bitten and maybe even the lady who was growled at and see what I can find out."

That was a great idea. A cop would be observant and able to report back details that could help us. "Let's go together."

He hesitated.

I didn't like the look on his face. "What?"

"You can be a little . . . confrontational in an interview situation." He winced a little as he said it, as if I'd already punched him in the arm.

I wiggled a little closer to him. "I swear, I'll keep my mouth shut and let you do all the talking. I'll be able to sense if there's anything hinky going on on the paranormal front, though. You won't have a clue."

"True that," he said. "Fine. But you follow my lead, okay?"

I held my hands up in front of me. "You're the boss."

He grabbed my wrists and pulled me over on top of him on the couch. "Ooh. I like it when you say that. Say it again."

Fire flooded through me and I leaned down and kissed him hard, pizza breath and all. "You're the boss."

"Mmmmm," he murmured, sliding his hands up the back of my shirt and popping the fastening of my bra. "Again."

"You. Are. The. Boss." With each word, I undid one button of his shirt, which left me with two still fastened. I unbuttoned those for good measure.

Then my shirt was off over my head and he began kissing his way down from my neck to my chest.

"Boss," I murmured.

Then I stopped talking.

"YOU LOOK CONTENT," NORAH SAID AS I STUMBLED INTO the kitchen the next morning.

I felt content. My man knew his business—and apparently mine—quite well. "You're looking well yourself, my friend," I said and plopped down on one of the kitchen stools.

"You want coffee?" she offered, holding out the pot.

I shook my head. "No thanks. I think I'll have some tea." The information I'd found on the Internet about being pregnant was pretty confusing, with each piece of guidance seemingly contradicting the piece I'd just read. Cutting down on caffeine didn't seem to be a bad idea, though.

I got up and pulled a mug out of the cabinet and started rummaging through the collection of boxes in there. Sleepytime. Nope. I'd been sleepy enough, thank you. Tension Tamer. I believe that was what Ted had provided last night. Morning Thunder. Sounded dangerous. Ah. I Love Lemon. I hadn't seen anything about the inherent dangers of lemon to pregnant women. I went with that.

Norah had put the coffee carafe back and was leaning against the counter watching me.

"What?" I said.

"Nothing." She straightened and grabbed a sheaf of papers that were on the corner of the counter. "See you tonight?" she said, slinging her bag over her shoulder.

"Is it Friday already?" I put my head down on the counter, on my pillowed arms.

"Oh, come on. It's not nearly as bad as it used to be." She poked me in the side.

"No. It's a totally different kind of bad." Friday night meant one of two things: sparring class or dinner at my mother's. Tonight was dinner. Although that reminded me. I should check with T.J. and see if he would be willing to take over the Friday night sparring group. If there was ever a group that might kick me in the stomach, it would be that one. The testosterone level got ratcheted up pretty high there and people forgot themselves on occasion.

Dinner at my mother's was a totally different kind of combat. It used to be a little slice of agony for me as I tried to dodge my mother's pointed questions about my life. Now, even if I wasn't an open book, I certainly did a lot less tap dancing there. It was still hard, though. Mom was the only one who knew about me. Grandma Rosie, my dad and my brother were still clueless and it still made for some awkward moments.

Norah had always been a frequent guest. Now I dragged Ted along with me, too, good sport that he is. Thank goodness my mother's fascination with my Messenger status had distracted her from how much she disapproved of my boyfriend. I suppose there were small blessings to be counted everywhere.

Speaking of small blessings, the fluttering in my lower abdomen was back. Without thinking, I pressed my hand to it. Could it feel me in there? Did it know my hand was there? I swear it felt like it moved to that spot the moment I put my hand there.

"Are you okay? Is your stomach upset? Is that why you're drinking tea?" Norah asked.

Uh-oh. I'd forgotten she was still there. I decided it was way better to cop to stomach upset than let her keep guessing. "Yeah. A little."

"I'm not surprised," she sniffed. "Your diet is terrible. Did you have pizza again last night?"

"Yes, but with a salad," I said with a smile.

She shook her head.

Normally I let Norah's advice about diet and healthy living wash over me like a pleasant waterfall that leaves no residue behind. It occurred to me that it could actually be useful at the moment.

"You know, I've been thinking about changing up my diet. Let's talk tonight at my mom's. You can give me some advice."

"Like I haven't been giving you advice about this for like the past decade?" she demanded, hands on hips.

"Yeah, but this time I'm planning on listening." I stood up and gave her a hug.

She blinked a few times. "Okay, then. Well, I guess I'll see you there."

She was out the door and down the stairs before I realized why she'd looked so stunned. That might have been the first time that I'd actually initiated a hug with her instead of the other way around. This motherhood thing was totally making me soft.

Somehow that didn't totally suck. Maybe this would be okay. A wave of nausea swept over me and I ran to the bathroom to barf.

"THIS IS KIND OF FUN," TED SAID AS HE EXITED OFF OF Interstate 80. "It's like a miniature road trip."

"Except we have to be back by dinnertime and there is no aerosol cheese in the vehicle. It can't be a real roadie without aerosol cheese." I was relatively certain that was actually a law.

"I think your decision to start revamping your diet couldn't come a moment too soon. That stuff is disgusting. It's like a petroleum product." He made a face.

"Disgusting in all the right ways," I contended.

He shook his head and tossed me a map. "Start navigating."

"We could have brought my GPS," I pointed out. "Then the navigating would have been done for us."

"And we would have become increasingly lazy and our map-reading skills would have become increasingly dulled," he intoned.

I held up my hand to stop the flow of the how-technology-is-ruining-us rant that Ted was clearly ramping up for. "Got it. Turn left at Clover. It should be two intersections up."

We pulled up in front of Leanne McMannis's house five minutes later. "Are you sure she'll talk to us?" I asked.

"Are you kidding? A police officer following up on a burglary? She'll probably make us coffee and offer us cookies." He got out of the car, straightened his shirt and walked toward the front door. I followed. I bet he got offered a lot of cookies. Almost no one ever offered me baked goods. It wasn't fair. I love baked goods.

"How's she going to know you're a police officer?" I asked. "You're not in uniform."

"I told you. I don't feel right wearing the uniform when I'm not really doing Sacramento police business. Doesn't mean I can't have my badge on my belt and let her fill in the blanks." He rang the bell. "And who's the boss?"

"You are," I said, smiling.

"God, that makes me hot," he said, then straightened as the door opened.

Leanne McMannis was a blonde of indeterminate years. She could have told me she was forty or fifty-five. Neither would have surprised me. Her hair was shoulder length and straight as a board. Her makeup was tasteful and she had on a pair of pressed jeans and a blue button-down shirt with a single string of pearls showing in its open collar. She had that casual but put together look that I never seem to be able to pull off. "How can I help you?" She looked from Ted to me, friendly but still clearly wary.

Ted stuck out his hand. "Hello, Ms. McMannis. I'm Ted Goodnight. I'm with the Sacramento Police Department and I wanted to ask you some follow-up questions about the burglary attempt on your home."

My baby knew his stuff. Her eyes lit up and she stepped back from the door. "Come in, then. I'm so glad. I figured no one really much cared about that."

"Our resources are stretched pretty thin these days with budget cuts and all, but we always care, ma'am." Ted followed her in and I trooped along behind him.

She turned to me, her brows drawn together. "And you are?"

"This is my associate, Melina Markowitz," Ted said.

I stuck out my hand like he had. Her grip was cool and firm with just the right amount of pressure. I recognized that handshake. It was like my aunt Kitty's handshake. I bet this woman sold real estate.

"Nice to meet you. Would you like some coffee?" She walked through her dining room toward her kitchen.

Behind her back, Ted gave me a thumbs-up. "Coffee would be lovely."

Once we were settled around her kitchen island with coffee and cookies (yes, cookies!), Ted asked, "So can you walk me through what happened that night again? I know you went over it with the other officers, but I'd like to hear it again from you firsthand."

"Of course. It's not like there's much to tell, though." She turned her coffee around in front of her. "It was a Friday night. I'd been out at the movies with friends and was getting home at about eleven o'clock."

Ted scribbled something down on his notepad. "I see."

"I pulled up to the garage, hit the button to open the door and there were these . . . people inside." She looked down at the plate of cookies on her left.

"Was there something strange about them?" I asked.

"Why do you ask?" She looked up at me and smiled.

"You seemed a little hesitant when you called them people." And she'd looked down and to her left, a classic sign of lying.

"You're going to think I'm crazy." She shook her head and nibbled off a minuscule bite of a cookie. No wonder she was still so trim.

Ted smiled. "I sincerely doubt that."

She looked at that smile and obviously melted a little. I didn't blame her. It had the same effect on me. "They didn't seem completely human to me. Something was wrong about them."

I leaned forward. "Something how?"

"First of all, their eyes. They glowed red. The other officer said that it was probably the way my headlights reflected in their eyes. You know, like when you take a flash photo, but this seemed so much more intense than that." She shook her head and folded her hands in front of herself. "Then there was something about their shoulders and their arms. Their shoulders seemed rounded over and their arms hung down farther than they should and their legs . . ." She trailed off.

"Yes," Ted prompted.

"I wasn't sure if their legs were bending in the right way."

"Interesting," Ted said, scribbling furiously on the notepad. I wished I'd brought a notepad. I could have written him a note right then. It would have said "werewolf in transition?"

But that made no sense. Werewolves change from human to wolf and back again. Sure there are a million steps along the way, but they don't pause in the middle of it, at least not that I knew. I'd seen one start to change from human to wolf and then choose to change back into human, but I'd never seen one walking around halfway in between.

"So I got out of my car . . ."

Ted set his pencil down and looked at her. "That was very brave, but possibly quite foolish. You could have been hurt."

"I know that now. I was just so surprised to see them in my garage, rummaging in my freezer." She leaned back in her chair and fanned herself as if she was going to get the vapors.

That was a new detail. "They were in your freezer?"

She nodded again. "My son's a bow hunter. He'd killed a deer and asked to keep the venison in my freezer. They had ripped all the packages open and were eating it." She shuddered. "Raw."

I couldn't help it. I looked over at Ted, my brows up.

"See. I told you you'd think I was crazy," she said, looking back and forth between us.

"I don't," I assured her. "I'm just glad you weren't hurt." Interrupting werewolves, or half werewolves, while they were feeding would be a dicey prospect indeed.

"Well, I can tell you, as soon as they growled at me and started toward me, I hopped back in my car damn fast and hightailed it out of here." She sat up straight and raised her hands as if she was surrendering.

"Smart," I said and was rewarded by a smile and her pushing the plate of cookies closer to me.

"Was anything stolen besides the venison?" Ted asked.

She shook her head. "My signs for my real estate business had been tossed around, but nothing else was missing."

Bingo on the real-estate-lady thing, but everything else about this situation surprised me. There was no need for a werewolf to break into someone's garage to eat frozen deer meat raw. It could hunt one down in no time and enjoy it warm. Why did I think that? My stomach rolled at the idea and now I couldn't get the picture of a werewolf with blood and tendons dripping from its jaws out of my head.

I swallowed hard and covered my mouth.

"Are you all right, dear?" Ms. McMannis asked.

I nodded, not trusting myself to open my mouth. Ted looked over at me, clearly concerned. I smiled and gave my head a little shake. He turned his attention back to Ms. McMannis, but with a sidelong glance at me.

"They haven't been back then?" he asked.

She shook her head. "No. I haven't seen hide nor hair of them again."

That seemed a little too appropriate, considering.

"Can you show me where they broke in?" Ted stood.

Ms. McMannis nodded, stood and led us out to the attached garage. "That side door was ripped completely off its hinges," she said, pointing at a door that led to the side yard of the house.

Ted ran his hand down the jamb. "Did you replace it with a heavier door?"

"No." She walked over to him. "I had a security door on it already. I couldn't believe anything could rip it down like that." She shivered. "It didn't even look like they'd used tools. It looked like they'd clawed the thing down."

"IT WASN'T PAUL," TED SAID, REACHING ACROSS TO FASTEN his seat belt.

Of course it wasn't Paul. I shook my head. Paul eating frozen deer meet from some lady's freezer? Not in this lifetime. I wondered if anyone else was missing from the Pack. That didn't sit right either, though. They certainly weren't behaving like werewolves. "Yeah, but I'm not sure what or who they were."

"You don't think they're werewolves?" He handed me the address for the cop's house.

"Not any werewolves I've ever seen. Or heard of. Or read about." I scanned the map. "Turn right on Jonquil Avenue."

Ted's brow furrowed. "Then what were they?"

"I don't know. I'll ask Alex about it. He knows some things I don't. I can get Sophie and Norah researching, too."

I glanced down at the map again and my stomach lurched. I tossed the map aside. "At least my GPS doesn't make me carsick."

"Are you sure you're okay?" Ted pulled over to the curb and put the truck in neutral.

Damn. I should have kept my mouth shut. "Lots of people get car sickness when they read in cars. It's a normal thing."

"Yeah, but you're not a normal girl." He looked hard at me.

"Gee, thanks tons. You sure know how to make me feel special." Deflect with sarcasm. A tried-and-true defense.

He shook his head. "You know what I mean. Did you see a doctor yet?"

"I haven't exactly had a lot of free time for that," I pointed out.

"How about we ask Alex to check you out when we ask him about the not werewolf thingies?" Ted suggested.

"Sure." Like hell I would, but it wasn't an argument I was going to win. I'd win through passive aggression, another tried-and-true defense.

He picked up the map, glanced at it and the address again and pulled away from the curb.

Michael Hollinger's house was a lot more modest than Leanne McMannis's. Then again, I was quite aware of how far a cop's salary didn't stretch. He wasn't doing too badly for himself. We did our march up to the door and knocked.

At first I thought the door had swung open by itself. Then I looked down. The little girl who had opened the door barely came up to the doorknob. She had on a pair of striped leggings and blue smock top with a big ribbon on the chest. She was, in short, adorable. "Who are you?" she asked.

Ted and I exchanged a look. He crouched down so they were eye to eye. "My name's Ted. What's your name?"

She pivoted back and forth on the ball of her right foot, then cocked her head. "Justine."

"Justine, is your dad home?" he asked with a smile.

She shook her head.

"How about your mom?"

This time, she nodded.

"Could you get her for me?" he asked.

Justine started to scamper back into the house.

"Justine," he called after her as he stood. "Close the door, honey."

She came back and slammed the door in our faces.

I shot him another look.

"She shouldn't open the door to strangers and she shouldn't leave them at an open door," he said.

"I know that, but we could maybe have learned a little something." Who knows what a person might hear through an open door? I admit that eavesdropping isn't the hobby I'm most proud of, but it is a useful one.

He shook his head. "Maybe we'll learn more if Ms. Hollinger knows she can trust us, that we have her family's best interests in mind."

Okay. That was a reasonable approach, too. The straightforward thing wasn't part of my usual playbook, but I'd told him—and told him and told him—that he was the boss today.

The door opened again, this time with a full-sized person behind it. Sarah Hollinger looked a little frazzled. Her ponytail was coming undone and her shirt was half tucked in and half hanging out. She was probably about my age, late twenties or so. She was carrying a few more pounds than she needed to, but even with the messy hair and total lack of makeup, she was still pretty. "Can I help you?"

"We were hoping to talk to your husband," Ted said. "I'm Ted Goodnight. I'm with the Sacramento PD."

"Is this a joke?" she asked, crossing her arms over her chest. "Because it's not funny."

Ted held his hands up in front of himself. "No. It's not a joke. I had some questions about a case he worked here that might relate to something I'm looking into in Sacramento. I was told he was out on leave."

She rolled her eyes, but dropped her arms back to her sides. "That's a nice way to put it. On leave. It sounds like a vacation."

Ted frowned. "I take it he's not at home."

"I couldn't keep him here. I was afraid he was going to hurt someone. I was afraid he was going to hurt Justine or the baby." Sarah shook her head and bit her lip. She looked like she might cry.

Ted's brow furrowed. "I thought his injury was a bite. I don't understand how that would make him want to hurt anyone."

Sarah Hollinger looked out her front door, glancing up and down the street as if she was checking to see if anyone was watching. Satisfied, she said, "I think you'd better come in."

The hallway looked like a Toys "R" Us had exploded in it. There was a trail of dolls and blocks and pretty little ponies up and down it along with one of those bouncy seats and some rattles. We worked our way through to the living room. Sarah picked up a little boy who was bouncing up and down in the playpen, and collapsed into an armchair. With her free arm, she waved at the couch. I picked up a little blanket and a sliding stack of picture books and set them on the coffee table to make room for us to sit.

"Why do you want to know about Michael?" she asked. The little boy bounced on her knee and drooled. Were all babies that slobbery? Eww!

"I had a similar case in Sac. The report from up here was pretty thin. I figured I'd come up and hear about it straight from him." Ted waved his fingers at the little boy and got a gummy drooly smile back.

"Was it you? Did you get bitten?" Sarah tried to tuck the hair that had come loose behind her ear.

Ted shook his head. "No."

"So is the person who got bit acting crazy?" she pressed.

Ted and I looked at each other. "I can't really discuss an open case," he said.

She waved her hand at him. "Yeah, yeah. Confidentiality. Blah blah blah. Well, whoever it was that got bitten, tell them it gets worse and not better."

"Worse how?" I asked.

"First of all, the damn thing never healed. It'd sort of scab over and then it would start bleeding all over again. Mike ruined like three uniform shirts because of it. Blood is hard to get out." She sighed.

That was true. Cold water. Hydrogen peroxide. Those were the only things that worked. Even those were not 100 percent reliable. I saw a little movement out of the corner of my eye. Justine was slipping into the room around the corner. I looked over at her and she made a mad dash for her mother, clinging onto her leg like it was a lifeline.

"Why is she here?" she asked, pointing at me.

Sarah gently pushed Justine's hand down. "Don't point, honey. It's rude."

"I don't like her. I don't want her to sit by my blankie," Justine whined.

I picked up the blanket I'd moved from the couch and held it out to her. She snatched it from my hand and darted back to her mother's side.

"Say thank you, Justine," Sarah said.

Justine shook her head and buried her face in the blanket.

"Justine," Sarah said, with that mom warning sound in her voice. I totally recognized it. It sounded like my mother. Was that a learned thing? Was there some kind of class? Or was it entirely instinctual? When would I start sounding like that?

"It's okay," I said. It wasn't, though. Why didn't Justine like me? What had I done to her? I realized she was only a little girl, but seriously, did I have cooties or something?

"So besides not healing, how did your husband get worse?" Ted smiled at Justine, who giggled and ducked behind her mother's chair. Oh, so that was the way it was. I was competition. Okay. I could see that. I settled back in the couch.

"Justine, honey, why don't you go watch cartoons?" Sarah said.

"Can I watch SpongeBob?"

Sarah sighed. "Yes. You can watch SpongeBob."

Justine slipped back out of the room. A few seconds later we heard that someone lived in a pineapple under the sea.

"At first, Mike just seemed a little tense," Sarah said. "He snapped at me and he wasn't as patient with Justine or Charlie as he usually is. He had trouble sleeping and . . ."

We waited.

"All he wanted to eat was red meat and he wanted it really really rare. Like bloody. It was gross." Sarah made a face.

"So where exactly is he now? You said you couldn't keep him here? I don't understand." Ted pulled out a notebook.

Sara's chin began to quiver. "That makes two of us. He got more and more tense and more and more angry. He was back at work, but he was getting into fights with other cops and . . . I think he might have beaten up someone he arrested. No one's saying anything, though."

They wouldn't say anything if they didn't have to.

"They locked him up now. In a mental ward." Tears welled up in Sarah's eyes. "I can't even take the kids to see him. I think it would scare Justine too much. It scares me. Half the time, I'm not even sure he knows who I am."

"What do the doctors say?" I asked.

"Bipolar. PTSD. Possibly schizophrenia. They don't know. They just keep throwing pills at him and nothing makes any difference." The tears spilled over now. "I don't know how I'm going to do this. I can't work. There's nothing I'm qualified to do that makes enough money to even pay for daycare for the two kids. We were just making it on Mike's salary and some extra work he'd get now and then as a security guard. The disability pay is about three-quarters of his salary. I had to go on food stamps."

The baby, who had been happily bouncing and drooling and waving a rubber Mickey Mouse toy in the air, turned toward his mother and patted her cheeks with both his chubby little hands. "Mama," he said.

Sarah pulled him closer to her. I tried to imagine what that would feel like.

"I'm so sorry, Ms. Hollinger. There are some funds set up for the families of officers hurt in the course of duty. I'm going to give them your name. Is that okay?" Ted said.

She nodded, grabbed a tissue from a box by her chair and blew her noise. The baby laughed and clapped his little starfish hands as if she'd performed some kind of trick.

"I'd like to talk to your husband, too. Would you give me permission to do that?" he asked.

She nodded again. "Do I have to sign something?"

"I think that would speed things along," he said.

5

THE NURSE HAD CURLY BROWN HAIR, CUT SHORT, AND A
round face. She was wearing scrubs that had pictures of
Hello Kitty on them. All that should have made her look
cheerful. I'm not sure a clown nose could have made her
look happy. She sat behind the desk, a sour expression on
her face, and looked at the piece of paper Ted had handed
her and then back at us. "You want to talk to Michael?"

"Yes, please." Ted gave her a smile, the one that seems to
open doors, especially when the doorkeepers are female.

"He's not having a good day." She handed the note back,
apparently immune to my sweetheart's smile.

Ted gave her an apologetic look. "We won't take long."

She snorted. "No. You won't. Not if you want to talk."
She stood up and came out from behind the desk. "Come
with me. He's in his room."

We walked down the hallway. I could hear a television
playing somewhere and smelled cigarette smoke. I wasn't

sure how that could possibly be legal. Smoking was banned pretty much everywhere in California. On the other hand, this place certainly wasn't new. Maybe I was smelling a few decades of accumulated smoke that had worked its ways into the cracked tiles and dingy baseboards. I looked over at Ted, but he didn't glance back at me. In fact, his gaze seemed oddly far away.

The nurse led us to a heavy metal door with a small window in it and gestured for us to look through. Ted took one glance and backed away. "Oh," he said. "I see."

The nurse gave him one of those world-weary I-told-you-so kind of looks. I stepped up to the window to see what they were talking about.

The man I assumed was Michael Hollinger was sitting on his bed. Well, sitting is sort of a misnomer. He was more crouching there, legs folded beneath him. I'm guessing he would have been using his arms for balance, but they were wrapped around himself because of the whole straitjacket thing he was wearing. As I looked through the window, his head swiveled slowly around so he could look at me. His lips pulled back and he bared his teeth at me.

Then he threw his head back and howled.

Ted jumped. The nurse shook her head and rolled her eyes. I stared back at him, right into his eyes that had a strange red cast to them. Then he leapt off the bed and hurled himself against the door.

I turned to the nurse. "This thing locked?"

"Hell to the yeah," she said with a snort. "He tried to bite Tyrisha last night. That jacket's staying on and that door is staying locked."

"How . . . how long has he been like this?" Ted asked. He looked pale.

The nurse shrugged. "It's been getting steadily worse.

When he first came in, he was a little oppositional, but mainly depressed. Now . . . well, you see what he is now."

"What are they doing to help him?" Ted finally tore his gaze away from the window and looked at the nurse.

"The usual. They're trying different drugs to see if anything helps. He can't do group therapy anymore, but the doc still goes in to talk to him one-on-one."

"Seriously?" I asked. They'd be better off sending in a wolf biologist than a psychiatrist at this point as far as I could tell.

"He's not the most extreme case we've ever seen. People come in here thinking they're all kinds of people or animals or angels or demons or vampires." She started back toward her desk and we trooped after her. "We get Jesus a lot. A few Napoleons. The occasional Queen of England."

"So he's not responding to anything? Not to the drugs? Not to the doctors?" Ted asked.

"A little when his wife comes in, but she's pretty freaked at the moment. Can't blame her with those two little ones to take care of." She plopped back down in her chair. "Is there anything else I can help you with?"

Ted shook his head and walked toward the door without a word. "Thanks for your time. We appreciate it," I said. This was a weird role reversal. It was usually Ted who made sure one of us observed all the social niceties.

The nurse buzzed us out and we headed back to our car. "Are you okay?" I asked.

He sort of grunted at me and kept walking, stretching those long legs of his enough that I had to scurry a little to keep up. I'm not a fan of scurrying. The fact that I was carrying his unborn child, and that apparently building a placenta had been making me tired and ill, did not make me any happier with him for making me scurry, even if he had no idea. "Yo. Slow down there. Where's the fire?"

He glanced over his shoulder at me, but didn't say anything. He did slow down his pace a little, though. We got back into the truck, still without a word from him.

"What the hell is going on with you?" I asked, buckling myself in with a scowl. Moodiness. Snippiness. These were all my bailiwicks. He was totally poaching on my territory.

"I need to get away from here, okay? Can we talk about it later?" He put the truck in gear and pulled out of our parking spot.

"Whatever," I said and slumped down in my seat.

Then it started to dawn on me. Ted's father had been in and out of mental institutions his entire adult life. Ted must have visited him in one at least once or twice as a kid. Watching Michael Hollinger growl and snarl and fling his trussed-up body against the door of his room over and over had been upsetting to me. What would it have felt like if I'd been his kid? Or even just a kid?

I turned toward Ted, horrified at how obtuse I'd been. "You visited your dad in places like that, didn't you?"

"A few times." He was doing that thing where his voice sounded normal, but I could see that he was clenching his jaw and his fingers were curled around the steering wheel so tightly that the knuckles were beginning to whiten.

"And sometimes he was like that? Like Michael Hollinger?" I asked.

Ted took a deep breath and then blew it out. "Not exactly. He didn't howl like a werewolf."

I guess he had that going for him. "But he was like an animal?"

Ted laughed, but it was an entirely humorless laugh. "Oh, yeah. Been there. Done that."

"I'm so sorry. I didn't think of that. We should never have gone." I twisted in my seat so I was facing him.

"I'm a big boy, Melina. I know those places exist. I know what the people who are in them are like. It was my idea, anyway." His voice sounded dull and flat.

That was true. At least I didn't have to blame myself for that. "I know you're a big boy, but it still must be upsetting." Well, duh, considering how he was acting now.

Ted sighed. "More than I expected it to be. Sorry about that." He shook himself as if he could shake off the bad memories. "It was a long time ago. It doesn't matter anymore."

"Yeah, I totally get that it doesn't matter by the way you're acting." I shifted back in my seat so I was looking out the windshield.

"Just give me a few minutes, please." He pleaded.

"Take all the time you want," I said.

That was it for the next ten minutes or so. Could silence actually suffocate a person? I was beginning to think it could. At the very least, it was making my stomach start to roll. I cracked the window open.

That made him look. He arched a brow at me. "You fart?"

I hit him. "No. I didn't fart. I needed a little air."

"I suppose a little air wouldn't hurt anything. I'm sorry. It's hard to explain. I didn't expect it to get to me. Then when I saw him in there, after having just seen his kids, it was like I was suddenly back there again. Seeing my dad, restrained, slavering, making animal noises."

"You could have said something. I would have understood."

He looked over at me and for the first time I really saw the pain in his eyes. "No. I'm sorry. I couldn't."

WE HAD A LOT OF INFORMATION TO PROCESS, BUT I didn't feel like any of it was going to give me any answers. What did it mean that Michael Hollinger went crazy after having been bitten by a suspect he was chasing? Why were there two of whatever they were in Leann McMannis's garage? I slumped down in the passenger seat of the truck to think as Ted drove us home. Then suddenly we were pulling up in front of my apartment building.

I sat up and checked my chin for drool. "When did I fall asleep?"

"Instantly," Ted said, turning in his seat to face me. "What is going on with you?"

"Me? You're the one who's actually having moods, sunshine." Sometimes the best defense is a good offense and I so wasn't ready to tell Ted that I was pregnant. I wasn't completely ready to admit it to myself.

He shook his head. "Fine. Whatever. We need to change to get to your parents' house on time."

I glanced at my watch. He was so very right. I hopped out of the truck, which was, of course, parked right in front of my building. I swear he has some kind of parking magic. Not only is there always a spot, he can maneuver his truck into spaces that I swear are smaller than the actual truck. We headed up the stairs. Norah was already in the apartment, waiting.

"You're late," she said as I let us in, immediately dispelling the relief I'd felt at the fact that she was no longer chaining the door when she was there alone with a healthy dose of irritation at being reminded that I was behind schedule. "I know. I'm moving. I'll make up for it by wearing a skirt, okay?"

"Whatever."

What was with everyone and the whatevers? "I'll be ready in five." I sprinted back to my room, dropped my jeans to the ground, tossed my jacket and tank top over the chair in the corner, grabbed a skirt and blouse from the back of the closet and threw them on. I breathed a sigh of relief when the skirt zipped with no problem. How long before the tiny Ted or minuscule Melina inside of me made a bulge that was hard to zip over? Weeks? Months? Days?

I grabbed a pair of boots from my closet because no way was I going to take the time to wriggle into a pair of panty hose and dashed back down the hallway. "See?" I said, bursting into the room.

Ted and Norah jumped apart as if they'd been kissing, except that they were sitting too far away from each other for that. I'd definitely interrupted something, though. I might not be the greatest at reading 'Danes, but I knew a guilty look when I saw one. I'd seen more than a few on my own face in the mirror.

"What's going on?" I asked, pausing to get my heel worked the rest of the way into my boot.

"What do you mean?" Norah asked, standing up and brushing off her skirt. She was wearing panty hose. Suck-up.

No way was I going to be distracted by her sartorial one-upmanship. "I mean, what were you doing when I came in?"

Ted stood now, too. "What makes you think we were doing anything?"

Had I imagined what I saw? Suddenly I felt unsure. Could pregnancy hormones make you bizarrely paranoid?

"Put on some lipstick, Melina. We need to go if we're going to pick up your grandmother," Norah pointed out.

As if I would leave Grandma Rosie in the lurch on a

Friday night. Pffft. I went to the bathroom, smeared on some lip gloss and walked out the door without another word.

"YOU LOOK TIRED," GRANDMA ROSIE SAID AS I WALKED her down the hallway toward where Ted and Norah waited in the Buick.

"I am a little tired."

Grandma Rosie stopped, which is never a good thing. It seems to take longer and longer to get her motor going these days. I took another couple of steps, hoping she'd move along with me, but she didn't. I turned around. "What?"

"You're never tired." She stared at me hard.

"Well, I am now. I'm tired and I'm hungry and Mom is making me brisket so can we get the lead out here?" I started walking again and was rewarded by the sound of the tennis balls on her walker legs shushing along the carpet.

"Brisket? What's the occasion?" Did she sound a little out of breath?

"No occasion that I know of. She asked me what I wanted and that's what I said." Because red meat sounded really good right now.

"You two seem to be getting along quite well lately." Did Grandma Rosie sound a little bit snarky?

I wondered how long that would last. I'm not sure my mother would be thrilled to know I was expecting a baby out of wedlock. Mom isn't a prude, but she does like it when things are done in the right order. I'm pretty sure in her mind that would put marriage before conception of progeny. "Yeah. Everything's great."

"Why is that?" Grandma asked.

I glanced over my shoulder at her and laughed. "Does a girl need a reason to get along with her mother?"

"A girl doesn't, but you do." She stopped again, this time clearly to catch her breath. "Watching the two of you try to communicate has been like watching two trains barreling down different tracks. Now all of a sudden you look like you're on the same one."

"Then we better be careful. That's how collisions happen." We were finally at the front door. It whooshed open in front of her and she stepped out to where Ted was waiting to help her into the Buick.

She let him hang on to her hands as she lowered herself into the passenger seat. She drew the line at letting him lift her legs in and pivot her in the seat. That was my job, after I folded up the walker. It had gotten to be like a dance, one where the steps got slower and slower every week.

It scared me. It's not like I didn't understand what life stage my grandmother was in. I got it. I understand that none of us get out of here alive. It was just that Grandma Rosie had been around my whole life. I had no conception of what my world would be like without her in it.

Without thinking, my hand went to my stomach again. Would Grandma Rosie be there for the little person that was growing inside me right now? Tears pricked at the back of my eyelids. Grandma had always been there for me. She'd been my ally and my playmate and my safety net. I wanted her to do that for my baby.

"Are you feeling sick again?" Norah asked me.

"So she has been ill," Grandma Rosie said.

"I'm not sick. I'm fine. I'm a little tired and I eat too much pizza and not enough vegetables." At least, that was my story for tonight.

Grandma Rosie said, "Well, duh."

Norah said, "True that."

Ted said, "No joke."

All in unison. Like a judgmental Greek chorus. "Anything else?" I asked.

"You should wear lipstick more often. It suits you," Grandma Rosie said.

"Maybe some yoga for relaxation," Norah said.

Ted was silent. He is a lot of things. Stupid is not one of them.

"Got it," I said. "I'll take it all under advisement."

We spent the rest of the ride discussing the new human resource person at Norah's office that she suspected might be bipolar and was either going to get fired soon or get the company sued. I was extremely happy to be discussing someone else's faults rather than my own.

Ted turned onto Florin Road and into the little U-shaped landmass known as the Pocket that extended into the Sacramento River. I felt like I could smell the brisket already. From there we turned onto Greenhaven. At that point, I was sure I could smell the brisket. I could possibly even detect onions and mushrooms sautéing to be mixed in with the couscous. Then we meandered through a few more winding streets and into my parents' driveway. By the time we did Grandma Rosie's walker dance in reverse, my father already had the door open and Aunt Kitty came flying out.

Aunt Kitty is just enough younger than my mom to make her automatically the cool sister. She's a total pit bull when it comes to making real estate deals, but when it comes to family, she's a total marshmallow. She also knows when to stop asking questions, something the rest of my family is not very good at. I adore her and somehow I hadn't seen her in weeks and weeks.

"Melina," she cried, giving me a hug and a kiss.

"Mama," she said, more quietly, kissing my grandmother on the cheek, careful not to knock her off balance.

"I didn't know you'd be here," I said. I would totally have put on more makeup if I'd known. Aunt Kitty is a girly girl and has tried to girly me up pretty much since my birth. I really try to humor her because I adore her, but I am way too old for rumba panties.

My hand went to my stomach again. What if I had a little girl? I sucked at girly. She'd have to rely on Aunt Kitty, who let's face it wasn't exactly au courant fashion-wise anymore, and Norah.

"I didn't know I'd be here either, but then I heard your mother was making a brisket. What's the occasion?" Kitty looped her arm through my elbow and started toward the house.

"I don't think there is one, except that I wanted brisket." And apparently, my mother loved me.

Aunt Kitty smiled up at me (she's also the shortest member of the family except Grandma Rosie). "I guess that's occasion enough."

It's not that brisket is so difficult to make, at least not the way my mother does it, but it is time-consuming. It has to cook low and slow and be sliced at precisely the right moment that it's still tender enough that it falls apart under your fork, but maintains its integrity as a slice and doesn't shred.

We all went inside. "Thank God you're here," my dad said to Ted. "The estrogen level was rising so fast I thought I was going to drown."

Ted laughed. "There are worse ways to go."

My father snorted—SNORTED!—and said, "Spoken like a man younger than I am. Beer?"

I looked around. "Where's Patrick?" My brother is almost always here for Friday night dinner.

"Traffic on the causeway," my mother said, sticking her head out from the kitchen. "Come in here and help."

My brother has been getting out of chores since he started college by blaming "traffic on the causeway." I'm not saying the traffic doesn't exist. It does. It sucks. You're trapped once you get on the causeway. I know that. I'm just saying that if a person always gets to not set the table because of traffic on the causeway, it's because they want it that way.

He's always been a little smarter than me. Traffic is only his newest ruse.

My father started pouring wine for the ladies. "None for me, Dad. Thanks," I said.

He froze for a second, the wine bottle poised over a glass. "Okay." The room seemed awfully quiet for a few seconds and then the bustle started up again. I was on salad, one of the few things I can be trusted not to screw up. Aunt Kitty was on cleaning green beans and Norah had to finish mashing the potatoes. Ted disappeared somewhere with my father.

I tried to imagine the scene with a baby on the counter in one of those holder things that people tote them around in. There was barely room for all of us who were cooking. And it's not like it would stay a baby for long. Pretty soon it would be running all over the place. I teach enough kids to know how active they are. My mother's house was totally not childproof.

Forget my mother's house, what about the apartment? My place had baby land mines everywhere. Open sockets. Sharp-edged tables. Actual weaponry.

"Melina, are you listening?"

My mother's voice broke into my reverie. "What? Sure. I mean, what did you need?" I asked.

"The tomato is not going to dice itself." She smiled, but with one of those tight smiles that let me know I was doing something to get up her nose.

I looked down. Apparently I was standing there with my knife poised over a tomato on a cutting board and not actually using the knife on the tomato. I got to work.

My mother shook her head and went back to making gravy, which I think is true magic. I've never been able to make it without huge lumps in it, except for one time when I went after it with an immersion blender which just made the gravy frothy in addition to being lumpy. Can I say that frothy, lumpy gravy is one of the most wrong substances on the planet?

My brother made his entrance about thirty seconds before the brisket hit the table. He didn't even have to carry so much as the horseradish from the kitchen. He and our dad did one of those shoulder to chest man hugs, he shook hands with Ted, kissed my grandmother and my mother and my aunt, beamed at Norah and gave me a quick hug. Then he did a double take. "You okay?" he asked me.

"Fine. A little tired." I was going to have to invest in some of that under-eye stuff that hides dark circles.

"You never get tired." He slid into his place and Dad set a beer down in front of him.

Luckily the conversation veered off from there. Patrick is working on his master's and he already talks like a professor, but truth be told, he always knew how to hold court. I used to occasionally resent his natural ability to command everyone's attention, but tonight I was grateful. I had way too much on my mind to keep up my usual façade with my family. Even so, I saw both Grandma Rosie and Aunt Kitty casting occasional glances my way. I didn't like that one bit.

One of the great things about being Grandma Rosie's ride is that she gets tired pretty fast these days. By eight thirty, she was yawning. She barely made it through her slice of yellow Bundt cake with the chocolate ganache icing, for which my mother is rightfully famous, before her head started to do the droop and jerk.

"Ready to go home, Grandma?" I asked as I picked up her plate, noting that Patrick suddenly had to make a phone call and was nowhere to be found right when it was time to clear the table. Plus he'd eaten the icing out of the center of the Bundt cake. It was where the icing was purely icing. It was like the tenderloin of the icing. I wondered if my mother would let me take some leftover cake home with me.

Grandma smiled up at me. "I am, dear. Just give me a second to powder my nose."

Grandma clip-clopped to the bathroom with her walker while I helped my mother pack up a little care package of leftovers to take home with her. My mother tucked a section of hair that had come out of my braid behind my ear. "Do you want to have coffee sometime this week?" she asked.

"Do you have a potentially demonic barista you want me to check out?" I asked, sealing shut the container of brisket.

"No. I just want to have coffee with my daughter."

I looked up. She looked . . . hurt. Damn. I'd missed something again. Truly, 'Canes might often be out to kill me, but they were soooo much easier to read.

"Sounds good, Mom. How about Wednesday? Does that work for you?"

She smiled. "It sounds great."

Grandma came out of the bathroom and the whole family shepherded her back out to the Buick. It was like the slowest moving parade ever. It was fine with me. It gave me a second to enjoy the night. There's nothing like a crisp fall night in a nice northern California suburb. It's all about the smell of fresh cut lawns and crisp leaves.

I sensed something else, too, though. I turned in a slow circle, trying to figure out where it was coming from. The signature was so faint, I could hardly make out if anything was there at all. Maybe I was imagining it. Although if I was, why was the hair on the back of my neck starting to rise.

My mother had my grandmother in the car and was helping with her seat belt while Aunt Kitty tried to put the walker in the trunk of the Buick. I started toward her, but Ted was already there. He took the walker away from Aunt Kitty and slipped it into the trunk. I imagine it helped to be over five feet tall and not to be tottering around on high heels. He definitely made it look easy, though.

Of course, Ted made everything look easy. He did everything with an easy grace, even tying his shoes. Would the baby inherit that? Would our baby come out genetically predisposed for that kind of athleticism? What would a baby that was half me and half Ted look like? I bet there was a website that I could look at.

"You ready, Melina?" Norah called out from the backseat of the Buick.

Everyone was standing there and looking at me. Great. "Sure." I flashed them all a big smile. "Let's roll."

I hopped in the back of the Buick with Norah, and Ted backed the car down the driveway.

"What were you looking for back there?" Norah whispered to me.

"I'm not sure. I thought I sensed something, but it was too faint to really get a sense of what it was. Whatever it was, I doubt it was powerful enough to do anything," I whispered back.

Ted pulled onto the freeway and headed back toward downtown Sacramento and then hung a right on Alhambra to get back to the Sunshine Assisted Living Community. We pulled up in front. Ted retrieved the walker while I helped Grandma out of the car, and then I walked her in.

The lights were all on, but the front lobby had the empty feeling of a business closed for the night. Of course, it was after nine. Pretty much all the residents were back in their apartments, either in bed or getting ready to get there. Sunshine residents were totally the early-to-bed type.

Grandma nodded at the girl behind the receptionist desk. "Good night, Maricela. I'm home for the night."

Maricela smiled and said, "Welcome back. I'll mark you back in."

We headed back down the hall. Grandma Rosie was even slower on the return trip than she'd been leaving tonight. I don't think the wine or the heavy meal was doing much for Grandma's speed. If we got much slower, I was pretty sure we'd actually be going backward. I tried to do some deep breathing and looked at the watercolors that decorated the hallways to stay calm.

She shuffled a few steps more forward. "So have you told Ted yet?" she asked.

"About what?" I asked, peering at a still life. Why did they always put one wilted flower in those paintings?

"About the baby?" she asked, shuffling a few more steps forward.

I froze. "How did you . . . ? I mean, what do you . . . ?"

She waved one hand at me and then put it back on the walker. "I'm an old lady. I know a pregnant woman when I see one."

I looked down at my stomach and she laughed.

"No. It doesn't show there yet."

"Then where does it show?"

"On your face, sweetheart. In your eyes." Grandma kept going, one halting step in front of the other. "I take it the answer to my question is no, then. You haven't told Ted."

"I haven't told anyone." I'd barely admitted it to myself.

Now Grandma did stop. "Are you thinking about . . . not having the baby?"

Was I? I supposed so. I'd always felt like the decisions women had to make about these things should be private and personal. I'd never wanted to join that particular debate. Now I was going to have to have it with myself. "I'm not sure."

Grandma nodded and started up again, heading toward her apartment. "It's not an easy decision to make."

"I don't know if I'm ready, Grandma," I admitted, falling into step beside her again.

She laughed. "No one ever is, especially not if they think they are."

"So what should I do?" I asked as we arrived at her door.

She handed the keys over to me to unlock it. "You have to do what's right for you and for Ted and for the baby." She looked up at me and smiled. "Although I wouldn't mind getting to meet my great-grandchild. No pressure, though."

"Thanks tons, Gram."

She laughed, then suddenly her face got serious. "This is going to be terribly hard on your mother."

I winced. "You mean the whole unwed-pregnant-daughter thing?"

"Heavens, no. She's just going to worry herself sick over you. You know you're her favorite after all."

"I am not her favorite. Patrick is. He always has been." Patrick who played soccer and went to prom and got good grades and never had weird unexplained absences.

"Pffft." Grandma walked into her apartment and clapped her hands to turn on the lights. "You only think that because she overcompensates. Trust me, a mother knows."

I was going to have to think about this one. Could that be right? I'd have to completely rewrite my whole relationship with my mother.

"I didn't think she would ever get over you almost drowning when you were three." Grandma plopped down into her rocking chair.

That was news to me. Of course, I'd had a whole lifetime to figure out myself after that. "I don't remember that."

"How could you? You were a baby. That was the thing. She hadn't protected her baby." Grandma frowned, then. "And afterward, you seemed so different. The doctors couldn't find anything, but your mother was sure that you'd changed somehow. Do you remember anything about that at all?"

We were definitely plowing into some deep water there. "Like you said, I was pretty much a baby." I kissed Grandma's cheek. "I gotta go. Norah and Ted are waiting."

"I understand." She grabbed my hand and held it. "Tell him, Melina. He's a good man. He'll do the right thing."

I was pretty sure she was right and that was part of my problem.

6

"YOU OKAY?" TED ASKED AS I SLID INTO THE CAR.

"Fine. I wish everyone would stop asking me that."

"Well, until you come clean, you probably won't get that wish," Norah said from the backseat.

Did they know, too? Was I broadcasting on some sort of pregnancy frequency without even knowing it? "What do you mean?"

"It means everyone knows there's something bothering you. Until you start talking about it, we're going to pester you. I don't get why you don't understand that by now." She yawned.

Great. My best friend found my life dilemmas boring. Then I yawned, too. I guess I was finding my dilemmas boring, too. "Nothing's bothering me that everyone doesn't know about. I'm worried about Paul. I'm working too many jobs. That's it."

"If you say so," Norah said, leaning back in her seat. Several pounds of brisket can do that to a girl. I knew that from a lifetime of experience.

We pulled onto my block and Ted parallel parked the Buick about two houses down from my apartment. I didn't even look at him, much less say anything. I was too tired for our regular argument over whether or not there was something weird about his ability to find good parking places. Besides, I could already see that Meredith was sitting on my porch, clearly waiting not so patiently for an update.

I looked over at Norah. "Is Alex on his way?"

She nodded. "I texted him when we left your mom's. He might be inside already."

Norah, before she realized what kind of fire she was playing with, had invited Alex into our apartment. That pretty much gave him carte blanche to waltz in and out whenever he pleased. It was a problem for a little while when he was getting all weird and stalkerrific with Norah. Once we got that worked out, however, he'd taken to actually knocking like a regular person. Still now that he and Norah were in what passed for a relationship between a vampire and a human, he occasionally still let himself in. I suppose Ted did, too. It was only fair, although sometimes I thought there should be some kind of vampire penalty.

"So what happened? What did you find out?" Meredith asked as we got to the steps.

"Let's talk inside," I suggested. It really wasn't the kind of conversation you wanted to have on a public street. If anyone overheard us, maybe they'd think we were talking about a movie or a TV show, but why take the chance?

"Right," she said. "Right. Inside. Where it's quiet."

She was so not doing all right. First of all, she looked like hell. I'd never seen her with her hair that twisted and uncombed and she didn't look like she'd slept much either. Her clothes were all wrinkled and she wasn't wearing any makeup either, which was really, really unlike her. Meredith was a relatively girly witch. I've never been entirely sure either that part of her magic wasn't sexual in nature. She was a powerful presence. Usually.

Not tonight, though. Tonight she seemed . . . diminished.

We trooped upstairs and, sure enough, Alex was waiting in the living room. He didn't miss the squinty glare I threw in his direction.

"I was invited," he said. "Specifically."

"I know. I'm still not used to it." I'd been incredibly careful not to invite Alex into this apartment for years—years!—just so he wouldn't be able to come and go as he pleased. Norah undid all that hard work one evening without ever consulting with me. Have I mentioned that I don't really like change?

We walked in and Alex and Norah went to change into comfier clothes. Ted headed to the bathroom. Meredith and I sat down in the living room.

"So have you had any more . . . episodes?" Meredith asked, making a zapping motion with her fingertips.

"Maybe." I wasn't sure I wanted to explain about being attacked by supernatural cattle, even to Meredith.

"That's evasive." She draped herself across the futon couch. "You know, this thing is spectacularly uncomfortable. Have you thought about purchasing real furniture?"

Real furniture. It was such a grown-up thing to think about. The futon couch had served Norah and me for years. Meredith had a point, though. It was hard as a rock.

"Sure. I've been thinking about redecorating the whole place. Maybe sewing some curtains and hooking some rugs."

"Very funny. You didn't answer my question, though."

"No. I haven't thought about buying real furniture. I will consider it."

"About the episodes, Melina. Have you had more?"

It would probably do me good to have someone to talk to about it. It was all pretty confusing. I nodded.

"When?"

I explained about taking the box we'd found on my doorstep out to the country and all that had happened after that.

"Demonic cows?"

"'Demonic' may not be the right word. Definitely Arcane cows."

"And you zapped them?"

"I knew I could, too. I felt it."

Meredith stared into space for a few minutes, clearly thinking over the situation. "You know, it could be why you're so tired lately."

I was pretty sure my new zapping powers weren't what was sapping my strength, but Meredith was not the person I wanted to tell first. I just didn't want to tell the person I wanted to tell first. Totally logical if you follow it through. Trust me. "Why?"

"A new power like that can be very energy draining. Everyone's noticed that you haven't been yourself lately. Maybe you should let them in on what's going on. People are worried about you."

It wasn't like I didn't know my friends were talking about me behind my back. It's kind of hard not to notice when all conversation stops every time you walk into a room. It also wasn't like I knew no one wanted to talk to me directly. "I know. I'd tell them if I understood it all completely." And if I knew what I wanted to do.

Everyone came back and we all settled down in the living room to pool our information. I filled the rest of the group in on what Ted and I had seen. I left out our little tiff after seeing Michael Hollinger in the mental ward. That was our business and nobody else's.

"Half werewolves?" Meredith asked when I was done. "Have you ever heard of anything like that?"

I shook my head and looked over at Alex, where he was lounging with one arm draped over Norah's shoulder. "No," he said. "Lyncanthropy is like a virus. It's not something that's genetically bred. It's not like if a werewolf and a human had a baby, you'd get a half-breed."

"Could you catch a mild case of werewolf?" Ted asked. He leaned forward, his elbows braced on his knees. "You know, like you catch a mild cold instead of a really bad one?"

"Not that I've ever heard of. It's an all-or-nothing kind of thing. You survive the bite and become a werewolf or you die of the virus before the next full moon. Has there been a full moon since this cop of yours was bitten?"

Ted and I looked at each other. "I didn't check," I admitted. "When was he bitten? Let's get a calendar out."

Ted pulled out his notes. "He was bitten on October fourth."

Norah consulted the calendar on her phone, which of course had moon phases on it. "No. No full moon yet. But there's only a few more days until the next one."

No wonder Hollinger was slavering and flinging himself against locked doors. The full moon can make werewolves pretty volatile. "What about when McMannis's garage was broken into? How close was that to a full moon?" I asked.

Ted looked up the date. Norah looked up the moon phase. "Two days before."

I didn't like the direction my thoughts were going. "Viruses evolve, right? That's why they're so hard to fight."

"In a nutshell," Alex said.

How successful could a virus that killed off a high percentage of its hosts be? "So maybe the werewolf virus has evolved. Maybe it's learned not to kill all of its hosts that aren't quite strong enough to withstand it."

Alex frowned. "That's a pretty disturbing idea, Melina."

"You didn't see Michael Hollinger. It would take some-thing pretty disturbing to make that happen to a regular guy." I felt Ted stiffen beside me.

"How bad was it?" Norah asked.

"Bad," Ted said and got up from the couch.

Alex gave me a quizzical look, but I ignored it. If Ted wanted to explain why he was so upset, he could do it him-self. Talking about his father was always a bit of a tightrope walk. He still loved the guy. I mean, it was his dad. But he had pretty much ruined Ted's childhood to a pretty spec-tacular degree.

"So what's next?" Meredith asked.

"I think I should go talk to Chuck. If he doesn't know what's going on with these half-werewolf thingies, he should. Maybe I'll learn something that will help us figure out what direction to take," I said. "Okay. We have a plan then. I've got Little Dragons first thing in the morning, but I've got a hospital shift tonight. I want to take a quick nap before I go."

Meredith shook her head. "No wonder you're exhausted all the time."

I shrugged. "It's what I've been trying to tell you. Even I have my limits."

That was for sure.

I WOKE UP FROM MY NAP FEELING SURPRISINGLY refreshed. I don't know if it was the sleep or the good effects of my mother's cooking. I wasn't sure I cared either. I was just glad to be rid of the logy, queasy feeling that had been dogging me for days.

I took a quick shower and changed into a work outfit. For

tonight, a pair of black pants and light cotton sweater with some flats. I wouldn't make anybody's top-ten fashion list, but I wouldn't stand out either, which was just as important to me.

There was no one in the living room. I heard a few bumps and sighs from Norah's room, but decided to ignore that, too. I really didn't want to know.

I slipped out of the apartment and went down the stairs as quietly as possible. It never did to annoy the neighbors. Then I was out the front door of the apartment building and on the street. The night was gorgeous. Perfect, even. The temperature had dropped into the sixties, and even though the air had that faint tinge of automobile exhaust that was inevitable in any city the size of Sacramento, it felt crisp.

I took a second to appreciate it, which is of course when I felt the tingle. Someone—something—was out there. It was faint, but it was there, much like it had been at my mother's earlier that evening.

That thought made me even more uneasy. Was something watching me? Stalking me? Waiting for a moment when I would be alone and vulnerable? Like now?

I hustled to the Buick and got inside. As always, I felt more secure once I swung the heavy door shut and locked it. I waited a second for my heart to slow back down. I looked around. It took a few seconds before I spotted them. Two huge crows in the ornamental plum that made a huge mess every fall in the yard across the street. Through the windshield, I waved my hands at them and yelled, "Shoo!"

They stared at me and didn't move.

I thought about honking the horn, but I figured that wouldn't be popular with the neighbors either. Instead I started the Buick and pulled out of my parking place. In my rearview, I saw the crows rise up out of the tree. Great. They were following me.

I tried to keep an eye on them as I drove, but I was often surprised at how much traffic there could still be on the streets of Sacramento this late at night. Where were all these people going anyway? Surely they had homes they could go to, didn't they? Regardless, the other cars made it tricky to keep an eye on the crows.

The silence in the car began to bug me so I snapped on the radio. The Buick was way too old to have an iPod dock or anything fancy like that. It did have a CD player that I rarely used. Generally, a good old AM/FM radio was enough for me. We'd had it tuned to NPR tonight for Grandma Rosie. She liked the news in the early evening and the classical music on the way home.

Something twinkly and sweet came out of the radio, but with a lot of static on its edges. I hit the button to advance it to the next station. Oldies. I sighed. Then that station started to go to static as well. I looked down at the radio as if that would actually give me any information, then I had to slam on my brakes to keep from rear-ending a Jeep in front of me.

I hit the button again as I merged onto the Interstate and a blast of sound came out of the radio that flung me back in my seat. I jammed my thumb on the off button, but nothing happened. The noise continued. I dialed the volume all the way down. The noise got louder. It sounded like some sort of PA system turned up to the max. I kept thinking I could hear words, make out fragments of sentences, but the volume distorted it too much to make it out clearly. I tried turning it up since turning it down hadn't worked. It got louder.

A car horn blared to my left. I'd drifted into the other lane while I was fooling around with the radio. I had to pay attention. I was hurtling along a road at sixty-five miles per hour in several thousand pounds of metal. I couldn't, though. The noise was deafening. It filled my ears and wormed into my brain. I kept poking at buttons and it made no difference.

Another car horn blared. This time to my right. At this rate, the cops would pull me over for drunk driving if I didn't crash first. I needed to get off the road. There wasn't much of a shoulder, though. The next exit was close to a mile away. That would only take a minute or so, right? I could do that. I tried putting my hands over my ears and steering with my knees. It didn't help much, but it was better than nothing.

Then my ears started to get really hot. I pulled my hands away. They were glowing. I swallowed hard, reached over and poked the off button of the radio with my index finger. The zap sent me flinging back against the seat again and earned me a third finger salute from the guy I almost side-swiped, but the noise stopped.

My ears rang like I'd been standing next to the speakers at a Manowar concert, but the loudest sound in the car was now my own breathing. A small wisp of smoke wafted around the edges of the radio. I left it alone until I got to the hospital parking garage. I wound my way up to the top level, my favorite place to park, and put the car in park.

Gingerly, I touched the power button for the radio. It was still hot. Nothing happened, though. No sound at all. Now that I could look a little closer, I saw that the edges of the metal had a singed look to them.

This was going to be hard to explain to the mechanic.

THERE DIDN'T SEEM TO BE ANY PERMANENT EFFECTS FROM my radio malfunction—and I so wanted it to be just a malfunction—except having to ask everybody to repeat things a little louder. Would it hurt people to enunciate?

I really didn't think so. I understand if you're in an emergency room at one o'clock in the morning, you're not at your best, but I don't think it would kill anyone to speak up. Still, it was a relief to go on an errand away from my little cube.

I felt the tingle as I headed down the hallway to carry to the charge nurse a set of faxes that had come in. I tried not to let my steps slow. After all, it might not have anything to do with me. If you think hospitals are full of germs, you're 100 percent correct. They are also full of all kinds of things that most people would have a lot more trouble accepting than a stray microbe or two.

Think about it. Do you know how many prayers are uttered in waiting rooms and ICUs and surgical suites? People who haven't believed in anything their whole lives, sometimes suddenly get religion when faced with illness, disease or disaster. If they don't themselves, then someone in their family will. That person will start praying and pretty soon everyone else is praying along with them.

All that beseeching and begging, desperation and torment, can be pretty darned attractive to ancient and Arcane beings.

"Hey, you. Messenger. In here," a voice rasped out of the waiting room.

I froze in my tracks and glanced around quickly to see if there were any 'Danes around. Everything looked clear.

"Yes, you."

I turned slowly. A dryad peeked out from behind the door, beckoning to me to come in. "What? Are you waiting for an engraved invitation?"

Okay. Something was not right here. I was totally getting a tingle and it had a decidedly woodsy flavor to it. The creature beckoning to me was a willowy woman, ethereal in her beauty. Everything was screaming dryad. Why the hell was she talking like a New York cabbie? Normally they don't speak above a whisper.

Then again, I reminded myself, mine was not to reason why. I sighed. "What do you want?"

"I want you to make a delivery. What did you think I'd want? A new carpet?" She rolled her beautiful moss green eyes.

Well, two could play that game. "Fine. Let me have it."

She gave a little snort, then handed me a piece of bark with an address scratched onto it.

"Seriously?" I asked. "You've never heard of paper?"

She pursed her full and luscious lips. "It needs to be of a tree."

"Whatever." I actually didn't care, so it wasn't difficult to feign indifference. "Who's it for?"

The dryad leaned back against the wall. "Chick up in the psych ward. Her name's Willow."

I couldn't help it. I snorted. "You've got to be kidding me. On the nose, much?"

The dryad cocked one hip and threw her head back. "Tell me about it. How ridiculous is that? A dryad named Willow? Can't really blame them, though. They didn't really know what they were naming."

Great. Now I was getting interested. No good ever came of that. "I don't get it. Who didn't know what they were naming? Why didn't they know she was a dryad?"

"She's not full dryad. She's not even half. Probably no more than an eighth. Her mother was probably about a quarter and she didn't even know what she was. Get this, though. The mother's name was Cedar." She barked out a laugh. "Who would name their kid Cedar?"

I had gone to school with several Cedars. "This is northern California."

The dryad sighed and coughed a little. "True that. Awful lot of tree huggers around here."

"Wouldn't you be one of them?" Dryads were all about trees and frolicking around them. That was their whole shtick. That and being all gorgeous and everything.

She slid onto the couch, folding herself into something that looked like one of Norah's yoga poses. "Absolutely. Love them. Great things, trees. Do you know how long a redwood tree can live, though?"

"Couple hundred years?" I guessed.

"Try a couple thousand for some of them. Know what they do during all those years? All those minutes and hours and weeks and days?" She stretched and yawned.

"I don't know. Grow, maybe?" Another guess.

"Bingo, Messenger girl. They grow. Roots go down. Trunk goes up. Leaves sprout." She leaned forward. "It's great for the first couple of hundred years, then it starts to get a little boring."

I could see that. Sometimes I could barely stand to wait at a stoplight. "So what are you supposed to do?"

"Whatever I want, really. I'm not a hamadryad. I don't live IN the tree. I live near it. I can wander a bit."

"So what's the deal with this Willow chick up in psych?" I sat down next to her. "And what's your name?"

The dryad stuck out her hand. "Jenny." Excellent. So much more sensible.

"Melina," I said and shook her hand. "Now about Willow?"

Jenny sighed. "Poor thing. She's got some dryad blood in her. We don't intermix much, but it happens. Anyway, it's a few generations back. No one in the family really knows about it. They just think they're woodsy sorts of people."

I could see that happening. I knew a few woodsy types

that didn't have a speck of dryad in them. "How'd that land her in the psych ward?"

"Long story short. Something happened to her tree." Jenny began twirling her long blonde hair around one finger.

"That made her go nuts?"

"It's a little more complicated than that and probably could have been avoided if anyone had been keeping track of her or her mother. They'd sort of slipped through the cracks. Again, it happens." Jenny shrugged, but she seemed a little less hostile.

I found myself fingering the piece of bark. It had a nice feel to it. "So they both went nuts?"

Jenny shook her head. "No. Somehow it's a little stronger in the daughter than the mother. I don't know why."

"Let me guess," I said. "It happens."

"You know it does. You've probably seen something like it in your family. You know, when someone seems like sort of a throwback to an earlier generation? Genetics are crazy."

I did know it. I was the throwback. I actually look so much like photos of Grandma Rosie's mother at my age that it even creeps me out, and I hang out with vampires and werewolves. I am relatively creep-proof. "Okay. Sure. I get that."

"So the redwood that this chick's like great-great-grandmother was tied to is finally dying and I guess she experienced some kind of, I don't know, psychic distress. If she'd known why, it'd probably have been okay. She could have probably handled it, but instead it made her sort of . . . crazy." Jenny made circles in the air with her finger by her ear.

"Hence her stay upstairs in a locked ward?"

"Let's just say she started acting out a bit. Apparently public nudity is frowned upon in midtown."

"And this?" I held up the piece of bark with the address on it.

"She's here for seventy-two hours. You know. The whole

5150 thing." Jenny pointed at the bark. "That's where she should go when she gets out. There'll be a couple of us there waiting. We'll be able to help her."

In California, Section 5150 was the part of the Welfare and Institutions Code that allowed someone—like a cop or a doctor—to involuntarily commit someone. It's kind of code for "serious whack job."

"What if she doesn't want to go?" I asked. I mean, why would she? Especially if she thinks she's already crazy. Why would a strange woman handing her a piece of a tree seem like anything more than another piece of the crazy?

"She'll want to. Once she holds it in her hand. She'll feel it. It'll speak to her." Jenny pressed her lips into a firm line and nodded.

"Got it." I did, too. Inanimate objects often had conversations with me, whether I wanted them to or not. I stood up. "It's been nice meeting you."

"Likewise." Jenny smiled. "Sorry if I was a little . . . sharp before. I didn't really know what to expect, given your reputation."

Well, wasn't that just the pot calling the kettle black. "What reputation?"

She gestured in the air. "You know. Word on the street. The down low. The four-one-one."

"Yeah. I know what reputation means. What's mine?" I wasn't sure I wanted the answer, but there was no way I was not asking.

She looked at me for a moment as if she was considering how much to say. "That you meddle. That you're a bit of a troublemaker."

I blinked a few times as I waited for that information to register. "I don't meddle unless I'm forced to. There's nothing I'd like better than to never meddle at all."

She held up her hands in front of her in a gesture of surrender. "Whatever, *chiquita*, I'm just telling you what the word on the street is. I get it. I'm not exactly what people expect either."

She could say that again. She was right, though. Whatever, indeed. People—or creatures—could say whatever they wanted. It didn't matter.

Except maybe it did when you were trying to find out what was going on with your friend, the disappearing werewolf. Would I get more cooperation if people didn't think I was going to stick my nose into business that wasn't mine?

I slipped the piece of bark into the pocket of the sweater I was wearing and headed down to the lab to see if they had some reports to deliver to the psych ward, to give me some cover for my visit up there.

THE LAB TOTALLY HAD SOME RESULTS THAT NEEDED delivering. It really wasn't a surprise. A huge amount of body fluids made their way there and, for some reason or another, someone somewhere always wanted to know what was in them. The tired looking man sitting behind the desk in the front seemed a little surprised when I offered to take the ones to the psych ward for him since I was headed that way anyway, but he wasn't going to argue with me. Most of the hospital staff spends a ridiculous amount of time on their feet. They'll do almost anything to get to sit for a few minutes here and there. Plus, I gave him one of my best smiles. The one where I cock my head a little to the side. I was hoping it was coquettish without being slutty. It worked, so it must have been okay.

I walked up to the door of the psych ward and waited to be buzzed in. It was pretty much the same setup as the place where we'd seen Michael Hollinger. I tried to imagine what it would be like to have been a little kid coming in here to see your father.

Say what you will about my mother—and I have said plenty at one point in time in my life or another—she has always been sane, if not reasonable, at least to my own vision of what is reasonable. What would it have been like if the adult you counted on couldn't be counted on to even take care of himself, much less you?

No wonder Ted had a great big hero complex. He'd been rescuing everyone around him his whole life, even when he was alone.

Could I be someone to count on for whatever little tadpole was swimming inside me right now? Would I be a source of security or a source of instability? I didn't exactly get to call the shots in my own life. How would that impact a kid who was counting on me?

The door buzzed open in front of me and I walked onto the ward. I dropped the stack of lab results off at the nurse's desk, made some small talk with the little Filipino nurse at the counter and looked around.

It didn't take me long to figure out which patient was my partial dryad in distress. First of all, she had that tall-slender-blonde thing going for her. Second, she was pressed up against the reinforced glass in the common room, staring at the leaves of the oak tree outside it as if they were communicating with her. Third, she gave me a tingle.

I walked up next to her. "Willow?" I asked.

She turned toward me, but it took a while. Willow's synapses weren't exactly firing at 100 percent efficiency. Whatever kind of joy juice they had her on looked like it was pretty powerful.

"Do I know you?" she asked.

"No, but I have something for you," I said, keeping my voice low.

Her brow furrowed and she stepped back. "What kind of thing?"

"Something good," I said. "Something that will make you feel better." I slipped the piece of bark out of my pocket and held it out toward her.

She looked at it, but didn't reach for it. "What is that?"

"It's a message from someone who wants to help you." I held it out a little closer to her, but tried to shield it from view from behind us.

"It's part of a tree." She stared at the bark, but didn't make a move to take it. Of course, her reflexes weren't exactly snappy right now.

"Yes, it is." I confirmed her statement of what was obvious to me, but might not be to her, given her present situation.

"They said that the tree stuff I've been seeing isn't real. Are you sure that's real?" She looked truly concerned.

Man, the docs were doing a real head trip on this poor girl. Not that it was entirely their fault. They thought they were helping. What's that saying about hell and good intentions and pavement? "They may not be one hundred percent right about that, but I don't think you should argue with them. The more you agree with them, the sooner you'll get out of here. I don't think you belong here, Willow."

She turned back to the window and pressed her hand to the glass. "I'm not so sure about that anymore."

That came close to breaking my heart. I'd been confused plenty of times, but never about whether or not I belonged locked up. "I am and so is the, uh, person who asked me to give this to you. Will you take it, Willow? There's an address on the back. You should go there when you get out of here."

"Are you real?" she asked.

"Yep. Absolutely. One hundred percent real." Of course, what would a hallucination say to her? I wondered what I'd have to do to convince her.

She thought about it for a few minutes more. I was starting to get nervous. The last thing I needed was for one of the nurses to come through and catch me trying to give tree bark with an address written on it to their weird tree girl. Finally she reached out her hand and took the bark.

And nothing happened. I'm not sure precisely what I expected. Maybe some sort of light breaking through the window and the sound of angels. Or a smile. Or the crackle of static electricity. There was nothing. Willow did smile a little bit, but only a little bit. Maybe, given all the drugs she was on, it was more like a big giant grin and I didn't know it.

"They're not going to let me keep this," she said then, looking down at the bark.

"Then you better hide it really well," I suggested. "I've heard the light fixtures in the bathroom aren't a bad spot for that kind of thing." With any luck, the bulb wouldn't get hot enough to burn the bark.

She nodded. "Yeah. Really well." Then she walked away toward the rooms.

I went back to the door, waited to be buzzed through and started back to the emergency room. I glanced at my watch. I'd been gone a little longer than I'd expected. Hopefully no one would have noticed yet. A girl can dream, right?

As I rounded the corner, I found Jenny lounging against the wall near the entrance. I glanced around, wondering what other people saw when they saw her.

Sometimes everyone can see the things I see. Everyone sees Alex and Paul and Meredith. I suppose I should say they see parts of them. I don't think they see them the way I do. Otherwise people would be running screaming down the sidewalks in front of them.

Sometimes people don't see what I see at all, though. Brownies are a good example of that. Gremlins also. People seem to notice movement, kind of like when you catch something out of the corner of your eye and then when you turn to look at it directly, there's nothing there. There probably was something there.

Judging by the way people glanced at Jenny, they saw her, if not everything she was. It was good to know because then I could talk to her in public without people locking me up next to Willow. The idea that I had imaginary friends was cute to people when I was six. Now that I'm staring at thirty, they don't find it as adorable.

"So?" Jenny asked.

"So I gave her the item."

"And?" She pressed.

"And nothing. She took it. She's worried that the nurses will find it and take it away from her." I grimaced.

"Crap. I hadn't thought of that." Jenny chewed on her lower lip for a second. "What do you suggest?"

I stepped back. "I have no suggestions. I delivered the item. That's what I do. I don't suggest."

"Oh, come on. Everyone knows you do way more than suggest. Help a sister out, will you?"

I'm not sure she realized her comments on my reputation weren't exactly winning her any favors with me. Some 'Canes don't have a lot of social skills. "I don't know, Jenny. You could come back when you think she's going to be released and see if you can intercept her as she's leaving."

She cocked her head to one side, her blonde hair

gleaming even under the fluorescent bulbs of the hospital hallway. "Not bad. It might work." Then she smiled at me. "Thanks, Melina. It's been a pleasure doing business."

I shook her hand and watched her go, then went back in to my desk.

7

I HAD TIME AFTER I LEFT THE HOSPITAL TO GET SOME coffee and change into a *gi* before I got to the karate studio. I found myself looking at my Little Dragons that morning with a completely different eye than I'd ever looked at them with before. Was the little person forming inside me going to be a completely fearless little person like Tiffany Gutierrez or a whiney little brat like Jackson Burton? I felt like I could handle either of those contingencies, but what if he or she was a sneaky mean little thing like Miles Watson? What would I do then? Was there something I could eat or take now that would keep that from happening?

I'd read some website that claimed you could determine gender, but I think you had to be doing all that during the conception portion of the proceedings. We were clearly well past that point. I wasn't exactly sure how far past, but definitely past. I wasn't far enough along yet that an ultrasound would tell me gender. Which didn't mean I shouldn't go get one. Or at least go to a doctor. Or something.

Then again, that meant telling someone and I still wanted to tell Ted first. I just had to work up the courage to do it.

I let Sophie take the Little Dragons through their warm-ups. She had a nice way with kids, way better than I had. She was easy with them, having fun without ever letting go of her authority. It wasn't an easy line to walk. It had taken me years of watching Mae and trying myself before I found it. Sophie had it naturally. Even with her hair pulled back and the scars on the side of her face from her car accident fully visible, she had a kind of un-self-conscious confidence that I still didn't have.

The group of twelve kids on the mat wiggled and hopped and giggled across the floor, stretching and warming up as they did. Then I stepped onto the mat.

Everyone went silent and the kids shoved their way into a straight line. Sophie bowed to me and then the kids did, too. It wasn't always a bad thing to be sensei.

It certainly made it easier to deal with the kids. They didn't expect me to be fun. I was the authority figure. The Big Kahuna. How would that work with my own kid, though?

I started the kids through a couple of drills, mainly stuff that we'd done before. It helped build their confidence at the beginning of a class to do a few things they were already familiar with before we started something new.

I thought about little Justine. I hadn't had much of a touch with her. She'd taken an instant dislike to me. What if it was like the trouble I had with dogs? What if all little kids instantly either disliked or feared me? What kind of parent would I be?

I added one new move to the series we'd been doing and about half the class managed to trip themselves and fall down. We started over.

The truth was, I still had options. No one knew, except Grandma Rosie and she clearly wasn't telling anyone. I still had a choice, although possibly not for a whole lot longer.

Before I made any of those choices, though, I was going to have to tell Ted. I really didn't want to think about that, so the lucky Little Dragons suddenly got my full attention once again.

I TOOK ANOTHER NAP AND THEN WENT TO FIND CHUCK. He wasn't at his house, but after a fair amount of wheedling, the man who answered the door told me he was at a job site and where to find him.

I wound my way through some back roads to a house that stood fairly far off the street. It was huge and new looking. I wondered what could possibly need re-doing in a place like this. I found him on the driveway, looking at some plans.

"Melina, so nice to see you again. To what do I owe the pleasure?" Chuck hadn't even turned around. He looked far more comfortable out here, a tool belt slung around his hips, than he did behind the desk in his office. Let's face it. He looked good in general. Werewolves age well and Chuck was no exception. It wasn't the first time I wondered how old he was now and how old he'd been when he'd been turned.

I don't exactly have a great eye for architecture, style or design, but even I could tell the remodel he was working on was going to be magnificent. Big and open and airy. Positioned on its lot in a way that made it look like the trees had grown that way to welcome it.

"Have you heard from Paul?" I asked, still hopeful that all my fears would prove to be ridiculous.

"Nope. You?"

I shook my head.

"Well, this has been nice, but it hardly seems worth the drive," he observed, still not really looking at me.

"I have some other questions, Chuck. Do you have a minute?" I scuffed my toe in the dirt.

Now he turned, watched me for a second and then turned away again. He put his fingers to his lips and emitted an ear-piercing whistle. "Yo, Sam. I'm taking a break. Melina's here with more questions."

Sam, the same werewolf that had been at the hardware store, poked his head out from behind some framing where I hadn't seen him before. "Hey, Melina. How's it going?"

"Great. You?"

"Couldn't be better."

Chuck and I walked away from the construction, down toward the street. "So what do you want to know now?"

"What do you know about Michael Hollinger and Leanne McMannis?" I asked, cutting right to the chase.

Chuck looked over at me, clearly confused. "Who?"

"Michael Hollinger and Leanne McMannis," I repeated, just in case he hadn't heard me correctly.

"I have no idea who those people are. Should I?" He sounded concerned.

"Yeah. I think you should." I outlined what had happened in both cases, as far as I knew.

"So this woman saw what looked like two creatures halfway between werewolf and human in her garage?" Chuck asked.

"That's what it sounded like to me, except wouldn't they have continued changing?" I still wasn't sure. I know a lot about werewolves, but I'm by no means as expert as someone who actually is one.

Chuck didn't answer. He kept walking. His pace sped up, though. I hurried myself a bit to keep up with him.

"Why am I only hearing about this now?" he asked.

It wasn't exactly my job to keep him posted on werewolf news you can use. "I just found out. How would you normally find out?"

He scowled. "It's part of Kevin's job to keep his ear to the ground and let me know about any werewolf activity in the area."

"You think these were werewolves, then?" I still wasn't convinced.

He stopped, thank goodness. I was getting out of breath. The air was thinner up here. "I don't know. I know we should have been checking into it. How long ago did this happen?"

"McMannis's house was broken into about two days before the last full moon. Hollinger was bitten about two weeks ago."

"And he's where? This Hollinger guy?" Chuck's foot tapped the ground.

"The psych ward." I shuddered a little bit.

Chuck rubbed his hand over his face. "That's not good. How are they containing him?"

"In a straitjacket in a locked room."

"That's not going to last. Someone's going to get hurt." Chuck's scowl deepened.

Duh. "I think someone already has."

Chuck shot a look at me. "I get that, Melina. No need to get on your high horse. No one in this pack bit that man. If they're the same things that were in that woman's garage, then I'm not sure we're even talking wolves here. I do know that if it's anything like lycanthropy, we need to get him out of that ward before the full moon."

I'd been thinking the same thing. "How exactly do you propose to do that?"

I got the look again. "Do you really want to know that?

Wouldn't it be better to have a little plausible deniability with that cop boyfriend of yours?"

He had a point there, but I didn't much like him bringing Ted into it. Between that and Jenny's comments, I was feeling like my personal business was a little too hot a subject on the 'Cane gossip channel these days. "I can handle my cop boyfriend."

"I have no doubt about that. I'm not so sure he can handle you." Chuck laughed.

His laughter rang in my ears all the way home.

THE NEXT AFTERNOON, SOPHIE AND I HAD FINISHED sweeping the back of the dojo when we both felt the presence of something. I felt it first and then saw Sophie's head shoot up. Then she got very still.

"What is it?" she asked. She still couldn't distinguish between different types of paranormal presences. Of course, I hadn't been able to before about six months ago either. I wondered if it was a talent she'd develop. I'd never developed a special skill for knife throwing, which she obviously had.

"Werewolf," I answered. Strong, musky, virile. For a second, my heart leapt. Could it be Paul? Was he back? I focused harder. No. Not Paul. It was familiar, though, a wolf I'd met. Still, it was probably better not to take chances. Just because it was a devil you knew didn't mean it was a devil you wanted to hang out with after dark in a strip mall parking lot.

We heard the first knock on the front door. Sophie jumped. I put a hand on her arm to steady her. She looked at me, her eyes wide. "A werewolf who knocks?"

The Pack wasn't exactly known for its manners. I figured this must be a good sign. "You stay here," I said. It's not like the Pack didn't know she existed. I'm pretty sure they did.

I hadn't exactly tried to keep her hidden. Even with a polite werewolf knocking on the door, I still wanted to keep her safe. That's me. Always thinking safety first. Maybe I wouldn't totally suck as a mom.

I walked out of the back and onto the mat, peering out into the dark to see who was there. I probably looked like I was on a stage set with all the lights on and the plate glass windows. I couldn't make out much of what was outside, though. A shape. Vaguely manlike. That's all I had.

I walked to the front door and the shape stepped into the light from the streetlamp outside in the parking lot.

Sam. I blew out a breath and a little tension with it and unlocked the door.

"Dude, you scared me half to death. What are you doing here?"

He stepped inside. Werewolves didn't have to wait for an invitation like vampires did. "Sorry. I was in the neighborhood and thought I'd stop by."

"In the neighborhood?" We were a good long way from his home.

He shrugged. "Kevin sent me down here to pick up some stuff from a tile place that's nearby. For the kitchen of that place you stopped by."

Okay. That sounded reasonable. "So this is a social call?"

Again with the shrug. "Not exactly. I was wondering if you'd made any progress on finding Paul."

"Come on in." I gestured for him to follow me into the office. Once we were settled, I said, "I haven't heard anything from Paul. Have you?"

Sam shook his head. "No. No one has. At least, no one who's talking about it."

"Who's talking?" I leaned forward on my elbows, eager to hear what he had to say.

He laughed. "Pretty much everybody. The Pack is getting restless. He's been gone too long without anyone hearing from him. They want someone to take some action."

That was news to me. Chuck clearly wanted me to stay away and I don't think Kevin could have been much clearer either. "What kind of action?"

"That's part of the problem. No one knows what to do. I figured I'd stop by here and see what you'd found out. I mean, I knew you'd been asking questions. Maybe if I knew what you knew, I could help." He glanced behind himself. "Is someone else here?"

I hesitated for a second and walked to the door of the office. "Sophie," I called.

She came out of the back of the dojo. "Yeah?"

"Come on in here. I'd like you to meet Sam."

She walked across the mat to the door, her long braid swinging behind her, her stride steady and sure. She'd come a long way from the shy little thing who had hidden the scars running down the side of her face with her hair when she'd come to the door. I felt a moment of pride.

I'd done that. Well, not alone, but still, I'd helped Sophie blossom into this confident young woman. I introduced her to Sam and they shook hands.

"Messenger in training?" he asked.

She smiled. "Basically."

"You like it?" He lounged back, his legs crossed at the ankle.

"It beats wondering why you're seeing weird stuff that no one else sees," she said with a laugh.

Sam laughed, too. "I suppose so."

Sophie flung her braid behind her back and I caught a glint in Sam's eye. Damn it. This was not what I needed right now. A Messenger/werewolf romance? No no no.

I broke into their conversation. "You can go, Sophie. We're done here. I'm just going to chat with Sam for a few minutes about Paul."

"That's okay. I have to wait another fifteen minutes anyway. Ben's picking me up." She smiled.

Great. I doubt Ben would be any happier to see the sparks flying between Sophie and Sam than I was.

"Okay. Go ahead and wait in the foyer, then."

Luckily Sophie took the hint and left the office. I pulled the door shut behind her.

Sam was watching me, one eyebrow cocked. "Don't you trust her?"

"Of course. She's young, though." *It's you I don't trust,* I thought.

He nodded. "I heard you were younger when you started."

Again with the gossip. I sat down. "Where'd you hear that?"

"Around." He shrugged.

Fine. Whatever. "So how restless is the Pack?" I changed the subject back to what I wanted to know about.

"Pretty restless. Folks are starting to grumble about Chuck not taking action. They think he should be doing something."

"Like what? Tacking up flyers to telephone poles?" I could just see it. A cute picture of Paul with "Lost Were-wolf" underneath it and those little tags to pull off with a phone number.

"Organizing search parties, maybe. Something."

"What does Kevin think?"

Sam sank farther back in his chair. "I don't know. He's . . . distracted these days."

"Distracted by what?" I wondered if Inge was part of

Kevin's problem. Someone who can make your brackets spontaneously go on sale could be an issue.

"I'm not sure about that either. I just know he disappears sometimes now, which he never used to do, and he doesn't seem very focused." Sam's fingers drummed on the arm of the chair.

That was interesting. "Disappears to where?"

"If I knew, it wouldn't be a disappearance. He doesn't have to check in with me. I just know that there are times when I expect him to be at the shop and he's nowhere around." Sam fidgeted more. Talking about Kevin was clearly making him uncomfortable.

"How often?" I asked.

"A few times a week."

"And you have no idea where?"

"Nope."

"And no one else does either?"

"Haven't asked."

I shot him a look.

He held up his hands. "How can you still not get this? I can't question Kevin. I can't question Chuck. Not unless I'm ready and willing to challenge them and I'm not. They're older, stronger and more powerful."

He was right. I did know that. "You can't even ask a guy where he's headed?"

He shook his head. "Some guys you might ask. Not Kevin."

I remembered the sense of Kevin's barely controlled rage at just seeing me in his shop and figured I could understand Sam's reluctance to quiz his boss on his comings and goings. "I'll see what I can find out on the down low."

"Thanks. You haven't learned anything yet?"

I hesitated. "Do the names Michael Hollinger or Leann McMannis mean anything to you?"

He shook his head. "No. Should they?"

"I don't know. I know they mean something. I'm just not sure what."

"I'll keep my ear to the ground."

I sort of wondered if he meant that literally, but decided not to ask.

He unfolded himself out of the chair and headed toward the door. "Maybe I'll go see if I can find anything at his cabin," he said.

Paul had a cabin? "Has anyone else been up there?"

"Of course. Chuck and Kevin both checked up there for him."

Damn it. Had they really? "Would you take me there?"

Sam looked a little uncomfortable. "They wouldn't say he wasn't there if he was. Or if there was some kind of sign that something else was wrong, they wouldn't hide it from the Pack."

"No, but sometimes I look for the ketchup in the refrigerator five times and don't see it and Norah can find it the first time she looks. We don't all see things the same way. I have some 'looking' skills, if you will, that you guys don't have."

Sam thought for a second. "Sure. Meet me tomorrow. I'll take you there."

We agreed on a place to meet and he left.

A cabin in the woods. Occupied by a werewolf. Nah. That didn't sound menacing at all.

MY FATHER HAS POINTED OUT THAT OUR FAMILY COMES by our general lack of sense of direction naturally. After all, our people wandered for forty years in a very small desert without ever figuring out how to get out of it.

I am the exception to the rule. It's like I have a compass in my head. Twirl me around blindfolded and I can still point which direction is north. I have no idea whether this is part and parcel of being a Messenger or if it's just me. I was too little when I slipped into the family swimming pool behind my mother's back and drowned to always figure out what's me and what's Messenger. I was only three at the time. At this point, it doesn't really matter anyway. I've been a Messenger nearly my whole life, so being a Messenger is being me, I guess. Or, at least, that's how I'm starting to feel.

I don't remember feeling all that different when I woke up after being dead for three minutes, but I was and nothing was ever the same again. I doubt I'll ever know if I could head east into the setting sun like my brother did recently if none of that had happened. It's one of the conundrums of my life as a Messenger and a Markowitz.

Regardless of that compass, I don't know if I would have been able to find Paul's cabin on my own. Between the turns on unmarked roads and the twists and turns those roads took once I got on them, I might still know which way was north, but I had no idea which way to go.

"Turn right here," Sam said.

I turned up the road that he indicated, although designating it a road was being extremely generous. Calling what we were on already a road would have been generous, and this was a little fork off of that. "So do you know the way here or are you tracking your way?" I asked.

"A little of both. I've been here a few times. Not always like this." He smiled at me as he gestured down at his body.

It took me a few seconds to get what he meant. He'd been here in his wolf form. He probably took a somewhat different route then, one that didn't require any roads at all. "Are you and Paul . . . close?"

He shrugged. "We're Pack," he said as if that was explanation enough.

It was, in some ways. It was a little like saying you were family, but with an added dose of violence. "I appreciate you taking the time to show me the way."

"I'm glad someone is doing something. He's been gone too long." He didn't turn to look at me as he spoke, but kept his eyes on the road in front of us instead.

"Has it been a problem?" I knew what Chuck had told me. It would be interesting to hear it from some other wolf's perspective. Chuck might have his extremely sensitive ear to the ground, but that didn't mean he knew everything that was going on in his pack.

Sam's brow furrowed. "It's not like we're not used to Paul being gone from time to time. He takes off all the time. We usually know when he's going to be back, though. And when he's around, he . . . balances things out. Things don't feel quite right with him gone like this. At least, not to me." Sam sighed and shifted in his seat.

I knew how he felt. It was like something in my life was a bit out of kilter with Paul not on the scene. "How about the other wolves, then? What is it like to them?"

"I don't think I can speak for anybody but myself. I know Kevin thinks everyone is overreacting, that Paul will turn up on his own and we'll all feel silly. I'm not so sure, though."

That sounded like an echo of Chuck's opinion. Maybe I was being an alarmist. Lord knows, my mother has called me a Negative Nellie more than once in my life.

"Are Paul and Kevin friends?" Paul had never really

mentioned Kevin by name, but he was pretty careful about who he mentioned. I never did hear a lot of names.

Sam looked over at me, his head cocked to one side as if he didn't understand the question. "They're Pack."

I wondered what it was like to have life be that simple. You're Pack or you're not Pack. I'm not sure if I've ever been able to view anything as that black-and-white in my whole life. I wasn't sure I wanted to either. Twenty-eight years of existing in the margins have given me an appreciation of the gray areas in both my worlds. Still, black-and-white aside, Pack politics could be complicated even if, in the end, they were usually resolved in the simplest of ways: by one werewolf ripping out the throat of another and feasting on his or her blood.

Just because you're Pack doesn't mean you like each other. It does usually mean you have each other's back, though.

"Can you track?" Sam asked, breaking the silence. He was a nice boy, making conversation like that.

"Some. Not like you guys. And definitely not from inside a car."

"I hear that." He nodded. "All those smells . . . the gas, the rubber, the electrical wiring. It scrambles me up. Paul's place is right up ahead."

Suddenly there it was. It looked exactly like a place where Paul would live. Clean, simple, but oh so very manly. It was truly a cabin. Moderately rustic. All rough-hewn logs with two Adirondack chairs on the porch. The area around the cabin had been cleared, but not planted. It looked like some place the guy on Brawny paper towels would live.

I stepped out of the car and stood for a second, trying to let my senses open, trying to feel some kind of pull in one direction or another that would tell me where Paul had gone.

"Wanna go inside?" Sam asked, stretching his arms and back. "He never locks it."

Why would he? Who would find it, much less burglarize it? I nodded and we walked up the porch steps and into the cabin. Inside there was . . . nothing. I mean, there were rugs and lamps and furniture, although not much of it. A couch. One chair. A coffee table. A small dinette set. A rug on the floor by the couch. There wasn't much else, though. There was certainly no sign of a struggle. If someone or something had taken Paul, they hadn't done it from in here. I can't imagine what it would take to move that man if he didn't want to be moved, but I'm pretty sure it would leave destruction in its path.

There also wasn't much of a residue of Paul-ness, for the lack of a better word. I didn't feel his presence here. He hadn't been here for a while. There was a slight scent of him, but no magical signature vibration, and the scent could be from anything. Clothes. Furniture. Sheets. Towels.

"Do you sense anything?" I asked Sam. "Smell anything?"

Sam lifted his head and scented the air. I'd seen Paul do it a hundred times. Maybe a thousand. I'd seen him do it when a familiar scent crossed his path, like when Ted or Alex or Meredith walked into his bar. I'd seen him do it when he was hunting for something, too.

Sam shook his head. "The bread over there is moldy. That's all I'm getting, though."

Bummer. "My turn," I said. I shut my eyes, tried to go to a place of calm and tranquility and opened my senses as far and wide as I could. I probably didn't look all that different than Sam had a second ago. I tilted back my head and breathed in. It was a totally different thing, though.

Werewolves hunt like, well, wolves. Their senses are

crazy sharp. Not quite as sharp in human form as they are in wolf form, but still way sharper than any regular person. They can smell and hear and taste and see with great acuity. Me? I can smell and hear and taste and see more sharply than most people, but not anywhere as well as a werewolf can. I also, however, sense magic.

I wish I could describe it. I've never been able to. Of course, until recently, there wasn't anyone I needed to describe it to. No one knew I was a Messenger except Mae, and since she was already a Messenger herself, I didn't need to explain much of anything to her.

Sometimes now, though, Ted would ask. Or Norah. They wanted to know what I felt. I didn't really have words for it. It was definitely like a vibration, but it was almost electrical in how it felt. Lately, too, there's been more of a flavor to it, but it was all mixed up. Like I could feel tastes in my flesh and smell the colors of what I was hearing.

At first, there was nothing. No buzz. No shiver. Then there was the tiniest of tingles. It was faint, but it was there. I opened my eyes and looked at Sam. "This way," I said and walked out of the cabin.

It's not like I knew where I was going precisely. I just knew which way to walk. We went out behind the cabin, away from the piddling excuse of a road. "Do you think it's him?" Sam asked, his voice tense and excited.

I shook my head. It didn't have the musky earthy feeling of a werewolf. It had magic to it, definitely. Although maybe whatever it was wasn't precisely magical, but had been made by something magical. Objects of power were funny like that. They might not be magical all on their own, but they held a bit of the tingle of whatever had made or wielded them. Whatever it was definitely wasn't alive. I wasn't sure if that was a relief or not.

"Where are you going? What is it?" Sam stayed behind me, but I could feel his excitement and it was distracting. I held my hand up to signal for him to stay back. I wasn't going to try to explain it to him now. He wouldn't understand anyway. Werewolves don't sense inanimate objects the way I do. Nor are they subtle, and whatever I was sensing was definitely that. Subtle. Delicate. Nuanced.

I kept walking. There was no path and I had to go slow to crawl over the occasional fallen tree and simply to watch my step. I didn't even realize I'd gone past whatever it was until it was well behind me. The vibration of it shifted, from a buzz that made me want to clench my teeth together, to a tension in my shoulders and back. I turned and headed back.

"Where are you going?" Sam demanded again. I held up my hand again to hush him. Whatever it was, it wasn't big and it wasn't strong. I needed to focus if I was going to find it.

He growled. Someone wasn't used to taking orders from those outside the Pack. Too darned bad. I glared. He hushed.

I headed back in the direction I'd come, but with slower steps. Again, I went past, but now in the opposite direction. It was like playing a game of Hot and Cold with a totally passive-aggressive playmate. I turned again, my steps even more measured.

Here. It was right here. But how? There wasn't anything. I stopped turning. Stopped looking. I opened my other senses. It was to my right. I shifted and opened my eyes again and saw a glint of something in the underbrush by some ferny looking plant.

I bent to look at it. It looked like a piece of netting, very fine and delicate. It glinted in the sun because it was made of metal. When I reached down to pick it up, I got an electric shock as if I'd been shuffling my feet across a carpet on a winter day.

8

"YOU OKAY?" SAM ASKED, AS I BACKED INTO HIM AND away from the shiny lace.

"Uh, sure," I said, shaking my hand to get rid of the pins-and-needles sensation touching the lace had caused. I squatted down to get a closer look at it.

"You want me to pick it up for you?" Sam offered, starting to reach for it as he asked. Then he snatched his hand back and yelped like a puppy who'd had his tail stepped on.

There are a lot of myths about mythological and paranormal beings. I've never, for instance, seen a vampire turn into a bat or recoil from garlic, and they totally have reflections. I have, however, seen a werewolf writhe in agony after coming in contact with pure silver. I didn't know how pure this was, but it was pure enough to have burnt Sam's fingers.

Sam gave me a hurt look. "Why didn't you warn me?"

I gave him my best apologetic look. "I didn't know. It zapped me, but not because it was silver."

"You think it's pure silver?" He squatted down next to me to look at the piece of lace, but kept a healthy distance from it.

I'm not a metalsmith, but I've seen more than my share of objects of power. In my experience, the purer the material the object is made from, the greater its power. This little piece of net had a fairly significant mojo to it, more than I thought it would if it was some kind of alloy. I sat back on my heels. "Maybe. Probably, even."

I glanced around. Objects tended to be more powerful if their makers were in close proximity, too. "Is there anything close to here? Another cabin? A town?"

Sam shook his head. "When Paul wanted to be private, he wanted to be really private."

That sounded like him. He wasn't a man of muddled motivations except for one area and that would be Meredith. I totally understood. Wanting someone or something that you didn't want to want wasn't a whole lot of fun and he definitely wanted Meredith and wanted not to want her at the same time. I often felt the same way about my mother's Bundt cakes.

I cast around. I didn't sense anything that could have made this lace. Of course, between Sam sitting right next to me and the lace sitting right in front of me, my Messenger senses were getting a little jammed. Plus the woods were full of life. Birds sang in the trees and squirrels chattered in the bushes, not to mention all the insects. Sometimes I felt like there were more distractions out in the country than there were in the city.

I looked around the area. I couldn't decide if the grass looked torn up or if that was simply its natural state of wildness. "What do you see?" I asked Sam.

He squinted in concentration. Then he pointed. "There and there." He pointed to a third area. "Maybe there, too. The grass seems more trampled and that branch over there is freshly cracked. I think there might have been a scuffle here. But, Melina, it would take more than a scuffle to take down Paul."

I nodded. "That's what I thought, too. Plus lace doesn't seem like much of a weapon, even if it is silver." If the mark of a true professional was the ability to play with pain, then Paul was definitely a professional werewolf. He could withstand a lot.

I pulled my sleeve down over my hand and picked up the piece of lace. I could still feel its buzz, but it wasn't strong enough to make me drop it. "Let's go," I said, standing up.

The world whirled, the edges of my vision went gray, and I nearly dropped the lace.

"Are you all right?" Sam asked, catching me by the elbow and steadying me.

I held still for a second. Everything righted itself and my peripheral vision returned. "Yeah. Just a little head rush. I guess I was squatting down there too long."

Sam nodded, but didn't say anything. I slipped my elbow out of his grasp and headed back to the Buick.

I was pretty sure I'd seen everything there was to see there, not that there was much. I was coming away with not much more than the vague sense of unease that I'd started with.

I knew what I'd been hoping. I'd been hoping we'd get to the cabin and Paul would be sitting on the front porch, drinking a beer and enjoying his solitude. That he'd chide me for worrying about him and send me back to town.

Failing that, I suppose I would have liked some clear-cut sign that something bad had happened to him. The presence of pure silver near his place wasn't a good sign, but the stuff looked so fine and fragile and it was such a little scrap of a thing, I couldn't imagine it being much of a deterrent for him. Sure, it would hurt like bloody hell if he touched it, but werewolves have a ridiculously high pain tolerance.

I was guessing it meant something, but hell if I knew what it was.

I LAID THE SILVER LACE IN THE MIDDLE OF THE COFFEE table so Ted, Alex and Norah could see it. "I found this up by Paul's cabin."

"Pretty," Norah said, reaching for it.

Ted grabbed her wrist before she touched it, then looked at me. "Is it okay for her to pick it up?"

"As far as I can tell. It doesn't seem to have any special power. I think whoever made it might have had a lot, though." There was an interesting buzz to it, but it seemed to hover around it rather than infuse it. The buzz had quieted some since I'd driven back down the hill from Paul's place.

Ted released Norah's wrist and she picked up the silver, apparently receiving not the slightest jolt from it. It really was beautiful. The silver had been stretched into a fine filigree, and even though this was just a fragment, there was clearly an intricate pattern woven through it. It reminded me of a snowflake.

"I'm pretty sure it's pure silver." I glanced over at Alex. He had a few hundred years on me of knowing what was up in the world, both Arcane and Mundane. "Have you ever seen anything like it?"

Alex shook his head. "Not that I can think of offhand. That's all there was of it?"

He was right. It wasn't much. It wasn't even the size of a handkerchief. I nodded and explained where I'd found it. "I can't imagine Paul wanting something like that around."

Alex took it from Norah and gave it a tug. "It's pretty tough for how delicate it looks. Still . . ."

"I know," I said.

"Care to let us in on the secret?" Ted asked.

I glanced at him to see if he was feeling testy. Ted took the whole protect-and-serve thing of being a police officer pretty seriously and it was darn hard to protect people if you had no idea what was out there. At the moment, however, he just looked curious.

"There's damn little in the world that can stop a were-wolf, but silver can definitely slow them down." Alex lifted it up into the light. "There's not much of it here, though."

Quantity definitely mattered nearly as much as quality when it came to how dangerous silver might be to a were-wolf. "It would have to be huge to bring him down. Plus I think I would have seen more of a sign of a struggle." A few beaten down clumps of grass weren't nearly enough.

"Maybe, maybe not. It doesn't feel right, though, does it?" Alex mused.

"Not in the least little bit," I agreed.

Norah looked over at me, eyes wide. "But you said that it didn't have any special powers."

"I don't think it does." It was odd to me, however, that whoever had forged it hadn't given it more powers than that. I have handled a lot of different kinds of objects during my years as a Messenger and there's a wide variety of them and the kinds of powers they can contain. Not everything made for a magical purpose was magical in and of itself. This lace or whatever it was being a case in point.

More often, though, objects made by supernatural beings had powers in and of themselves. It made them more useful. Even 'Canes liked to multitask. Why not have a net that could maybe put someone to sleep as well? Or make them tell the truth? This seemed to be just a net. I turned to Alex. "Why not give it more powers than that, though?"

He shoved his dark hair off his forehead. "Good question.

Maybe they didn't want whoever got hold of it to have too much power."

"It looks like a net to me," I said, expressing my worst fears about it.

"It does," Alex agreed.

"I happen to know someone who knows a lot about nets." I didn't like to hang out with her much, but I could find her if I needed to.

Alex couldn't keep the smile off his face. "You're going to see Cordelia? For a favor?"

"Information is not a favor." Of course, Cordie might not see it that way. I'd better go prepared with something she'd like.

"Good luck with that."

He was right. I'd need it.

SO IF I DON'T MAKE A DELIVERY, THERE ARE REPERCUS-sions. I've only deliberately not delivered something once and quite honestly that was plenty for me. I didn't think anything would happen to me if something was taken away from someone after I delivered it, but quite honestly, it was bugging me. I couldn't stop thinking about Willow up on the psych ward, and something Sophie had said the night before to Sam had really brought that home.

There'd never been a time when I'd had to question what I was seeing or hearing. By the time I'd figured out how abnormal I was, abnormal was my normal. I'm sure there was a time that it was confusing, but I was too little to understand how confusing it was.

I've always been a little jealous of Sophie. I feel like coming into being a Messenger as a teenager has given her some opportunities and perspective that I didn't have coming into it as a toddler. I'd been so busy looking at how much greener her grass was that it hadn't occurred to me that I was rolling in some pretty verdant stuff myself.

What would it be like to suddenly start seeing things no one else saw, or hearing things that no one else heard? I figure it could make somebody bat-shit crazy.

Willow hadn't had anybody at all and look where she was, all 5150ed up in a locked ward.

I found some more lab results that needed delivering. "Hey, Connor," I sang out as I breezed into the lab. "I was passing by. You have anything that needs delivering up on seven? I'm headed there next."

Connor leaned over the counter and stared at me with a really funny expression on his face. "Oh, you are, are you?"

He looked pained, like maybe his stomach hurt really bad. "Um, yeah. Are you okay?"

"Oh, I am fine, Melina. Absolutely fine." He held a handful of folders out to me, just a little bit out of my reach.

Now, in all fairness, I could have been over the counter and back with the folders in my hands before Connor even recognized that my feet had left the floor. At least, I thought I still could. I didn't think the whole bun-in-the-oven thing had slowed me down too much yet. While it would be fun, it didn't seem wise, so I just put my hand out.

Connor didn't budge with the folders. "Do you want me to take them or not?" I asked.

"Oh, I want you to take them, sweetheart." He leaned even farther over the counter.

Was he leering? Over lab results? Why wasn't he looking at my face? I'd had enough. The folders were within reach without jumping the counter. I snagged them from his hand. "Great. See you later."

I left him staring at his empty hand.

I WENT THROUGH THE DOUBLE-BUZZING ROUTINE AGAIN and dropped the folders off. I'd already seen Willow in the common room looking out the window. I slipped in while the nurse was busy filing the lab results.

"Hey, Willow," I said, sitting down next to her.

She turned toward me before I even spoke. She didn't even look like she was moving underwater anymore. "Hi. Melina, right?"

"Yeah. That's right. How are you feeling?"

"A lot better. Thanks." She glanced around the common room and then stretched the cuff of her sweatshirt out a little bit so I could see the edge of the bark against her skin.

"They didn't take it?" Wow. I was surprised.

Willow smiled. "I hid it really well."

She must have. If there was anything the staff of the psych ward was good at, it was figuring out who had contraband and where they'd stashed it. They had to be good at it. The people up here were here because they were a threat to themselves or others. It was amazing what they could turn into weapons. The staff had to be super-vigilant. "Nice work."

She slid it back up her cuff. "It's like I knew where to put it. It's almost like it told me itself."

I knew how that felt, too. I had a pretty good rapport with inanimate objects. I didn't know too many other people who did, though. Was this another burgeoning Messenger? "Has that happened to you before?"

She shook her head. "No. Just this. I really appreciate you getting this to me, though." She leaned toward me and whispered. "Before I had it, I sort of thought I might really be going crazy."

I could see how she could have come to that conclusion,

what with the special jacket that made her hug herself and the padded room.

"I'm glad you're feeling better. How much longer are you here for?"

"One more day."

"You have a ride when you get out?"

She nodded. "So what exactly are you?" She cocked her head to one side and looked me up and down as if really seeing me for the first time. It was good to see how much more alert she was than when I first met her. Her eyes were clearer and her blonde hair was a lot cleaner.

The extra alertness came at a price, though. I didn't really want to explain too much about myself. Willow had enough to absorb at the moment. "I'm just the Messenger. No one to worry about."

She wrapped her arms around herself. "But there are things to worry about, aren't there?"

My mom was always honest with me. I didn't always like it, but I always knew that I could trust her. At this point in my life, I'd rather be trusted than liked. I didn't want to freak Willow out any farther than she'd already freaked herself. I mean, she'd managed to freak herself all the way into a locked ward. On the other hand, I didn't want her to think there were nothing but rainbows and unicorns awaiting her when she finally got out of the locked ward. "Yeah. There are things you should definitely be afraid of."

"How will I know?"

"Jenny will explain a lot of it. Some of it is a matter of experience, though. It's a pretty gray world out there. Things aren't completely black-and-white." Wasn't that an understatement? I was actually happy that my roommate was dating a vampire. That was confusing. One of my best friends was a werewolf. Neither of those groups made it onto anybody's "good guy" list, but both of those examples definitely made it onto my list of people to trust. More than trust. I relied on them.

"That sounds . . . scary." She folded her hands carefully in her lap as if to consciously keep them still. I wondered if she was trying not to finger the piece of bark she had hidden up her sleeve.

"Sometimes it is," I admitted.

She blew out a breath. "I suppose not as scary as not knowing if any of it was real or not. That sucked."

"I can only imagine."

She looked over at me. "Were you born knowing?" Again, she cocked her head to the side, almost like a bird.

"No. But I was pretty young. I can only imagine how weird it must have been to suddenly have things change for you."

She turned away from me, as if it was too difficult to look at me while she spoke about it. "I was pretty sure I'd lost my mind. Then I tried to talk to some people about it and they were pretty sure I'd lost my mind, too. Hence the whole 5150 thing."

"I'm so sorry." I was, too. I couldn't imagine how much that must have sucked. Perhaps I shouldn't whine so much about my situation.

"It's okay. It's all getting better now. Of course, I'm not entirely sure that you're real or that any of this stuff about wood nymphs and trees is real or if my craziness is really layered and realistic. I figure I'll go with it for a while anyway. It's better than staying locked up here, drugged out of my gourd." Again, she smiled.

I thought about Michael Hollinger. Maybe he would be better if he knew he wasn't losing his mind, too.

"Well, I just wanted to check in. I work downstairs. You'll be able to find me if you need me." I stood up.

"Thanks." She looked up at me and then her forehead

furrowed. "Did your boobs get bigger since the last time you came up here?"

I looked down. My shirt was tighter than it usually was and my boobs totally ached. No wonder Connor had been so glad to see me.

THE SACRAMENTO DELTA IS A STRANGE LITTLE PLACE. IT'S hard to believe you're only a few miles away from the capital of the seventh largest economy in the world when you wind along the river looking at houseboats and funny little bait and tackle shops. Stray a mile or so in any direction and you'll be in the middle of acres of vineyards with grapes that bask in the heat of the summer sun and sweeten in the cool air of the nights once the Delta breezes sweep through. Come through in the fog like I was and the place was downright creepy, with almost a southern Gothic feel about it.

The Valley is famous for its fogs. Ask any resident about tule fog and you'll get an earful about being stranded someplace, unable to see the hand in front of your face. I was lucky. This wasn't a tule. They're kind of a winter thing. This pea soup was just business as usual in the fall in the Central Valley.

I wound down River Road past Clarksburg. I was looking for someone in particular, someone who knew about nets. Her name was Cordelia and she was a mermaid.

I'd met Cordie when I was in high school. I'm not sure if she'd taken up residence in the Delta before that or if that was just the first time I'd been called on to take something to her. Regardless, it was our first encounter. It definitely hadn't been our last. I'd been coming down here probably once every month or two since then.

I'm not sure how exactly she wandered into the Delta or

why she decided to stay, but she clearly wasn't going anywhere. I suspected she liked the solitude and lack of competition. Mermaids can be totally cutthroat.

Cordelia had a few favorite places to hang out. I knew a few of them. With any luck, I'd catch her at one of those and be able to show her the net. The pattern of knots in it was so intricate, I felt like it had to be unique. If anyone might recognize who had made the net by this small piece of its pattern, it would be Cordelia.

I shuddered at the thought of how the net might have been used, at the agony it might have caused. All that silver on werewolf skin.

Maybe I was wrong. Maybe it wasn't a net at all. I knew I was jumping to conclusions, but I didn't know what else to do. So I jumped. I pulled over to the side a little south of Scribner Road and got out of the car.

There's something about being near water that's soothing to me. It's completely counterintuitive as far as I'm concerned. Having drowned once, I would think I would be afraid of water or at least tense around it. Instead I have the complete opposite reaction. I can sit and watch water go by for hours. Put me on a beach with ocean waves and it's probably one of the few times I'm able to sit still for long periods of time without wanting to jump out of my skin.

I let all my senses open—the Arcane and the Mundane— and drank it in. I could use a little soothing these days.

I soaked in the smell of the river, the dank chill of the fog and listened to the swish of the water. Unfortunately, that's all I got. Cordie wasn't there. I sighed, got back in the car and started driving again.

I went a few more miles south and pulled over to go through the same routine. Nothing. Not the faintest tingle. It took me two more tries before I finally found her.

I hadn't seen Cordelia since before I started being able to differentiate between different types of 'Canes with my senses, so I took a moment to really get a feel for what kind of impact a mermaid had on me. Her presence was a bit tangy with a hint of salt to it. I walked down to the water humming under my breath, finally starting to sing as I got to the river's edge. "Ask any mermaid you happen to see, what's the best tuna?"

Then I sat down and waited, still singing. She surfaced about five minutes later.

"You know that song bugs the crap out of me, don't you?" Cordelia asked, water cascading down her long blonde locks and over her bare breasts.

I smiled. "Yeah. I know. I needed to talk to you. I figured getting you to tell me to shut up was the most surefire way to get you to surface."

"That's not nice, Melina." She reached over her shoulder to gather her hair up and wring it out.

"But it was effective," I pointed out.

She laughed. Cordelia wasn't bad. I actually kind of liked her. I also knew I couldn't totally trust her. Mermaids are some of the most selfish beings out there. Honestly, they make vampires look like philanthropists.

"So what was so important that you had to talk to me right away?" she asked, swimming closer to the shore. Well, swimming isn't exactly the right word. Cordelia more undulated through the water.

I pulled the silver netting out of my bag. I'd wrapped it in some fabric and fully expected it to be a tangled mess. I mean, if I set the earbuds to my iPod down on the counter and walk away for twenty-five seconds, the cord is tied in about fifteen knots when I come back. Not so for my silver net. It slid out of the fabric flat as a pancake without a single tangle. I held it up so Cordie could see it.

She reached her hand out for it and I yanked it back. "No way, José," I said. "This is not a gift."

She pouted. "But it's pretty."

"And shiny. I know. It's still not yours."

"What is it?" she asked.

"I was sort of hoping you could tell me." It is why I'd driven down here in the fog after all.

"Why would I be able to tell you anything about that?" She crossed her arms over her breasts, which was kind of a relief. I'd started to feel like her nipples were staring at me. I so wish mermaids really wore coconut bras like they do in Disney movies.

"Because you know more about nets that anyone else I know." Mermaids were well-known for tangling up fishermen's nets and for occasionally getting tangled in them. "These knots look really unique. I thought you might know who made them."

"It's sort of hard to see them from a distance. Just let me hold it for a second." She smiled at me with a sweetness that almost had me believing that she wouldn't snatch it up and dive down to the bottom of the river. Almost being the key word there.

"No. Squint. Maybe it'll help."

"If I get wrinkles in my forehead, it's your fault." She sighed and complied. "It's not like any net that I've ever seen," she said finally. "No one knots a net like that. In fact, those don't even look like knots. Are you sure it's part of a net?"

I wasn't sure. I was afraid. I didn't care if she knew the former. I'd prefer to keep the latter to myself. "No. It looked like one to me."

"Not to me," she said. "And I've seen a lot of nets in my day."

True that. Cordie's alabaster skin might be as smooth as mother of pearl, but that didn't mean she hadn't been around the bay a few times. "So what do you think it is?"

She tilted her head to one side. "I really couldn't say. I like the pattern, though. It looks like something you might find on the back of a chair at your grandma's."

Cordie clearly did not know my grandma Rosie. She abhorred anything "froufrou" as she called it. She liked everything simple, unadorned and clean. I totally got it. My mother, on the other hand, would probably have BeDazzled our entire house if my father hadn't put his foot down.

I wondered if it would be possible to search for the pattern somehow. Maybe that would give me a clue as to who could have made it. I stood. "Thanks, Cordelia. I appreciate the help."

She hissed at me. Everybody thinks mermaids are all beauty and seduction. Trust me, they have a mean side. Their teeth are sharp as knives and they can entangle someone in their hair and drag them down to their death. Plus they'll do it without batting a long, beautifully curled eyelash. "That's it? You take and you don't give?"

I dug in my bag for what I'd brought for her. "You know that's not my way."

"I know you'd try to get away with it, though." Her eyes narrowed into slits.

Hard to argue with that. I pulled out the box of chocolates I'd bought and tossed them to her.

She ripped the box open and popped one of them into her mouth. Her head fell back and she made a moaning noise. "Oh, yes," she murmured.

Cordelia had a wicked sweet tooth, something that was fairly difficult to indulge when you lived in the water.

Chocolate was her special obsession and this was damn fine chocolate. I buy it from a funny little candy shop in Davis that makes the most outrageous truffles I've ever tasted.

"You made that look dirty," I observed.

"It is. It's very dirty." She smiled at me. "The most delicious things always are."

I got back in the Buick and turned on the radio. I'd left a news station on. "Authorities say that a man has escaped from a locked ward at a local mental hospital. Michael Hollinger is to be considered a danger to himself and others. Authorities do not think Mr. Hollinger was armed at the time of his escape, but other sources claim Mr. Hollinger is a police officer with easy access to weapons. The circumstances surrounding Mr. Hollinger's escape are under investigation and authorities would not comment on how he escaped or if he had assistance."

"Damn it," I said, pounding the steering wheel.

I STUCK MY BLUETOOTH IN MY EAR AND STARTED CALLING people as I drove. First on my list were Sophie and then T.J. That covered the dojo. Next up was Ted.

"Michael Hollinger escaped from the psych ward," I told him.

"Duh," he replied. "Trust me. I've heard. Pretty much everyone in law enforcement has."

"I don't think he managed this on his own." I chewed on my lip as I drove. I suppose it was possible that whatever was possessing him could have given him the strength to bust out of that straitjacket and out of the locked room and ward, but I didn't think it was likely.

"So you think he had accomplices?" Ted sounded skeptical.

"I think Chuck broke him out. I'm headed up there now to find out what's happening."

"Do you want me to meet you?" he offered.

"No. I did want you to know where I was going, though." It was always prudent. There might well come a day that it did make a difference. I hoped today wasn't the one.

"Are you sure that's safe?"

I wasn't, but he didn't have to know that. "It'll be fine. I'm just taking precautions."

"Call when you know something. Or when you don't. Just call, okay?"

I assured him I would and hung up. I figured I'd head into town first. Maybe Sam would be at the hardware store and I could get a little background info. He seemed to be on my side. Or, at least, Paul's side. It might not be my brightest move to burst into a group of werewolves who may or may not have just broken a werewolf halfling out of a psych ward.

A week ago, I might have done it anyway. What was a little danger to life and limb when one of my friends might be in trouble? Now, though? Now it wasn't just me. It was me and the tadpole. I had precious cargo onboard. Just thinking that made me want to gag a little and I hadn't barfed in days.

I had thought it, though. Maybe I wouldn't be quite the disaster of a mother that I thought I might be.

I spent the rest of the drive chewing the thoughts over. I pulled into town and parked down the street from the hardware store a few spaces down from the yarn shop. I got out and started walking toward Kevin's store, and then turned on my heel and started back toward the car when I saw him walk out of the store and flip the sign in the window to Closed.

Either I moved too quickly and the motion caught Kevin's

eye, or I didn't move fast enough and was spotted. Either way, he caught up to me in a few energetic strides.

"Do you have a message for someone?" he asked.

"Nope." In my pocket, the scrap of netting or lace or whatever it was started to vibrate a little. That was interesting.

"A package?" Kevin pressed and stepped a little closer to me.

I shook my head and backed up a step or two. The silver in my pocket vibrated a little more.

"Why are you here?" He jutted his chin out.

Man, this guy really didn't like me. I wondered what I'd ever done to him. "I was in the area and thought I'd come through again. It's really a nice little town." I smiled.

"Then don't spoil it. Go back where you belong." He glared at me.

"I was going to stop by the yarn shop." I glanced over my shoulder at it. We were practically at its door. "I was thinking about taking up knitting. I've heard it's very relaxing."

Kevin growled a little. "Leave Inge alone. She's had enough trouble in her life. She doesn't need you poking around." He stood in the center of the sidewalk and glared at me. No way was I getting past him to the hardware store, and even if I did, it's not like Sam would be able to talk to me at all. Besides, the lace was beginning to vibrate hard enough and heat up sufficiently that I seriously wanted it out of my pocket as soon as possible.

I held up my hands in surrender and went back to the car. I dug the silver out of my pocket before I got in, and then I spread it out in front of me on the dash. It was down from frantic vibrating to emitting only a tingle.

I tried to imagine Kevin carefully weaving or knotting it. It wasn't easy. It was so delicate and fine. It wasn't out of the question, though. I remembered pictures of Rosey Grier doing needlepoint. You really can't assume anything about the crafts anyone wants to do.

If Kevin was the one who'd made this silver, it raised a whole new host of questions, though. Why had he made it? How? When? And what the hell had this fragment been doing up by Paul's cabin?

The answers didn't set well with me. Kevin was Chuck's second. His second is sort of like the vice principal at a high school. He's the disciplinarian and often is in charge of training. He'd be the one to calm everyone down if there was an emergency, and maybe that was all he was trying to do by discouraging anyone from looking for Paul. Maybe.

Or maybe he didn't want anyone looking for Paul because Paul was a threat to him at this point. If Kevin was going to make a play to take over the pack from Chuck, Paul could be an irreplaceable ally or a formidable opponent. I'd bet on the latter.

So why not challenge Paul directly? Why all the treachery?

I didn't much like the answer to that either. If Paul had somehow caught wind of what Kevin was up to before Kevin was ready to put his plan into motion, a direct challenge would have been too public. Plus this served the added benefit of making it look like Chuck was possibly the weak one who had removed Paul from the scene with treachery instead of trying to rip out his throat with his teeth in the time-honored werewolf way.

9

THERE WAS NO WAY I WAS GETTING ANY INFORMATION from Sam tonight, but there was also no way I was going home without stopping at Chuck's. If I had to go in blind, so be it. I'd go in blind.

I pulled into the driveway. There were close to a dozen vehicles parked around the house. Whatever was going on apparently called for the Pack to assemble.

Poor Michael Hollinger. I knew Chuck had a place where he kept werewolves that were out of control. I didn't want to think about what that would be like. I also knew Chuck had his methods for dealing with wolves he couldn't control. It was also something I didn't particularly want to think about. It hadn't been my problem before.

Strictly speaking, it wasn't my problem now. My only interest in Michael Hollinger was to find out if he had anything to do with Paul's disappearance. His shell-shocked wife and his bratty little girl were none of my business. So why the hell did thinking about them make me so uneasy. It had to be the hormones.

The door opened before I could even knock on it. Sam stood in the doorway, arms folded over his chest. He looked down at me. "Now is not a good time, Melina. Chuck is kind of busy."

"I only need a minute," I said. I looked up and fluttered my eyelashes the way I'd seen Norah do it when she was trying to get something from Alex. "It's for Paul, Sam."

His shoulders dropped. "I'll ask. I'm not guaranteeing anything, though."

I stepped inside the house and shut the door behind me. "Thanks."

I cooled my heels in the hall. Although cool was about the last thing I was. There were so many wolves in this place, I felt jumpy in my own skin. The air was thick with worry and tension.

Whatever Michael Hollinger was, it wasn't soothing to the Pack. After about fifteen minutes, Chuck finally came into the hall. He sat down next to me on the bench where I'd been waiting.

"You broke Michael Hollinger out of the psych ward, didn't you?" I said, by way of a greeting.

Chuck shrugged. It was answer enough for me.

"What is he? What's going on?"

"I'm not sure what's going on, but I know that man is not a werewolf." Chuck looked weary. He had that weight-of-the-world-on-his-shoulders kind of slouch. No wonder the Pack was getting restless. A tired Alpha wasn't going to be able to maintain discipline.

I slouched right along with him. No one cared if a Messenger was tired. "Then what is he?"

"I'm not sure. There's definitely some elements that are

totally like a new wolf at the full moon, but it's not quite the whole enchilada."

"I'm not sure Mexican food metaphors are appropriate here."

"Why? Because everyone thinks the dude is a few tacos short of a full combination plate?" He tilted his head back against the wall.

"Actually, no. It's because right now the thought of Mexican food is making me a little nauseous."

He smiled at me. "I've heard the first few months can be kind of rough."

"Yeah. You knew that first day I came up here looking for Paul, didn't you?" That had been what Chuck had been lying about. He'd congratulated me and then had to lie about why.

He nodded.

I wasn't sure what had tipped him off. "Heartbeat?"

"Nah. It's more of a pheromone thing. I didn't realize you didn't know. Sorry about that." He rubbed his hand across his face.

"Yeah, well, I figured it out soon enough. No harm. No foul." I leaned back against the wall. "So what do we do with Hollinger?"

Chuck straightened his legs in front of himself as if they were stiff and sore. "That's a good question. He's not going anywhere until after the full moon. We'll keep an eye on him through this one and see what happens."

I shivered. "What made him become like this?"

"Well, it's obviously that bite," he said.

"So he was bitten by a werewolf?" Could Paul have done this?

Chuck snorted. "Not bloody likely. Not unless he was bitten by a werewolf in human form and I have never— never—heard of a werewolf biting someone in human form."

Absolutes always make me uneasy. "Never?"

"Look. It's not like I know of every single thing that has ever happened, but I've been around the block a few times. The biting instinct . . . well, it's strongest when we're in wolf form. It abates when we're in human form." He smiled, showing his perfectly even white teeth.

"Let's say that it didn't abate for somebody. Could a bite from a werewolf in human form cause what's happening to Michael Hollinger?" There had to be some sequence of events that got Hollinger to this place.

Chuck sighed. "It's a reasonable question. I'll see what I can find out. It doesn't seem likely, but I don't have much else to go on at this point."

"What about finding out who did the biting? Any luck there?" I pressed. At this point, I wasn't sure if I wanted it to be Paul or not. If it was him, at least he wasn't being kept captive somewhere under that silver net.

He shook his head again. "Nope. I don't think it's anyone in the Pack. Actually, I'd pretty much swear to that."

"Which leaves us where? Lone wolves traveling through?" It happened. If they came through someone's territory, they were supposed to sort of check in, but let's face it, there's a reason a lone wolf is called a lone wolf. Rule following is not their strong point.

"It's possible, but everything you're telling me about it is so urban. If there were lone wolves hunting around here, I think we would have some sign of them in the wild."

"It's a pretty big wild out there." Acres and acres and acres of it around here.

"True enough. Again, I'll see if I can find anything out from anyone else."

"Meanwhile, what do we do with Michael Hollinger?" I asked, looking toward the door.

"There's no 'we' here, *kemo sabe*," Chuck said. "We'll get him through this full moon, then we'll see if he calms down. We can't exactly have a conversation with him right now."

"And then?"

"Then we'll see if we can teach him to control himself." He grinned. "We have our methods, you know?"

I did. Sort of. I'd heard rumors. "Not exactly. Care to share?"

"Nah. I'd like to keep a few of our secrets intact."

Secrets. Everyone seemed to have them these days. Apparently it was what all the cool kids were doing. "Do you think it has anything to do with Paul?" I asked.

Chuck looked over at me, clearly surprised. "What on earth could this have to do with Paul?"

I shrugged. "I'm not sure. I know he's not around and there's weird stuff happening. I don't like coincidences."

"No one does, but sometimes they're just that, Melina. I can tell you one thing for sure. Paul did not bite Michael Hollinger. In human form or in wolf form."

"How can you be so sure?"

Chuck snorted. "If Paul had bitten him in wolf form, he'd be dead or he'd be a werewolf."

"And if Paul bit him in human form?"

"It would never happen. Paul has too much control for that." Chuck stood. "Go home, Melina. Leave this to us. If we need your help, I'll let you know."

I opened my mouth to speak, but he held up his hand. "Go home. Take care of your own problems. Michael Hollinger isn't one of them." Then he turned and walked away.

I WAS BACK THE NEXT DAY LIKE A BAD PENNY. I JUST wasn't going to make myself known. I had done surveillance with a werewolf before. It was awful. The ability to sit still

in a confined space—like a car—is not intrinsic to wolfiness.
This, however, was going to be the first time I'd done surveillance on a werewolf. Maybe Chuck was right. Maybe Michael
Hollinger was not my problem. Maybe Paul was fine. On the
other hand, that scrap of silver had nearly jumped out of my
pocket when Kevin was nearby. That meant something and
the only way to figure out if it was my problem or not was
to figure out what the hell Kevin was up to.

So here I was getting ready to do surveillance on a
werewolf.

The pitfalls were numerous and many of them were obvious. There was that heightened sense of smell. Was he going
to be able to catch a whiff of me? How far away did I have to
stay to keep him from doing that? Paul was the person I
would have asked, but that wasn't going to happen.

Then there was his hearing. Would he be able to pick out
the sound of the Buick from other cars? Would he notice
that?

Plus, most werewolves were pretty wary, in wolf or
human form. They walked around a little bit like cops, now
that I thought about it. They stayed very aware of their sur-
roundings, recognized cars and patterns of behavior. I wasn't
sure if they were looking for threats or prey, but either way,
Kevin could well notice me or my Buick.

I was going to have to fight fire with a little flicker of
flame. I had pretty badass hearing and vision, too. Not as
badass as a werewolf, but then again, perhaps the element
of stealth would work in my favor.

Knowledge was definitely going to be power in this situation. Or at least I hoped so. If it came to pound-for-pound
strength, I was going down and I knew it. Kevin could rip
me apart with his bare hands, or paws, depending on whether
he was man or wolf at the moment. I parked the Buick a few

blocks away from the hardware store, off the main drag on a side street. Then I strolled down the sidewalk, trying to blend in with the window-shoppers on the street.

I am not much of a stroller. As lazy as I am, it's a little surprising. Mainly I find time spent getting from one place to another to be a waste of said time, so I try to make it go as quickly as possible. That often takes the form of walking with both purpose and determination and driving a bit over the speed limit.

No one else on the sidewalk was walking with purpose and determination unless their purpose was to annoy me and they were determined to do it as quickly as possible. On the other side of the street, I saw a woman with an actual stroller. She looked like she was having nearly as much trouble as I was navigating through the random clumps of people who stopped abruptly in ways that can only be described as both arbitrary and capricious.

Wow. How much worse would this be with a kid? I'd have to get one of those sling things. I couldn't see myself using a stroller unless it doubled as a battering ram. Maybe I could get a custom stroller with some sort of front apparatus. Preferably something sharp. Wow. Was I seriously mentally stroller shopping? I guess the reality of the situation was truly starting to sink in.

There was a truck parked behind the hardware store that I was pretty sure had to be Kevin's. It had that battered contractor look to it, plus I'd seen it parked at Chuck's the night before. The alley behind the store was narrow and it looked like traffic moved pretty much one way. So far, this was all working in my favor. That made me nervous. Clearly the universe was setting me up for a colossal fall.

I moved the Buick over to the side street that Kevin would have to come out on if I was right about the truck and the one-way traffic. I found a spot where I could see him when he came out and crossed my fingers that he'd head away from the main street with its stop-and-go traffic and irritating pedestrians. It's what I would do, and I personally don't think Kevin was any more of a people werewolf than I was a people person.

Or maybe it was me he didn't like. That was unfortunately a distinct possibility. He wouldn't be the first person and I'd be stunned if he was the last.

I slid down in the seat of the Buick. It wasn't as good as being in the back of a van, but I figured I wasn't too noticeable. Plus I was super-comfy. The seats in this thing were like a couch. Better than some couches, especially futon couches. My stomach rumbled. Hungry again. This kid was definitely demanding. I reached in the back and grabbed the bag of food I'd packed this morning.

I unwrapped my turkey sandwich and opened a bag of chips. After carefully inserting several potato chips into the sandwich, I took a big bite and sighed with contentment. I could spend an afternoon like this, having quality time with myself and a turkey sandwich. All that camaraderie and sharing stuff was overrated.

It hadn't been that long ago when none of these people were in my life. Well, they were in my life, but not with the kind of presence they had now. I walked alone then and things were a lot less complicated.

I had also been a lot lonelier. I'm not sure I would have couched it that way at the time. I probably would have talked about being frustrated or angry or irritated. Loneliness was the root of it, though. Perhaps complication was the price one had to pay for that.

I sunk even lower in the Buick, took another bite of sandwich and nearly jumped out of my skin when the pickup truck from behind the hardware store rattled past me. I tossed my sandwich back in the bag with regret. We'd have to get someplace damn fast to have the chips stay crunchy in there with the turkey and the cheese and the tomato, and it wouldn't be the same with soggy chips. Then I started the Buick and headed down the street after the truck.

Truth be told, I couldn't be sure Kevin was driving. I hadn't seen the driver's face and it could easily be Sam or one of the other younger members of the Pack who worked at the hardware store when they weren't working on one of Chuck's construction sites. So far I'd been lucky. I'd guessed right on where the truck would come out and which way it would go. I needed a trifecta, though.

The truck went a few more blocks up Main Street, then made a left onto Bennett. I hit the accelerator. This was where things got tricky. It would be all too easy to lose him on the bigger busier street, but I hadn't dared to be too close behind him on the little side street for fear of being noticed.

I made the left turn on Bennett just in time to see the pickup go through a light at Richardson. There was no way I'd make it, so there was no point in pushing the pedal to the metal. I glided up to the light and idled there, trying to crane my neck to see the pickup ahead of me around the conversion van that had pulled onto Bennett from another side street.

I shut my eyes and tried to pick out the truck's particular engine noise from the others. It wasn't going to work. There was too much other noise. Than a horn honked behind me and I realized I was sitting at a green light with my eyes shut. Whoever said I wasn't a total ace at surveillance?

The Buick leapt forward and squealed a bit. Yeah. I was slick. No doubt about it.

Still, I managed to catch up to the truck at the next light, which was a damn good thing because Kevin—or whoever was driving, I still wasn't sure—turned onto Highway 49. If I hadn't been one car behind him, there would have been no way to catch him without risking life and limb, which these days, I wasn't that interested in doing.

Kevin turned out to be one of those guys who used cruise control. We hit the highway, he started going seventy-two miles per hour—a socially acceptable seven miles over the speed limit—and kept it there. My attitude toward him softened a little. If he'd been one of those guys who switch lanes every ten seconds, racing up people's backsides and then slamming on his brakes, he would have seen me for sure. This way, I could hang back a bit. There was something to be said for a predictable man.

Kevin pulled off at Brunswick Road and I pulled off a few seconds after him with a little green Camry between us. I hoped that was enough cover for the Buick. We all turned right at the stoplight, crested up over a rise and went about a mile. Kevin and the Camry turned right into the entrance of Sierra College. What the hell? Kevin's nefarious and mysterious disappearances were in the service of higher education?

I went down a different aisle in the lot and parked near the end. I could see Kevin walking toward the campus. I waited a few minutes and then walked in after him, knowing I'd be able to track him by his magical signature. For the record, community colleges are not hotbeds of paranormal activity. I was getting one very wolfy tingle and that was it.

I wound up in building N7 205, lurking outside of room 207B, home of Advanced Calculus. I thought about poking my head in, but nothing clouds my brain faster than advanced mathematics. Everything made sense to me up until Algebra II, then someone started talking trigonometry and it was as if the mental rug was pulled out from underneath me. I went back to my car figuring I could keep an eye on Kevin's truck and pick him up from there. Maybe he'd go someplace more interesting after class.

I got back to the Buick, finished my sandwich, soggy potato chips and all, and slid down in the seat. The afternoon sunlight slanted into the car and within a few minutes I was toasty warm. The combination of toasty warm and full stomach was more than I could fight off and I felt myself dozing. I glanced at my watch. Surely I could close my eyes for a few minutes? Those classes were long, weren't they? Fifteen minutes was all I needed. Then I'd be ready to face the rest of the day. I shut my eyes.

I WOKE TO SHARP RAPPING ON MY WINDOW AND performed a complicated maneuver that had me both choking on my own spit and cracking my head against the window.

Kevin was staring in. He made a rolling motion with his hands.

I rolled the window down.

"I'm leaving now. I didn't want you to miss your chance to follow me." He leaned his elbows against the Buick's door.

I rolled my eyes and fell back in my seat. "How long have you known I was there?"

He shrugged. "Before I got on the highway. Not until after I was on Bennett, though, if that makes you feel any better."

It didn't. "So what's up with the self-improvement?"

"The drive for learning is part of the human spirit," he said, straightening up.

"You're not human," I reminded him.

That earned me quite the nasty look. "You're following

me because you think I have something to do with Paul not being around, don't you?"

I nodded.

"Let's go have coffee. I'll explain a few things to you."

It was better than a poke in the eye with a sharp stick so I agreed. He gave me directions to a coffeehouse a few blocks away and I met him there. I sat down at a table with him with my cup of tea. This baby better appreciate what I was giving up for it.

"What the hell is the matter with you?" Kevin asked as I sat down.

His instant and constant antipathy to me was starting to grate. What had I ever done to him? "Back atcha, big guy. What's your problem?"

"My problem? My problem is that I've got a meddling Messenger hanging around my pack at a time that's very delicate."

"Delicate because a Pack member is missing and no one's doing a damn thing about it? Which leads me to believe that someone in the Pack wants it that way?" I countered as I sat down.

He crossed his arms across his chest. "You really think I'd do that? That I'd do something like that to Paul?"

"Yeah. I do. You're confrontational. You're aggressive. You're strong and smart, but your chances of becoming the Alpha of this pack are diminishing every year. You're not getting any younger, Kevin. Neither is Chuck, but he's not getting old that fast either."

"Exactly. I see I don't have to explain my position to you. Maybe you're not as dumb as you look." He snorted.

I just love it when people say things that are both insults and compliments at the same time. It makes me want to smack them right across their kissers. That did not seem like the right course of action at the moment. I decided to keep my eyes on the prize instead. "What do you mean?"

"My position in the Pack. That's why I'm taking classes. I'm going to get my engineering degree so I can get out from under Chuck financially and start up someplace on my own. Be my own boss. Start my own pack."

I wasn't buying it. "Why start a new one when you could take over this one? And what better way to do it than get rid of your competition and throw suspicion on your Alpha all at the same time. I have to admit. It's a hell of a plan. If someone from the outside wasn't looking at it, you'd probably get away with it, too."

Kevin's hands tightened so hard on the edge of the table, his knuckles went white. "How dare you," he growled at me.

"I dare because someone has to." I leaned forward and looked directly into his eyes. "Paul has been there for me in so many ways, so many times. I am not backing down until I find him, and if that means going through you, then you'd better put on a cup, mister."

For a second, I thought he was going to reach across the table and grab me by the throat despite all the witnesses that were around. I think he thought he was going to do that, too. Instead, he stared at me long and hard and then he started to laugh. "I'm beginning to see what Paul saw in you. You've got potential to do more than tote and carry, don't you?"

Frankly, I didn't even think I was all that good at the toting and carrying, so suggesting that I had potential for more sort of surprised me. It surprised me even more that the suggestion had come from Paul. He'd always had my back, but I thought it was kind of the way a big brother had the back of his idiot baby sister. Damn it. Had he been manipulating me even more than I'd thought he was? I was totally going to twist his ear once I found him. "I don't know about that," I said. "I do know that something's not right here and I want to know how you're involved in it."

"I'm not," he said, flatly. "I see how I could have tripped your suspicions, but let me be clear. I wouldn't sabotage Paul, or Chuck for that matter. What kind of wolf sneaks around behind his Alpha's back like that?"

"One that might not be able to seize power any other way," I suggested.

"Okay. You've got a point. In a head-to-head challenge against Chuck, I'd lose. I don't have enough backing in the Pack or the physical strength to take him down and keep him down." He looked down into his coffee. "I don't have the heart to tear his throat out either, if the truth be known. If that makes me weak, well, so be it."

Oh, crap. I was starting to like Kevin. "So why do you have to do anything?"

"I'm stagnating. I have nowhere to go in the Pack. I've risen as high as there is to rise. It's time to start out on my own." He leaned back in his chair.

"And what about Paul?" That was my real concern, whether or not I liked Kevin.

He shook his head. "I don't think you understand the role that Paul plays in this pack. I would never leave Chuck without someone like Paul in place. He's a leader, but not by brute strength, although he's got plenty of it."

"I thought that was what Pack politics were all about. Who could dominate whom." At least, that's how it always seemed to me.

"You should know better. We're not that simple. If we were, we'd just rip each apart and live by ourselves. There's a drive within us to be part of a community. It's how we survive. More than that, it's how we thrived. We need wolves like Paul that can lead and assert a calming influence."

That was for sure. They were all a bunch of hotheads. "So why were you so eager to get rid of me? All I'm doing is trying to make sure Paul's okay. It sounds like you want the same thing."

"Because you don't belong. It's Pack business and the Pack will take care of it." Again with the crossed arms. It was a little intimidating. It made his biceps pop.

"But the Pack isn't!" I practically shouted. "The Pack is sitting around with its thumb up its collective ass."

Kevin bared his teeth at me. "Settle."

"Like a good dog," I shot back, although I did lower my voice.

"Don't get your hackles up. The two of us getting in a shouting match about werewolves in public isn't going to help anyone. What I'm trying to tell you is that there is no one in the Pack who has any reason to get rid of Paul. Certainly not me. If anything, his not being around is slowing my personal plans down. So you can stop following me around, okay?"

I sat back in my chair, deflated. I could see Kevin's point. Damn. I'd thought I had something. "Fine. Go sharpen up your math skills. But help me, too. Where do you think Paul could be?"

Kevin's grip on the table loosened and he leaned back in his chair, too, although there was still plenty of starch in his spine. "Wherever he wants to be. Why can't you accept that his Alpha told him to get his head on straight and he went somewhere to do just that?"

"Why can't you accept that he would not do that without letting . . . someone know?"

"You mean the witch, don't you?" He made it sound like he was calling Meredith a totally different word, although it did rhyme.

"Yes. I do mean the witch. Her name is Meredith and he cares about her. He would not go without telling her." I ruminated for a moment or two. "Plus, it seems like there might be somebody trying to scare me off."

Kevin snorted. "Well, whoever would be trying that certainly doesn't know you well."

I started to laugh and then froze. He was right. Anyone who knew even a little bit about me would know that trying to scare me off would be like waving a flag in front of a bull. So it would have to be someone who didn't know me, not even by reputation. Which mean that it couldn't be someone in the Pack. I'd been following the wrong person entirely.

Who else's attention would I have come to, though? I thought about it for a minute. Then I dug the silver lace out of my backpack. It had no tingle to it at all. I tossed it toward Kevin. His hand went up to catch it instinctively. The second it hit his skin, he nearly howled and dropped it.

"What the hell?" he demanded. "What are you trying to do?"

"Eliminate you as a suspect," I said.

"IT'S NOT KEVIN," I SAID AS I COLLAPSED ONTO THE futon couch.

"What's not Kevin?" Ted asked.

I was so happy to be home in my own apartment. I might sing the praises of the comfort of Grandma's Buick, but it was really only comfortable compared to other cars. Sleeping in the Buick had left me with a crick in my neck and a pain in my back. "Kevin didn't kidnap Paul to try to take over the Pack."

"And you know that how?"

"I followed him and the silver stuff didn't tingle at all,

which is weird because it did tingle the other day when I was standing next to him on the sidewalk." I rolled my head and listened to my neck make popping sounds.

"There are so many parts of that sentence that I have questions about that I'm not sure where to start." He frowned at me.

I yawned. "Pick one."

"You followed a werewolf that you suspected of kidnapping Paul?" He held up one finger.

I nodded. "I wanted to see what he was up to. Turns out he's taking calculus."

"Well, sure. That makes perfect sense. Higher mathematics would seem to be a natural thing for a werewolf to study." He was still frowning and holding up the one finger.

"Don't be a smart-ass. He wants an engineering degree. He wants to start his own business and then start his own pack." I stretched my arms.

"The silver tingled around him." He held up a second finger.

"Yeah. The other day on the street. It was in my pocket and we were standing on the sidewalk near the hardware store and then it practically burns a hole in my jeans." I stretched. "I've told you objects of power react when they're near their maker."

"So if Kevin isn't the one who made that silver lace, who else was nearby who could have?" The frown was gone. Now he looked thoughtful.

I didn't have an answer for that one. "I don't know." No way was it Sam. It would have vibrated like crazy when we found it.

He pressed. "Who else was there?"

I closed my eyes and tried to re-create the moment. "I don't know. People."

"Okay. Try not to think about what you saw. What about what you sensed with, you know, your other senses?" He leaned toward me.

"Nothing. I had those locked down pretty hard." I shook my head.

"Why? Is Kevin that overwhelming?" He sat up straighter now.

Was he a little jealous? "No, but that chick at the yarn store is."

"She's Arcane?"

"I can't really say. Her grief is too overpowering. I had to slam everything shut just to stay on my feet." I shivered thinking about what it felt like to get even a whiff of Inge's grief.

His eyes widened. "Have you always sensed emotional states like that?"

I shook my head. "No. It's a recent thing."

"Kind of like the zapping." He didn't ask that as a question. It was a statement of fact.

I looked over at his handsome face, at the way his jaw ran so true and square. I had to tell him. It was time. "There's something else new."

He turned to face me, head cocked to one side. "Yeah? What?"

I ducked my head. This was so hard.

He lifted my head, fingers gentle under my chin. "Hey, it's okay. Whatever it is, we'll figure it out."

I so hoped that was right. "Ted, I'm pregnant."

I had imagined this scenario and how it might go. I had imagined the possibility of Ted immediately dropping to one knee and proposing to me. I had imagined him pulling me into his arms and telling me he loved me. I had imagined tears filling his eyes as he contemplated me carrying his child. I'd imagined my protests. I'd imagined how I'd tell him he didn't have to marry me. I'd imagined doing my usual standing-brave-and-tall thing.

I had not imagined him pushing himself back into a corner of the couch and going a whiter shade of pale than any Procol Harum song could ever conjure.

I had also not imagined Norah and Alex walking in the door two seconds later.

"Hi, guys," Norah sang out as she flounced into the living room and then froze, staring at Ted. "What's wrong?"

"How do you know something's wrong?" I asked.

"How could you look at him and not know?" she countered, pointing at Ted. "Are you sick?"

He shook his head. I saw his Adam's apple bob up and down a few times, but he still hadn't said anything.

"Is someone else sick?" Norah pressed.

More head shaking. More not speaking.

Then Norah turned to me. Or on me. "What did you do to him?"

I took a deep breath and said, "I told him I was pregnant."

I hadn't realized how spiteful I was feeling until the surge of satisfaction ran through me as I watched the wind taken neatly out of Norah's indignant sails. "You're what?"

"Pregnant. With child. Knocked up. Preggers. I have a bun in the oven. I'm gravid." I ran out of ways to say it. It's not like I had a lot of practice.

Alex flopped down in the armchair. "So you finally told him, did you?"

Now Ted found his voice. "You told him before you told me?"

"You are absolutely the first person I told," I said and turned toward Alex. "How did you know?"

He tapped his ears. "I have really acute hearing. I heard the heartbeat."

"When?"

"Last week some time." He shrugged.

"And you didn't tell me?"

"I knew you'd figure it out eventually. You're not that un-self-aware," he said, smiling.

"Thanks tons."

Alex turned toward Ted. "Are you okay?"

Ted stared at me, blank-faced. This was so not what I'd thought would happen. "We never talked about having children. I didn't think we were at that stage yet."

"Yeah, well, apparently your sperm and my eggs thought differently," I said, feeling more and more disgruntled and, frankly, butt hurt. Where was the grand proposal gesture that I could turn down? Where was the overflow of emotion that I could stem?

"You look like you could use a drink," Alex said to Ted.

"Yeah, well, I can't have one so he can't either," I snapped.

"You realize that makes no sense, right?" Alex said, leaning back in his chair, a bemused smile on his face.

"I'm not supposed to make sense. I'm hormonal, remember?" I looked over at Norah, who hadn't said a word in a few minutes. She looked just as poleaxed as Ted. Norah loved babies. I'd have thought she'd already be planning my baby shower and trying to dress me in smock tops. "Don't you have anything to say?"

"Have you been to a doctor?" she asked.

That was the last straw. I stood up. "Good night. Thanks for all your support." I walked down the hall and went into my bedroom. For the first time possibly ever, I locked the door.

10

APPARENTLY BUILDING A PLACENTA IS SUFFICIENTLY
exhausting that I fell asleep despite the rage and hurt that
was roiling inside me. That was something to be grateful for.

"Thanks, baby," I said, putting my hand on my stomach.
"It's good to help each other out because it looks like each
other is all we're going to have."

I rolled out of bed and considered my schedule. It was
pretty clear today. T.J. and Sophie could cover the classes
at the dojo and I wasn't due back at the hospital for a few
days. I decided to call Meredith and see if she wanted to
help me look for Paul. Surprise surprise, she totally did.

She arrived at the apartment an hour and a half later,
dressed for action. Her auburn hair was pulled back into a
thick braid and she was wearing a cotton jersey shirt, leggings and soft black boots with no heel. In fact, she looked
suspiciously as if she had dressed up as me for a costume

party. She took one look at me and said, "What's up with you? You look different."

I sighed. I'd hoped to keep this quiet for a little while longer, but apparently my friends were a little too observant for that. "I'm pregnant."

Meredith's eyes went wide, her hands flew to her mouth and then she threw her arms around me. "Congratulations! How wonderful! How are you feeling?"

Well, finally, someone gave me a decent reaction. "I'm okay. I think it's why I've been so tired."

Meredith sat down on one of the stools by the breakfast bar in the kitchen and looked me up and down. "That would explain that." Then she stopped and stared right through me. "It might explain some other stuff, too."

"Like what? Why my boobs hurt?"

"Well, yeah that, but also the, uh, zapping thing."

Yeah, right. "Look, Meredith, I've been doing a lot of reading up on pregnancy and nowhere does it mention that expectant mothers suddenly develop the ability to channel electricity."

"Yeah, well, you're not just you anymore, now are you? You're kind of two people at the moment. Maybe the zapping thing isn't your ability." She smiled as if just the thought of it amused her.

I saw where she was going. If I was eating and drinking for two, maybe I was also being magical for two. "I don't think I'm that far along. Right now it's probably barely a collection of cells." A collection of cells that responded to me when I put my hand near it or thought about it a lot, but still a collection of cells.

Meredith waved her hand in the air. "What are any of us but a collection of cells? Do you think having Arcane abilities is something that comes along later in life? We're all born into it one way or the other."

"Not me." I hadn't been. I'd been a normal three-year-old. It had all come down to that one afternoon when I was supposed to be napping and had opted to go for a swim instead.

"Are you so sure about that?" She leaned forward on the counter. "You were really young. Do you remember what you were like before that day?"

"Of course not. I was three. I barely remember that day." Actually, I didn't remember that day. Everything I knew about it came from other people's accounts: my mother, my father, my grandmother, Mae. They'd all been the ones to tell me what happened and what the consequences of those occurrences had been. My father can't talk about it without shaking, so he's pretty useless as a source of information.

Meredith straightened up and lifted her hands, palm up. "See my point? You might have had something magical about you already that you don't remember."

"What about Sophie, then? Wouldn't she have had something about her, too?" If there was a reason that I was a Messenger, then it would stand to reason that it would apply to Sophie as well.

Meredith shrugged. "That would make sense. Have you ever asked her?"

I sat down next to her. "No."

Meredith shrugged and said, "Maybe you could inquire."

I shook my head again. "No. I'm pretty sure if I started zapping people in the womb, someone would have mentioned it by now."

"Still. It wouldn't hurt to ask Sophie."

Although, come to think of it, Sophie had sort of asked me. Maybe the conversation we'd had about why we had become Messenger when others hadn't had been a way to open the topic.

I supposed it wouldn't hurt to ask her. I finished drinking my tea and we headed out the door.

I AM GENERALLY A LITTLE MORE AWARE OF MY SURROUND-ings than most people. I figure it's a combination of having some extra senses, some extra sharp senses, and wanting to stay alive. It's a potent blend. I was feeling a little extra aware because of my bun in the oven. Was my present state of knocked-uppedness contributing to my abilities?

Regardless of why, I felt a tingle almost the second we walked out the door of the apartment. I put my hand on Meredith's arm to slow her down as she strode toward the Buick. "What?"

"Do you see something? Hear something?" I asked.

She stopped, then shook her head. "What am I supposed to be seeing or hearing?"

"I'm not sure. The tingle's too weak." I turned in a circle looking around my neighborhood. Damn it. The crows were back. "What about them?" I asked, pointing.

One of them cocked its head at me and winked. Cheeky bird.

"They're kind of big, but otherwise they look like crows. It's that time of year, Melina. You know there are a ton of them around here in the fall."

True enough. Every fall there was a massive influx of crows into the area. They'd hang out, roost, caw obnoxiously loudly and cover cars parked under trees with poo. Not exactly my favorite thing. I turned and started again to the car and stopped. "But there are usually hordes of them. I'm just seeing two of them all the time and they're huge." I'd been meaning to look them up. They just never seemed to rise high enough on my to-do list, I guess.

"There are hordes of them over at my place. Does that make you feel any better?"

"No. It makes me a little more concerned. Why are there only two here at my place?"

Meredith turned to look at them again. "You know you are a little sensitive on the subject, right?"

Like I needed to be reminded. "Humor me a little. Do they mean anything in particular?"

She shrugged, but didn't take her eyes off the crows. "I doubt there's a culture on the planet whose mythology doesn't have a crow in it somewhere. Japan, China, the Norse tradition, the Greeks. They've all got crows."

"How do I find out whose crows these are?"

"If they're even somebody's crows and not just two particularly big birds that have bullied all the other ones out of the neighborhood?" Meredith asked.

"Yeah, if that."

"I don't know. I'll look into it, okay?"

"Okay." I guess I couldn't ask for much more than that.

We turned back toward the Buick again and that's when I saw the package sitting on the hood and sighed. "We might have to make a slight detour."

"Seriously?"

"Generally, the faster I deal with these things, the better off I am." I'd found that delays meant tempting Messenger fate. The longer I put off delivering a package, the more likely I was to run into a string of bad luck. It was like asking to step in dog shit in your favorite boots. The consequences were simply not worth it.

"Where's it going?" she asked.

"I won't know until I get closer." We walked up to the car and looked at the address.

Meredith looked from the envelope to me. "Well, at least that shouldn't take long."

It was addressed to me.

"ARE YOU GOING TO OPEN IT, OR JUST STARE AT IT?" Meredith asked after a few minutes.

"I'm going with open, but not out here on the street."

"In the car, then?"

I shook my head. "Let's take it back up to the apartment."

"Whatever you say. You're the expert."

That's the thing, though. I wasn't. Not on this. No one sends me packages. At least, not meant for me as their final destination. Giving a package to me was like dropping it off at the post office, in more ways than one. I'm pretty sure I had the postal worker attitude down to a science.

I took a second to examine the envelope before I picked it up. It registered as ordinary to all my senses. Plain old manila. Finally I plucked it out from behind the windshield wiper where someone had put it and held it in my hands. Holding it, I finally got the tiniest vibration off it, but not much at all.

"Anything?" Meredith asked, keeping an eye on the crows.

I shook my head. "Not really. Let's take it upstairs."

Back in the apartment, I set it down on the kitchen counter to examine it more thoroughly. It was the type of manila envelope you can buy anywhere. Grocery store, drugstore, Costco if you want a lifetime supply. Anywhere. It had been folded shut and the little metal tabs had been flattened down to keep it shut, but no one had put a wax seal on it or anything interesting and unique like that. They hadn't even licked the envelope to moisten the flap. It was dry as a bone. Not that I had the resources to track DNA or anything, but it would have been something.

I know it's gross, but body fluids do help with identification. I'd love to see what would happen if some DNA lab got hold of vampire saliva or something like that, but that's not the kind of identification I mean. Think of it this way, there's nothing more essentially us than the very substances that our bodies create. They can be like distilled essences of ourselves. I am not by any means advocating using vampire saliva as a perfume unless you have a pretty profound death wish. Still, I could often get a read off of what has been left behind.

No one had left anything behind on this particular envelope, which, in itself, felt like an important fact.

I was, however, getting something, but it didn't seem to be coming from the envelope. I glanced around the apartment, trying to figure out what it was. I was going to need to shut it out if I was going to get anything off this envelope at all, but I didn't see anything obvious.

"Now what?" Meredith asked, leaning over the counter on her elbows.

"Now we open it." I straightened the metal tabs, unfolded the flap and shook a piece of paper out onto the counter.

We both stared at it as if we expected it to spontaneously combust or maybe fold itself into a paper airplane. It didn't. It just sat there.

"That was kind of anticlimactic," Meredith observed. "I expected something more grand. Maybe some smoke or a big popping noise."

I didn't say anything, but I totally agreed with her.

I picked up the piece of paper and turned it over. Things seemed suddenly much more climactic. The letter was from Paul.

Dear Melina,

I've heard through the grapevine that you've been look-ing for me. I'm writing to tell you to stop. I probably should have told you I was leaving town for a while. I'm sorry if I worried you. I'm fine and will be home soon.

Paul

I slid the piece of paper across the counter to Meredith and watched her read it. I didn't want to say anything until I heard her verdict on the letter. I already had my own opinion.

She read it, slid it back to me and said, "Paul didn't write that."

"Nope. At least, not under his own steam." It did look like his handwriting, but that was about it. Everything else about it screamed fake.

I carried it into the living room and sat down on the futon couch. Meredith sat next to me. "Something's definitely wrong," I said.

"Yep." Meredith sat down next to me. "No way would he have written you. He'd have written me."

She wasn't being conceited or jealous. She was right. He wouldn't have written me. Or if he had, the letter would have held a lot more insults and been a lot ruder. And absolutely no way would he have apologized.

"It's all weird and stilted," she said.

That was true, too. Paul had a poetic side and it tended

to come out when he held a pen and paper. This thing didn't flow.

As I held the letter, trying to open myself to anything else on it that might be a clue, whatever else was in the apartment that was vibrating started sending out a stronger tingle. I was going to need to go find it to keep it from distracting me. If I shut it out, I shut out the vague signals I was getting from the letter.

"Hold on a second," I told Meredith. I stood up, still holding the letter. The tingle was definitely coming from my room. I walked down the hall, motioning for Meredith to follow me.

There wasn't much on my desk. My laptop, a sorter thing for my mail and a basket with a few papers in it. Nothing looked like it might be the source of my discomfort, although it was definitely stronger now that I was closer to the desk. I set the fake note from Paul down so both my hands would be free and the tingle got stronger. I opened the top drawer. The silver I'd found at Paul's cabin was there and it didn't take me more than a few seconds to realize that it was causing my problems. I went to pick it up and got a shock strong enough to make me yelp.

"Did you just zap that?" Meredith asked from the doorway.

"No. I think it might have zapped me." I stared at it. "You pick it up."

"You know, that's a little like handing me something, saying it smells bad and asking me to sniff it."

"So sniff it. I don't care. But let's take it into the living room. Something's going on with it and I think it has to do with this fake letter from Paul."

We headed back into the living room. The closer the letter

and the lace were, the stronger the signal was. The most obvious explanation was that somehow the two objects were related. The most obvious relationship was that they had been made by the same person.

The most obvious conclusion to come to—from a piece of silver and a letter trying to convince me not to look for Paul, both coming from the same person—was that Paul was indeed in trouble and it was time to shift into high gear and come to his rescue.

Oh, boy, was he ever going to hate that.

WE LAID THE SILVER OUT ON THE BREAKFAST COUNTER and the letter next to it. The low-level tingle from both of them was making me clench my teeth. Meredith seemed unaffected. I wondered what that would be like.

"So Cordie said this stuff was not a net." Meredith nudged the silver with the end of a pencil.

"No and I figure she would know."

"So what is it?"

It was the most pertinent question. "I'm not sure. Cordie said it looked like a doily."

Meredith cocked her head to one side and looked at it from that angle. "She's got a point."

I fetched my laptop from my room and fired it up. I plugged doily pattern into Google and then clicked on the images. There were pages. And pages. And pages. We started scrolling through.

"There," Meredith shouted.

I looked at her. "I'm right next to you."

"Sorry. I got excited."

I clicked on the image she pointed to. It did look a little like our silver fragment. The page loaded. There were ten other examples, all of which looked a little like our fragment.

"It's hard to tell which one since we only have a piece of it." I peered closer at the screen. It wasn't helping.

I could see how it could be the first one. The geometric pattern seemed pretty similar.

"Or it could be that one." Meredith pointed to a second image and held the silver up next to it. Okay. It totally could be that one, too.

"Is it this close to all of these?" I pushed back from the screen.

She nodded. "You've seen one doily, you've kind of seen them all. Except they're all different."

"Like snowflakes, huh?"

"Exactly."

"The ones that are closest seem to be that Norwegian Hardanger lace." I checked the name of the website to make sure I had that right. Terrific. Half the area around Chuck's place was Norwegian. I'm not sure that narrowed anything down at all.

"Maybe somebody who knew more about Norwegian fiber arts could help you pinpoint the pattern," Meredith suggested.

I froze. "You mean like maybe somebody who had a yarn shop with a Norwegian bent to it?"

"Yeah. Exactly. You know someone like that?"

I put my head down on the counter. How blind could I be? Inge. She had to be involved. The lace had been buzzing in my pocket because I'd been standing next to her store, not because Kevin had been standing next to me on the sidewalk.

Inge, who whenever she was around made me slam my senses shut as hard as I could because of her grief.

But why? If the silver lace was a fragment of a much larger piece I could see the how, but the why completely escaped me.

I turned to Meredith. "I think we need to find out more about the yarn shop lady and I'm going to need your help to do it."

"SO WHERE EXACTLY ARE YOU GOING TO BE?" MEREDITH asked as we pulled into town.

"Nearby. It depends on where I can find parking." A Messenger's days were full of details like parking and other issues like that. It really was kind of ridiculous. I could be driving around northern California with a magical sword or a charmed chalice and still have to look for two-hour parking on the street before I could deliver them. "Are you nervous?"

Meredith rolled her eyes. "I don't do nervous."

I waited.

"I just want to know where you are in case I need to make a quick exit."

That seemed reasonable. "I don't think I can be closer than maybe a block away without slamming everything shut pretty hard." Inge's effect on me was profound and deeply disturbing. Just thinking about having to be around that melancholy made my stomach twist. Of course, I hadn't been my usual rock-solid self in the gastrointestinal area.

"That's fine. What do you want me to look for when I'm in there?" Meredith asked, fiddling with her braid.

"I'm not even sure. I just know that she has to be involved somehow." My cell phone buzzed. I glanced at the number and hit the reject button.

"Who was that?"

I didn't answer.

"You're not going to talk to him?" She shook her head. Not fair. "I did talk to him."

"Are you not going to talk to him ever again? Are you kicking him to the curb?"

Was I? I didn't know myself anymore. I knew that he'd disappointed me and hurt me. Although, really, whose fault was that? I'd let him in, hadn't I? I'd invited him into my life in a manner that was way more profound than the way Norah had invited Alex into our apartment. I was still pissed at her about that and I was beginning to see I should be pissed at myself as well. No hypocrisy here. Well, not much. "I don't know. Maybe he's kicking me to the curb. He didn't exactly drop to one knee and propose when I told him I was carrying his child."

Meredith's eyebrows went up. "Did you just drop it on him like a big bomb?"

"Yep. It's kind of my way."

"And what has he said since then?"

I shrugged. Ted had now left me at least six voice mails and sent me about a dozen texts, none of which I'd listened to or read.

"He hasn't said anything?" Meredith's brows climbed higher.

"I haven't been taking his calls," I admitted.

"Melina, Melina, Melina. What are we going to do with you?" She chuckled. "You should cut the guy a little slack. Impending fatherhood is kind of a big deal. It might have taken him a minute or two to let the news sink in." She stopped and then gave me a very piercing look. "He didn't ask if you were sure the baby was his, did he?"

I shook my head. "Nope."

"Well, okay, then. That's sort of a deal breaker. Unless, of course, you've given him reason to ask."

I punched her in the shoulder.

"Ouch."

I didn't apologize.

"Give him another chance."

"I'll think about it." I pulled the Buick into a parking place a block down and around the corner from Inge's shop and Kevin's hardware store.

Meredith flipped the vanity mirror down and checked her hair and makeup. "Can you keep your senses open here?"

I experimented. I could feel Inge's presence, but it wasn't overwhelming me. Distance indeed made me fonder of her. "Yeah. I should be okay here."

"Good. Then you should be able to sense it when I'm coming back to the car." She flipped the mirror shut. "You know, just in case I'm in a hurry."

I gave her a long hard look. "What is it that you're intending to do in there?" Our plan had been for Meredith to do a little reconnaissance. I wasn't exactly a great candidate to do it. First of all, Inge had seen me before in Kevin's shop. I didn't want her to get suspicious if she did indeed have something to do with Paul's disappearance. Second, being near her weakened me to the point where I was practically on my knees.

Reconnaissance, however, generally didn't require you to beat a hasty retreat to a getaway car, which sounded like what Meredith was planning.

She turned to me all wide-eyed and innocent. "I don't know. I don't know what we're looking for or what we're getting into here. Neither do you. I want to be prepared."

"No spellcasting," I said, trying to sound stern.

"Of course not," she said as if she wouldn't have dreamt of it, which had to be a bald-faced lie.

"Okay then. Beat it. I'll be right here." I leaned the seat back in the Buick.

"Don't fall asleep, Melina," she warned.

"I wasn't planning on it."

"Don't do it anyway."

Whatever.

Meredith got out of the car and disappeared around the corner toward the yarn shop.

I sat in the car and stewed. This was a fool's errand. What had I been thinking? If Paul had been at Inge's store, I would have felt him by now. I was 100 percent sure of that. Even with Inge's masking melancholy and what felt like a few stray brownies around, I knew I would pick his signal up. I hadn't. Besides, who would hide a werewolf in a yarn shop? I don't care what you were using to keep him subdued, it wasn't going to work. It took the bull in a china shop metaphor to a whole new level.

There were other werewolf vibes around. I had to assume it was Kevin and Sam and whoever else was working in the hardware store. Not Paul, though. I would have recognized Paul.

Speaking of werewolf, however, there was one getting pretty close. I slid down in the Buick, but it didn't help. Sam leaned in the open window on the passenger side. "Melina, what are you doing here?"

Great. I tried to keep track of Meredith's signal as the powerful presence of a young vital werewolf filled all my senses. "Oh, you know, just hanging out." Lame. I know. I should have had a lie prepared.

He cocked his head to one side. "Do you have a lead on

Paul?" He opened the door and slipped into the car, his big brown eyes wide and interested.

"I'm not sure. Maybe." There wasn't a whole lot of point in lying, but I wasn't ready to tell anyone besides Meredith about Inge yet. It could be totally a false direction. The last thing I needed was for a bunch of werewolves to be breathing down her neck if she wasn't involved. Or, for that matter, if she was. I had no idea where Paul might be or what she might be doing with him, after all. If he was in danger, I didn't want to make it worse.

"What is it? Is there some way I can help?" he asked.

I bit my lip. As much as I wanted to keep my own counsel, I needed more information. Sam would know plenty. "What can you tell me about Inge?"

If possible, those wide brown eyes got wider. "Inge who runs the yarn shop? That Inge?"

I nodded.

"You think she has something do with Paul?" He pressed.

"Honestly, I don't know yet. That's why I'd like to know more about her."

"Well, she's sure had her share of trouble." Sam sat back in the seat.

"What kind?"

Sam squirmed a little. "The car accident kind, I guess. Her husband and her youngest son were killed in a one-car accident on State Route 89 last year."

No wonder this woman had melancholy rolling off her like stink off an ogre. That would devastate anyone. "That's terrible."

"Yeah. Everybody said it was just a matter of time. Still, nobody really expects that." He looked pained.

"I'm not following."

"The husband. He was a drunk. He'd had like three DUIs in the past two years."

"How did he still have a license?" I asked. That was ridiculous.

"He didn't. He was driving without one." Sam shook his head. "Some people just don't care, Melina."

"But he had one of his kids in the car with him? How could he not care about that?" I was starting to feel sick. What kind of father was that? My father would never NEVER have put me in danger that way. And Ted? I knew through every fiber of my being that there was absolutely no way that he would do that to our baby even if he didn't want him or her.

Oh, God, our baby. His and mine, even if circumstances were forcing us into parenthood before we were ready. I gripped the steering wheel to keep my hands off my stomach.

"It's hard to fathom, I know, but it happens all the time, Melina," Sam said.

No wonder Inge walked around like a black cloud. What a hideous combination of grief and guilt and regret must she carry around with her? Wait. I knew exactly what kind of hideous cloud it was. It had nearly choked me to death the first time I'd come in contact with it. "How does she keep going?"

"She's got two more sons. That's a pretty powerful incentive to get out of bed in the morning," Sam said. Then suddenly he bared his teeth and growled. I stared at him. "You brought her with you?"

I looked down the sidewalk. Meredith was coming back to the car. He must have sensed her.

"I did. She's a friend." I did not like the turn this was taking.

He snorted. "Not in my book, she's not."

I got out of the car and held up my hands, hoping to slow Meredith down. She was doing her typical sexy stride back to the car and didn't even break her pace by one step, waving to me instead as if she thought I'd gotten out of the car to greet her.

I ducked my head back into the Buick. "Don't start anything."

"Don't worry. I won't. I'm leaving." Sam got out of the car, striding with his long legs. As he passed Meredith, the two of them glanced at each other. I could see her eyes narrow and his lips pull back from his teeth. I held my breath, but the two kept on walking.

"Consorting with werewolves the second my back is turned?" she asked as she got to the car.

"Consorting isn't exactly how I'd describe it," I said, getting back into the Buick, relieved that they hadn't started actual combat on the street.

"Probably just as well. He looked like a baby and a woman in your condition shouldn't be flirting."

I looked down the street where Sam had turned the corner. He did look young and I tended to treat him like he was, but that was a mistake. There was no telling how old he was. I needed to keep that in mind when I was dealing with him. I opted to ignore the remark about my condition. Flirting wasn't my strong suit even when I wasn't knocked up. I doubted the whole swelling waistline and intermittent nausea would create any great coquettish moments. "What did you find out?"

"That I'd really like to learn to make broomstick lace, real wool makes me sneeze and Inge worships at an altar to Frigga in the back of her shop." Meredith smiled. "Now start driving."

11

"WHAT DID THE ALTAR LOOK LIKE?" I ASKED, NOSING THE Buick into the street and back toward the highway.

"Like an altar." Meredith pulled an emery board out of her purse and started to file her nails.

"Could I have a few more details, please?"

Meredith sighed as if the breath was coming up from her toes. "It had a white and blue cloth and white and blue candles arranged in a circle. Then there was some yarn on a spindle and a jug of something."

"Something?"

"I'd guess mead or something like it. I don't have your nose. I can't walk by and sniff something and know what it is."

"So where was it?" I was trying to imagine a shrine like that in the middle of a yarn shop. You'd think people would mention it.

"Tucked in the back of the shop in the storeroom."

"How did you get back there?"

"I pretended like I was looking for a bathroom."

"Do you think she bought it?"

Meredith made a comme ci, comme ça gesture with her hand. "Maybe. I think she'll remember me if she sees me again too soon, but she didn't seem overly suspicious. She was pretty quick to hustle me out of there, though."

"Did she at least let you pee?"

"No. Not very sisterly, was it?" Meredith shook her head.

No. It wasn't. What the hell was Inge up to? Meredith was clearly worrying at the same problem, chewing at the edge of her thumb while she did it. Suddenly she turned to look at me. "You were saying that there have been two crows—big crows—hanging around outside your place all the time lately?"

"Yep. I've seen them at the hospital and at the dojo, too."

"Always two of them?"

"Only always two."

"And then there were demonic cows?"

"Yep."

"Anything else?"

I told her about the episode with the Buick's radio.

Meredith whipped out her iPhone and started hitting buttons.

"There's an app for witches?" I asked. "What is it? iSpell?"

"No. There's not an app for spells, although sometimes I still feel like this thing is magic." She went silent as she pushed a few more buttons. "I think your crows are Muninn and Huginn."

"Who?"

"Odin's crows. They roam the world and report back to

him. And I think those cows might belong to Odin and be reporting to Frigga. The cows could belong to Gefion."

"Who the hell is that?" I didn't like this at all.

"One of Frigga's handmaidens, and the thing with the words blasting out of the radio? Totally could be the work of Saga. Another of Frigga's handmaidens."

"So what you're saying is we've somehow gotten ourselves tangled up in the doings of a bunch of Norse gods." Crap. This was not good news. As much as I didn't like fooling around with supernatural denizens of the night, dealing with the gods and goddesses of various cultures invariably led to trouble. It's the stuff myths are made of, after all.

"It's possible."

"Why would they be following me around?" That was the part that made no sense.

"It started when you started looking for Paul, right?"

"Yes."

"So it stands to reason that they have something to do with his disappearance, doesn't it?"

My heart sank further. It was bad enough to just be skirting the edges of the business of gods and goddesses. If Paul was in the middle of it somehow, we'd be in serious trouble. What on earth—or off of it—would a Norse god need with a werewolf, though? And what did Inge have to do with it? "So what next?"

"I think we should take a look at Inge's house," Meredith said, waving her phone at me. "And I have the address right here."

"How'd you get her address?"

"I did a little scrying. You'd be shocked at how well a smartphone can simulate a crystal ball." She smiled.

"Technology is indeed a wonderful thing."

———

"WHAT ARE WE LOOKING FOR?" I ASKED AS I PARKED down the street after driving past Inge's house at a snail's pace. It wasn't anything special. Your basic blue ranch house with white trim, probably built in the late seventies. It had a small front yard, a concrete pad of a front porch and an attached garage.

"I don't know, but I didn't know what I was looking for when I went into the shop either."

She had a point. We watched for a few minutes in silence. Nothing happened.

"How long are we going to wait to figure out what we're looking for?" I asked.

"I don't know that either. Can you sense anything?"

I didn't from this distance, but thought I'd try to open my senses a little further. After all, Inge was back at the shop. Chances of her melancholy slapping me around here seemed slim. I shut my eyes and tried to relax my defenses. At first, it didn't feel like I was getting anything except a slight residue of Inge's sadness. Then I felt something else.

"There's someone—something—in there," I said, finally.

"What kind of something?" Meredith sat up straighter in her seat, eyes bright.

I tried to focus on the sensation, to get its flavor. "I'm not sure. It's really faint."

"Is there anything familiar about it? Anything at all?"

I shook my head. "Maybe. Maybe something a little wolfish about it, but it's not a werewolf and it's definitely not Paul."

A little starch went out of Meredith's shoulders. It would be a little too much to hope that Inge was keeping Paul in her basement or attic, subdued by a silver net that the two of us could whip off to rescue him.

"Is it another werewolf?"

I shook my head slowly. I wasn't sure what it was. Just that it was something. I didn't think I could get much more from it at this distance either. "Let's get closer."

She turned to look at me. "Do you think that's wise?"

I threw my hands up in the air. "I'm not sure any of this is wise. If we're meddling with Norse gods we're pretty much asking to get a lightning bolt up our asses. I don't see that we have any choice, though. No one else is looking for Paul. No one else thinks he's in trouble. His only chance is us."

Meredith frowned at me. "I meant is it wise to do this in broad daylight. Maybe we should wait for nighttime."

She had a point there. It was unlikely that darkness would protect us from anything in the house. If it was a supernatural creature, it most likely had supernatural senses that would know we were coming. Darkness could, however, keep nosey neighbors from calling the cops on us. I was only planning on a brief reconnaissance mission, though. No breaking and entering. At least, not for the time being.

"Let's just take a stroll past and see what we can see. If we want to do more serious snooping, we can come back later."

Meredith agreed and got out of the car, stretching her shoulders and arms.

"Hey, no yoga poses on the sidewalk. That will totally make people talk."

She shook her head, but stopped. "Fine. Let's take our little stroll."

We headed up the sidewalk toward Inge's house. As I got closer, the sense of whatever it was in the house got stronger. It didn't get any clearer, though. Not at all.

"This is weird, Meredith," I whispered to her as we walked.

"Tell me about it. We look about as natural as elves at a goblin festival."

"No. Not that." Although she had a point. We looked ridiculous. If I was a neighbor, I'd be calling the cops right now, but that wasn't what I'd meant. "I can't tell what's in there."

"It's not like you've been able to do that for a long time. It's kind of new, right? You're not exactly an old pro at it."

"Yeah, but this isn't like it's something unfamiliar. It's like it's all muddied up." I tried to think of a way to describe it. "You remember when you were a kid and at a restaurant with a self-service soda thing? How you'd mix a bunch of different sodas together and you could sort of taste all the different sodas in there together, but it was something else altogether now that you'd mixed them?"

"So we've got a mixed-blood thing in there?" Meredith kept strolling, even though I was slowing down and pulling back on her arm.

"No." I'd encountered a few of those before. They still were what they were.

"Then what?"

"That's what I'm saying. I don't know for sure." Now I did come to a stop, because regardless of what I didn't know, I knew that something was about to come out of that house. "He's coming," I whispered.

"Who?"

"The thing. It's coming out." I turned her so we were walking back toward the car.

She started frantically glancing over her shoulder. I yanked her arm. "Cut it out. You're being conspicuous."

"How am I supposed to see what's coming out of the door if I don't look?" she whined.

"Wait until we're at the car." We were only a few feet away by then.

"This is killing me," she hissed.

"Stop being so dramatic," I hissed back, but it wasn't easy for me either. All the hair on the back of my neck was prickling to a salute.

"Pregnancy is making you really bossy." She got to the car and walked over to the passenger door which allowed her to turn and look at what had come out of Inge's house. I turned, too.

"It's just a kid," she said, clearly disappointed.

I squinted. She was right. It looked like . . . a kid. A tall, thin blond kid. I bet he looked a lot like what Ted had looked like at sixteen or seventeen. Would that be what my child looked like sixteen years from now? I couldn't help it. I stared.

"Who's being conspicuous?" Meredith asked as she slid into the car.

I shook myself out of my reverie and unlocked the door and slid in, too.

Then I saw him lift his head and scent the air. He stopped in his tracks and turned to look right at our car. For just a second, his eyes blazed red.

I started the engine and got the hell out of there.

"WHAT THE HELL WAS THAT?" MEREDITH DEMANDED.

"How am I supposed to know?" I shot back, although I had a sinking feeling I knew exactly what it was. It was one of the things that had been in Leanne McMannis's garage and one of the things that had bitten Michael Hollinger.

"Because it's your thing."

"No. My thing is delivering stuff to things like that, not to necessarily know what they are."

Meredith opened her mouth, but before she could complain more, my cell phone rang. This time, it wasn't Ted.

"Hello?"

"I hear you've been hanging around town again."

Chuck. Great. Sam must have ratted me out the second he got back to the hardware store. "What can I say? It's such a cute little town and I find I'm totally getting into rosemaling."

"Cut the crap, Melina. I don't know what you were doing there and I'm not sure I want to know. I think you should come by my place before you head home, though." He sounded impatient.

"I have, uh, company with me." The idea of taking Meredith to Chuck's was unappealing on so very many levels. I wasn't sure if I was worried about them ripping her to pieces or her cursing them to kingdom come. It seemed like a lose-lose proposition to me and those are my least favorite of all the propositions.

"The witch?" he asked.

I sighed. There didn't seem any point in trying to get him to use her name and to not make "witch" sound like that word that rhymed with it. "Yes."

"Drop her somewhere."

"Like where? On the side of the road?" There wasn't a whole hell of a lot between town and Chuck's place. Not even a bar.

"Fine. Bring her. But she stays in the car."

I cut my eyes over to Meredith. Could I get her to stay in the car? "I'll talk to her," I said and hung up.

"What?" she asked, her tone already sharp.

"Chuck wants me to stop by before I go home." I squirmed a little.

"Why?" Her tone was flat. She really didn't like Chuck

any more than he liked her. Although honestly it was both of their losses. They would like each other, if they didn't have to play tug-of-war with Paul all the time.

"He didn't say." He hadn't, had he? He'd just summoned me and then hung up. It must be good to be the Alpha.

"And you're going to go running because he called?" Her tone had gotten very acid.

"Yep. Pretty much." It didn't make me feel good about myself, but pretending it wasn't true wasn't going to make me feel any better.

"Fine then. I've always wanted to see the seat of power of the Pack." She settled back in her seat, arms crossed over her chest.

"Yeah, about that . . ." My words drifted off.

"What?"

"He wants you to stay in the car." There it was, out.

She exploded. "He wants what? You cannot be serious. You cannot. He expects me to stay in the car like a pet that can't be trusted in the house?"

I didn't think his view of her was that benevolent, but that didn't seem the right tack to take. "Look. Could we maybe not take the most confrontational stance at the moment? You could take a little nap while I see what he wants. It might not take long."

"How would you feel if you had to wait in the car while I went in?" she demanded.

"Like it would be a good time to take a nap." That part was actually true. I really felt like I could go to sleep instantly whenever.

She sunk lower in the seat. "Fine."

"Just don't chew up my seat covers while I'm in there, okay?"

She shot me such a dirty look that it actually made me laugh.

THE MAN SITTING AT THE TABLE IN THE KITCHEN OF Chuck's house eating meatloaf and mashed potatoes didn't even look familiar. The idea that he was the same man that I'd seen hurling himself against a locked door while giving himself a straitjacket-induced hug was nearly inconceivable. Yet both he and Chuck swore that he was that Michael Hollinger.

I sat down across from him and stared.

He waved his fork at me. "Sorry," he mumbled wiping his mouth with a napkin. "I'm starving."

Chuck poured me a cup of coffee and set it down in front of me. Even the smell of it made me a little queasy. I shook my head and pushed it away.

"Morning sickness?" he asked.

"It would be nice if it confined itself to mornings." The queasies seemed to attack me at all times of the day and night. Certain things I knew would set me off. The smell of coffee. The sight of raw meat. The sound of people eating crackers. Other times it sneaked up on me.

"You're pregnant?" Hollinger asked. "Congratulations! Kids are the best. My two little ones . . . well, they make everything worthwhile. You're gonna love being a mom."

I looked at his beaming face. I wasn't entirely sure this man understood how irrevocably his life had changed. Assuming Chuck was going to let him hold on to that life. The Pack hadn't survived this long without a pretty ruthless policy about secrecy. "Thanks." I smiled at him, but knew it was pretty weak. I looked back over at Chuck.

"Come on, Melina. I want to show you the new truck." Chuck motioned toward the door with his head.

I stood up and followed him out the back door. We didn't speak until we were a fair distance from the house. Then Chuck said, "I have never seen anything like it."

"What did you do to him? He seems . . . normal." I sat down on a stump in the clearing we'd come to. The sun was warm on my face and I took a second to drink in the clean, fresh scents of pine needles and leaves.

"I think he might be. Now." Chuck leaned against a tree next to where I sat. "I didn't think he was going to survive the full moon. When he couldn't get out of that cell, I thought he might literally rip himself limb from limb. There wouldn't have been a damn thing we could have done about it either. No one could get close to him. At least, not without fear of getting bit."

I could understand why no one would want that. Hollinger had contracted whatever he had from a bite. Still . . . "You don't think your natural protections would have warded off whatever he has?" Assuming this acted like a virus, wouldn't being a werewolf be like an immunization against Hollinger's strain of lycanthropy?

Chuck shrugged those massive shoulders. "I honestly don't know and I had no intention of risking any of my Pack to find out."

"Does he remember anything about the guy who bit him originally?" I was as interested in how this all started as in how to deal with it once it happened.

"That he remembers a little bit more about. It wasn't one guy. It was two."

I almost rolled my eyes. We have a standing joke in the ER. No one who comes into the ER is ever the one who started a fight. It's always "Some Dude" or his cousin "Two

Dudes" who came out of nowhere and made all the trouble. "Two dudes, then."

"Yeah. Two dudes. In an alley behind the grocery store."

"What were they doing?"

"Hollinger's not sure, but he said it looked like they had turned over a Dumpster and were trying to break into the store."

I tried to imagine how much force it would take to tip a Dumpster and shook my head. "So what happened?"

"He shone his flashlight on them, identified himself and they rushed him. One of them bit him."

"He didn't fight back."

"Oh, he fought. In fact, he's pretty sure he hit one of them with his Taser. Didn't even slow him down."

"Would a Taser slow you down?"

Chuck raised a brow. "In wolf form? No. In human form? Some."

"So were these wolves?"

"Not exactly wolves. More wolflike. Kind of like what your friend McMannis described in her garage. The red glowing eyes. The fur. The growling. But still walking upright."

I chewed on my lip. The story was beginning to sound so familiar. "Chuck, what do you know about Inge?"

"Inge with the yarn store?"

"Yes. That Inge."

"How could she possibly be involved?"

"I'm not sure." I explained about the silver lace and the shrine to Frigga and the way her son's eyes had glowed red at us this afternoon.

"You think her kids are the ones who bit Hollinger?" He looked skeptical. "Based on one sighting of a kid who's eyes glowed at you? That could just have been a trick of the light."

"I don't think so."

"I've been around those boys dozens of times. There's nothing Arcane about either of them."

"Have you been around them recently?"

"No, but Kevin has. He'd have noticed something and he would have reported it." Chuck was adamant.

Darn. I thought I might have started to figure this out. "Are you sure?"

"Yes. I'm sure. Are you? Maybe your senses are off because of being pregnant. It's got to mess with your systems."

I glared, even though I wasn't totally sure he was wrong. Maybe I just saw those glowing eyes because I wanted to resolve the situation. I was glad he was sure. I wasn't sure I was. "What about Hollinger now?"

"It's like whatever was in his bloodstream burnt itself out during the full moon. He's back to being who he was before."

I thought of his wife and those two little children and my heart clutched a bit, even if one of the kids was a brat. "Are you going to let him go back to being who he was before?"

Chuck blew out a long breath. "There's been some discussion about that. Not everyone is comfortable with the idea."

"Where do you stand?" I held my breath while I waited for his answer. Chuck might be an embattled Alpha at the moment, but he was still the Alpha. His vote would count more than anyone else's.

"I think there are worse things than having a cop who owes us his life. He doesn't remember much about what happened, but what he does remember isn't pleasant. He knows without us he might not have survived. Or he might have survived, but other people might not have." Chuck straightened up and then squatted down next to me. "Besides, I don't think the Pack is going to stay here much longer. I'm starting to get itchy feet. It's time to move on."

"You said that before. Would you really leave all this?"

"I have before and quite likely I will again. It's the way it works. I'm starting to see suspicion in a few people's eyes. It's best to go before that spreads."

He would know. He'd certainly been around the block more times than I had. "And would the whole Pack go with you?"

He shrugged. "Some will. Some won't. A couple of the members of the Pack think I'm being soft with this Hollinger fellow. It'd be easy enough to kill him and make it look like he had an accident out in the woods after escaping from the ward."

That was certainly true. It wasn't exactly compassionate, but it was true. "You think he'll be able to keep his mouth shut?"

"Try to imagine what your average person would say if a police officer starting talking about his time among the werewolves."

"He'd be right back in that locked ward."

"I don't think Michael likes what he remembers of that place. I think we can trust him."

I took a deep breath. "I'm so glad. What's his story going to be?"

"We're sticking pretty close to the truth. He's going to tell people that he doesn't remember how he got out of the psych ward. We're going to tell people we found him wandering in the woods, sick as a dog and took care of him until he could tell us who he was." Chuck stood and extended his hand to me.

I took it and stood, too. "What about the part of the Pack who thinks this isn't the right move?"

Chuck frowned and started walking. "I've dealt with dissension in the ranks before. This has a slightly different feel to it, but I've weathered other storms. Worse storms, to be honest."

"What do you mean it has a different feel?"

"There are always politics being played in the Pack. I know that. Everyone's always jockeying for position. It's the downside of having so many strong dominant personalities together. Something's off about this, though. I catch these undercurrents that don't add up." He waved his hand in the air. "It'll pass. It always does. And if it doesn't, I won't be around to worry about it."

"Because you'd leave?"

Chuck stopped and looked at me. "No, Melina. I'd be dead. I'm not leaving this Pack voluntarily. Ever."

That froze me. "Is this really the hill you want to die on?"

He sighed. "I'll eventually die on one hill or another. I think protecting an innocent man who was in the wrong place at the wrong time might be an okay one with me." He cocked his head. "Speaking of innocents, do you have a plan for . . . uh . . . you know." He gestured at my stomach.

"Not yet." That unfroze me. I started back toward the house. I really didn't want to discuss this.

"What does the father say?"

I didn't answer.

"You told him, didn't you?"

I stopped and turned. "Yes. I told him. And he sat there gulping air like a fish on a dock."

"What did you expect? A proposal?"

I didn't answer, which was apparently answer enough.

Chuck took my hand and led me back toward the house, chuckling. "Give him some time. It's a lot for a man to take in all at once."

"And it's not for a woman?"

"I didn't say that. He didn't ask if you were sure it was his, did he?" Chuck glanced over at me.

"No!" What did Chuck think I was?

"Good. That might be a deal breaker. Other than that, though, I think you should give him another chance."

"I'll think about it," I grumbled.

WE GOT BACK INTO THE KITCHEN AND FOUND MICHAEL Hollinger mopping up the last of his meatloaf with a piece of bread and chatting with Meredith. I thought Chuck's eyes were going to pop right out of his head.

He turned to me. "I thought I told you that she had to wait in the car."

I held up my hands in front of myself. "That's where I left her. I swear. But she does have thumbs, you know. She can open a car door by herself."

Meredith smiled sweetly at Chuck. "Melina had been gone for so long. I was worried. What with her condition and all."

I glared at her. She was so not worried about my "condition." She just wanted to piss Chuck off.

Mission accomplished, as they say.

"Get out," he growled.

Hollinger looked from Meredith to Chuck to me, clearly confused. She pushed back her chair and stood. "I'm going."

She took her time walking to the door, though. I followed, making sure I stayed between her and Chuck. She turned as she opened the door. "We're on the same side, you know."

"Which side is that?"

"Paul's side."

12

I KNEW HE WAS THERE BEFORE I SAW HIM. IT WASN'T LIKE sensing Alex or Paul or even Meredith. It was a quickening of my heart, a leap in my stomach, a feeling of both excitement and tension. Damn him. He'd totally made me fall in love with him, and then when he found out he'd knocked me up, he disappeared on me. Although I suppose it was hard to fault a guy for disappearing when he was sitting on your doorstep, but I wouldn't be me if I didn't attempt the difficult.

I took my time gathering my garbage up from the inside of the Buick and locking it before I walked up to the steps to my apartment, where I knew he was waiting.

His blond hair shone in the gathering gloom and I swore I caught a whiff of his cookies-and-vanilla scent from halfway down the block. My eyes started to fill. We'd been through a lot. A couple of near-death experiences. A lot of suspensions of disbelief. Confusion. Chaos. Would this ever-so-normal couple dilemma be the thing that killed this relationship faster than a mongoose would kill a snake?

"Melina, thank God!" He sprang to his feet as I approached. "I've been so worried. Where have you been?"

"Chasing Frigga-worshippers into their lairs." I walked past him and unlocked the front door of the building.

"Here," he said, taking a bag from me. "Let me carry something."

I let him take it, but didn't comment. He followed me into the building and onto the stairs.

"I've been calling and texting you all day," he said from behind me.

"I know." I kept walking.

"Why didn't you answer?"

"I guess I was shocked speechless. It happens to some people sometimes, you know?" Ha.

"Melina." His voice had a warning tone in it. What the hell? He was pissed at me? I was clearly the injured party here.

"Don't 'Melina' me." I unlocked the door to the apartment. Or tried to. Norah had the chain on again. I did not feel like fooling around. I lifted up my foot and gave the door a swift kick just to the left of the chain. It flew off.

"Melina!" This time it was Norah.

"What?" I marched through the door and tossed my stuff down.

"You could have called for me." She stood with her hands on her hips staring at me.

"And you could have made it easy to get into my own apartment," I countered.

"I didn't know when you were coming home. You haven't been answering anyone's calls or texts all day."

"I was busy." I started to walk around her, but she moved

to block my path. I stared at her. On a bad day, I could probably toss Norah halfway down a football field. I knew that. I was pretty sure she had figured that out herself by now, too. Yet, here she stood, blocking my way.

"What is your problem?" she asked.

"My problem? What is yours? You're not the one who's pregnant." I moved to go around her on the left, but she shifted to block me again.

"That's what this is about?" Great. Ted had shifted around me and was now standing next to Norah.

"Maybe." I looked from one of them to the other. I had trusted them. I'd come to rely on them. I'd thought they'd have my back. Based on their reactions the other night, I'd apparently been wrong. They'd led me to have certain expectations, then they'd dashed them.

"Melina," Ted reached his hand out to take hold of my arm.

Without hesitation, I snaked my arm around his and broke his grip. "What?" I asked, my voice flat.

He held his hands up in front of himself in a gesture of surrender. "I'm sorry. I wasn't prepared for the news. I needed some time to adjust."

"You think I was prepared? You think I planned this?" I stepped toward him and he dropped back a step. Good. He should be a little afraid of me right now.

"No. Of course not. That's not what I meant."

"Then what do you mean?"

"I mean that we need to talk about it." He reached for me again, this time with both hands.

I was so not in the mood to be held and mollified. I shoved back with both my hands and as my hands hit his chest, a shock traveled up my arms with such force that it literally set me back on my heels and then, unfortunately for my dignity, on my ass.

"What the hell was that?" Norah gasped.

I held my hands up in front of me and watched the faint blue glow around them fade. I looked up at Ted. "This is totally your fault," I said.

NORAH HAD WISELY GONE TO BED WITHOUT ANY MORE commentary and left Ted and me alone to talk. Or whatever.

After managing to shock myself back on my ass, I was now apparently in the mood to be mollified. Maybe there was something to that whole electric shock therapy. It had certainly taken the wind out of my own personal sails.

I wondered what it would have done to Willow if they'd tried it on her. I looked over at Ted. "Did they ever do electric shock therapy on your dad?"

He gave me a quizzical look from in the kitchen where he was making me a cup of tea. "What?"

"Just curious. Did they ever, you know, zap him a little bit to see if it would make him better?"

"I don't really know. I was a kid. They didn't really discuss treatment plans with me." He went back to focusing on the tea. It didn't smell as good as the stuff Meredith made.

"What all did they do to him?"

He set the mug down in front of me, put a tea bag in and then poured the boiling water over it. "Why this sudden interest in my father?"

I shrugged. "I'm working on a theory."

"What kind of theory?" He sat down next to me at the counter. I noticed he kept a few inches of distance from me.

"A theory about the, uh, the baby."

"Our baby," he said.

I didn't dare look at him. Not for a few seconds at least. I felt something inside me melt a little, though. Maybe I wasn't going to handle this alone. "Yes. Our baby."

"So tell me about this theory." He shoved the jar of honey over toward me.

"It's going to require a little backstory," I warned.

"I can be patient."

That was true. He'd been patient lots of times. Patient with me, with Norah who had hated him at the beginning, patient with my mother who was still suspicious of him. So I told him about Willow.

"Okay. So she's actually not crazy. She's a wood nymph and didn't know it," Ted said.

"Yeah. But that made her think she was crazy and it made everyone else think she was crazy, too." I sipped some tea off my spoon to see if it had cooled enough.

"I can see how that would have happened. She's going to be okay now, though, right?"

"I think so. She's in good hands." I thought about Jenny for a second and amended, "Reasonable hands, at least."

"What does this have to do with our baby?" There it was again. Our baby. Something tight in my chest loosened a little bit.

"I'm getting there. Remember when we saw Michael Hollinger up in that locked ward?" I looked down at my tea. I hadn't exactly handled that moment all that well either.

"I do," he said, his voice quiet.

"Well, Hollinger isn't exactly crazy either."

"I wouldn't call him sane," Ted protested.

"You would now. Besides, he wasn't going crazy for no reason. He was going crazy because he was infected with something and he didn't understand what was happening to him and neither did anyone around him. Now that he's with Chuck, he stands a chance of figuring it all out and being able to handle it." I took a sip of the hot sweet tea. I didn't see any way I wasn't going to miss coffee, but this really wasn't so bad if you doctored it up right.

"Okay," he said tentatively. "Are you suggesting that my father was a wood nymph or was infected with some kind of werewolf venom?"

"Yes and no. I mean, not precisely those things, but maybe he had something a little tiny bit Arcane about him." I pinched my fingers together to show how much. "And that somehow got triggered and sent him over the edge."

Ted sat with that for a moment or two. I drank more tea and waited. It was entirely possible that two could play at this patience game.

Finally, he spoke. "So that would make me a little tiny bit Arcane as well."

"Even less so than your dad, which might explain why you don't give me a tingle."

He grinned. "I don't make you tingle? That is not the impression that you have given me in the past."

"I didn't mean like that." I thought about punching him, but didn't want the baby to zap me again. I was pretty sure that that was what had happened before, though. I'd been about to shove Ted pretty hard with the total intent of sending him back a few feet and our baby—his baby—had zapped me before I could hurt him.

He put his hand over mine. "I know. This isn't about me being able to find parking spaces again, is it?"

Was it? "Sort of. I mean, maybe that's some funny little way that your magic manifests itself. Maybe not. I do think it explains some of this electricity shooting out of my fingertips, though."

"You're losing me," he said.

Funny, based on the way that his hand had gone from mine to rest possessively at the small of my back, I didn't think so. Regardless, I backtracked again and explained some of my thoughts. Sophie had started me thinking, about how I might have become a Messenger.

"So you're saying that there's something magical about you, innately so, that meant that you were Messenger material." His hand was rubbing slow circles on the small of my back now. It felt good. "And maybe there's something magical about me, too, that was passed on by my bat-shit-crazy dad."

"Allegedly bat-shit crazy," I amended. "All combining in my uterus to make a baby that's zapping things when they're a threat to someone or something it cares about."

He smiled. "Like me."

"Like you. And Sophie, too. So don't get all cocky, okay?"

"I wouldn't dream of it." He paused, his hand still on my back. "I'm really sorry about how I reacted the other night when you first told me about the baby."

I froze, really hoping that he didn't say anything stupid right now. I was starting to forgive him, but it was a fragile state at the moment. He didn't say anything more. I looked over at him. He looked back at me with those ridiculously blue and serious eyes.

"I know I disappointed you. I never want to disappoint you. I love you."

Okay. How was I supposed to stay mad at him?

"In my defense, at least I didn't ask if you were sure the baby was mine." His face split in a grin.

This time, I did punch him, and the baby let me do it, too.

———

I HAD COME DAMN CLOSE TO FORGETTING MY PROMISE to meet my mother for coffee. Luckily, she knew me all too well and called in the morning to remind me. There was a time in the not all so distant past that those reminders irritated the bejeezus out of me. I was not a child anymore. I didn't need to be told when to go to bed, reminded to file my taxes or to turn my clocks back and/or spring them forward depending on the season.

Now, however, they didn't seem so awful. In fact, it was kind of nice to know that she had my back. Would I be that kind of mother? The one who, despite massive discouragement from her daughter, kept helping day after day, month after month, year after year? A stab of regret slid through my heart like quicksilver. I'd been an ungrateful brat for most of my life. I was still resentful, disaffected and withholding. How would I feel if the tables were reversed?

She was already at the Temple coffee shop when I arrived, sitting in the corner, reading a book, prepared for me to be late or not show at all. I waved, but went directly to the counter to order . . . tea. Before I could pull out my wallet, my mother was next to me handing a five to the barista. She looked at my cup and said, "Tea?"

"I'm trying something new," I said, the cover-up lie out of my mouth before I even thought about it. I'd been lying to my mother for so much of my life that it was more of a reflex than anything else. This time it left a bad taste in the back of my throat.

We sat down. "Was there something you wanted to talk about?" I asked.

She shook her head. "No. Just wanted to have a little girl time."

An awkward silence stretched between us. We still weren't good at this. It was quite possible we would never be. I'd seen other mother/daughter duos out for coffee. I knew what we were supposed to look like. We were supposed to be laughing and gossiping. We were supposed to be having fun. Not sitting across from each other grimly trying to come up with something to say. Something to share.

Not that I didn't have plenty to share. So whose fault was it that we were sitting here with pleasant smiles plastered on our faces and a lot of dead air between us?

I took a deep breath. "Mom, I'm pregnant."

I might as well have held up Medusa's head and waggled it in her face. She totally turned to stone. After a few seconds, I finally asked, "Mom, are you breathing?"

That snapped her to attention. She grabbed both my hands as if I wouldn't be able to hear her words unless we were in physical contact. "Tell me what you want to do."

"I'm keeping the baby," I said. I knew I'd made my decision. It was the first time I'd said it aloud. Damn it, it might well be the first time someone actually asked me. I'd thought about the alternatives. As unexpected and shocking as the news had been that I was pregnant, it had taken a while for me to really know what I wanted. I wanted this baby. I wasn't going to have an abortion and there was no way I was giving this baby up for adoption. A 'Cane baby raised by 'Danes? Well, I had a feeling that would be worse than what had happened to Willow. I wouldn't curse any child to that kind of life.

I knew damn well that I didn't have to have the baby at all. While I blanched at the thought of what this fetus might do to any doctor attempting to abort him or her, I knew it could still be done. I was all about choice. This was mine, though. I already admired the spirit this stubborn little collection of cells inside me showed. I'd do anything I could to blow the flame of its being higher and not to snuff it out.

My mother's hands covered her mouth and there was no way to miss the tears springing to her eyes. "And Ted?"

I squirmed. I wasn't sure what to say about Ted. I couldn't help but notice that even with all the talk of "our baby" and being together and having each other's back, Ted had yet to get down on one knee and make an honest woman out of me. "We're talking."

"What does that mean?" My mother's hands were off her mouth and palm down on the table now. Her tone was a little sharp.

"I'm not sure, Mom. He . . . he kind of freaked out when I told him. He's a little better now, but he hasn't really said too much." He hadn't either. He'd been all warm and cuddly, but there had been no talk about what we were going to do or how or anything else. It was, to be honest, wildly un-Ted-like. Then again, he'd been decidedly un-Tedly through all of this.

Mom's eyes narrowed down to slits. I knew that look. I'd seen it before. It didn't bode well. "We'll see about that!"

I reached across the table and put my hand over hers. "No, Mom. Give him some time. We didn't plan this. It's throwing both of us for a loop."

She put her free hand over mine so my hand was the meat in a little mom hand sandwich. "Here's the thing, dear. This doesn't get to be done on your timetable or his. Not anymore. If you're keeping this baby, your schedule is now the baby's schedule."

"And we have like seven months before the baby needs to take over that." Although even I knew that wasn't precisely true. Wasn't it the baby's schedule that was making me need to sleep for eight hours a night? Wasn't it the baby's needs that were making me devour meat and crave vegetables? It was already taking over my life. What would it be like when it was on the outside of me and could actually scream and kick to get its way?

"Are you getting medical care?"

"Not yet, Mom. This baby is special."

"All babies are special, Melina."

I knew that. We are also all gifted, just some of us open our presents later. I'd heard that all before. "I mean really special, Mom. It can already do things."

Obviously the Medusa effect on my mom's face was gone because her eyebrows climbed right up to her hairline. "Like what?"

"Like, uh, zap people."

"How do you know it's the baby?"

"Because I've never zapped anyone before in my life."

"Could it be a new power? You said you had some new things happening?"

"Yes, but they're all more like other levels to skills I already had. This is totally new."

"Hmmmm." She chewed on her lip.

"Mom?"

"Yes, Melina?"

"Did I do anything when I was still, you know, inside you?"

Mom got very still. "It was a long time ago, Melina."

That wasn't a yes or a no. "I know. I'm betting you remember at least pieces of it." Like I'm pretty sure she'd remember if she shot lightning bolts out of her fingertips even if it had been even longer ago. It wasn't something you forgot.

"Well, this is going to sound crazy," she said.

I glowered at her. "Really? That's what you're going to lead with?"

She laughed. "Okay. Maybe not as crazy as some of the things you've told me recently. Still, I never really told anyone about it."

"Tell me now, okay?" I was dying.

"You used to glow."

"Like a light?"

"Sort of like when you shine a flashlight through that real thin skin between your fingertips. I'd turn out the light to go to sleep and could swear I could see my stomach glowing." She laughed. "Your father thought I was nuts. He never could see it."

"That's it?" It was hardly a lightning bolt from the fingertips. It wasn't even finding good parking spaces or smelling like cookies.

"That's it. Sorry. Was that not what you were looking for?" She grimaced.

What had I been looking for? Proof that somehow this baby I was carrying was going to be greater than the sum of Ted's and my parts? What baby wasn't? "No, Mom. It was exactly what I was looking for. Thanks."

She beamed. Then leaned in toward me and whispered, "Do you want to go shopping for maternity clothes?"

NINETY VERY LONG MINUTES AND TWO COMPLETELY ridiculous smock tops with giant bows on the back later, I was back in the Buick and ready to take my search for Paul to the next level.

Inge had him. I was sure. The question was where. There was also the question of why, but it seemed secondary. There'd be plenty of time to ask her why after we got Paul. I wasn't even sure how to begin my search. He wasn't at her shop. He wasn't at her home. I would have sensed him when I was there. Where else could she have stashed him?

Meredith called before I started driving in circles in my frustration.

"I think I may have figured out something about Inge's sons. Can you come over?"

"I'm already in the car. I'll see you in ten."

Meredith lived in a loft in midtown. I got there in ten and then cruised for parking for another five minutes. I looked down at my stomach. "Perhaps you could have some of your daddy's parking luck, too. It would help." I knew it was a coincidence, but just then I saw a Suburban pull out of a space half a block ahead of me on my side of the road. At least, I think it was a coincidence. Regardless, I patted my stomach and said, "Thanks. Strong work there, fetus."

Meredith buzzed me into the lobby of her ever-so-modern glass-and-steel building and I took the elevator up to the seventh floor. She was hanging out of her doorway, beckoning for me to hurry when I got out of the elevator. "You've got to see this. Come on."

Inside her apartment, she hustled me over to where her laptop sat on a coffee table by the couch. She clicked a button to wake it up and then turned it toward me.

I was looking at a page about Ulfhednar. "I can't even pronounce that. What are they?"

"Just read," she said and sat back on the couch.

Ulfhednar were warriors. They were kind of like berserkers, but instead of taking on bearlike qualities, they took on wolflike qualities, but more likely just wore wolf skins. Just in case I wasn't sure from their entirely unpronounceable name, the page told me they were Norse.

"No one said anything about anyone wearing wolf-skins," I said, pushing the computer back at her.

"I know, but we have reports from two people who saw humans with wolflike qualities, but that weren't werewolves. Put that together with that shrine to Frigga in the back of Inge's store and you have to consider that there are Ulfhednar around." Meredith looked very smug.

"What do Ulfhednar have to do with Frigga?" The connections were too fragile yet.

She sighed. "Frigga is Odin's wife. The Ulfhednar are associated with Odin. Inge worships Frigga. Maybe Frigga is helping her out somehow." Meredith snapped her fingers. "Frigga is a weaver! She could have woven that silver net to snare Paul."

"That's another thing. Why the hell do they have to snare Paul? What does he have to do with any of this?" I still wasn't completely sold.

"I don't know. Not yet. But there are too many little things stacking up here to ignore. Don't you think?"

I did think. I just didn't know what made sense. "So what do the rest of the werewolf pack have to do with this?"

"Maybe nothing. Maybe all the maneuvering in the Pack is just a distraction." She tapped the pen she was holding against the tablet of paper where she'd been taking notes.

"Like some kind of smoke screen? Who could set up something like that?" It was possible. It seemed tricky.

She shook her head. "Not deliberately. There's always maneuvering in the Pack. You know that. Someone's always jockeying for position. It's one of the things that makes Paul so different from the rest of them. He's happy where he is. Or was."

"That whole calming-influence thing." I chewed on my lip. Had I let myself be distracted by what was essentially standard operating procedure in the Pack? "Fine. Let's focus on Inge, then. Where the hell would she have him?"

Meredith's face fell. "I don't know, Melina. I just don't know."

WE DECIDED THAT OUR NEXT STEP WAS TO TAKE A GOOD hard look at Inge's kids. If they were Ulfhednar, at least the mystery of who bit Michael Hollinger and ransacked McMannis's garage would be solved. Maybe watching would help me figure out what connection there might be to Paul, as well. Was Inge forcing him to give them wolf lessons?

Whatever it was, was going to have to wait. I'd dumped my responsibilities at the dojo on Sophie and T.J. for long enough. Ulfhednar stalking was going to have to wait for tomorrow.

I pulled into the parking lot and did a double take. My mother's Volvo was parked there already. What was she doing here? She never—and I do mean never—came to the dojo. It wasn't precisely that she disapproved; it was simply a part of my life that she'd never understood. My mother prefers to stay away from things she doesn't understand. Yet here she was, sitting in her car, right in front of it.

When I was little, a lot of what I learned at River City Karate and Judo was a secret from my mom, which had been exciting. When I was a teenager, it was a place to escape her. Okay. It had still been a place to escape her in my early twenties. This place was mine. Mine and Mae's.

My first instinct was to go park a block away and sneak in the back, but it wasn't like she wouldn't see me once I got inside, what with the big plate glass windows on the front of the place. Plus, we had been breaking down a lot of barriers between us. Maybe it was time to at least ease this barrier down a few notches.

I parked right next to her and she was out of her car like a shot. "Melina!" She trotted around the car and hugged me.

I allowed it. I am not a hugger. I don't know if I was cuddly before I was three, but I know I wasn't after. I was not the kind of little girl who snuggled into her parents' laps or held hands walking down the street. I had a very defined sense of personal space. My mother had generally respected that. Now, however, she had both her arms wrapped around me, trapping my arms at my side, and I'm pretty sure she was sniffling.

"Mom, are you okay?" I asked.

She gasped in a wavery breath. "Fine. I just haven't been able to stop thinking about . . . about what you told me at coffee this morning."

Oh, that. The knocked-up thing. I should have known there would be repercussions.

"I'm fine, Mom. A little tired. That's all."

"I know. I know. And I'm sure you know everything you need to know. You kids are all so clever today and everything's on the Internet. Still, I thought you should read this. It explains a lot of stuff." She thrust a copy of *What to Expect When You're Expecting* into my hands.

"Mom," I gasped, turning the cover toward myself. No one at the dojo needed to know yet.

She glanced around and then whispered. "Is something watching? Something that might steal the baby?"

"No, Mom. I'm just trying to keep this quiet for as long as I can." I wasn't exactly sure how the parents were going to respond to Sensei showing her integrity, self-respect and discipline by getting knocked up out of wedlock. I had some doubts it would be good for business.

She nodded quickly, brushing at her cheeks. Dear Lord, was she crying? "Oh, sure. Got it. Who knows?"

"Ted. Norah. You. Grandma guessed. I didn't tell her," I added quickly.

"Grandma guessed. When?" Her eyes went wide.

"Last Friday night." Wow. That seemed like months ago. It had only been a few days.

Mom's lips tightened. "I can't believe she didn't tell me. My own mother." Then her face softened and she brushed at my cheek with the back of her hand. "And my own daughter."

"Mom," I pleaded. "Can we take this down a notch?"

She took a step back. "Sure. Absolutely. But read the book, okay? It's stuffed with good information. And call me if you have questions. I've done this twice, you know."

Her face looked a little pinched. "Mom. It's okay."

"Yes, yes, I know." It was no good. She still looked pinched.

I took a deep breath. "And I will call you. And I will ask questions. I promise."

She looked a little less pinched. "Good. The first trimester is so important. You're not drinking, are you? Not that you were a big boozer, but you know it's better to stay away from it entirely."

"I'm not drinking." Then I thought of a question I did have. "But can I really not have sushi?"

Fifteen minutes later, after getting a very long list of what I should and should not eat, I finally got my mother back in her Volvo and headed for home. She and Sophie crossed paths in the parking lot. Sophie got out of her Camry and walked over to where I was still standing in front of the dojo.

"Was that your mom?"

I nodded.

"But she never comes here."

"I know." I sighed. "I think those days are over."

13

THROUGH THE COURSE OF THE AFTERNOON, MY MOTHER left me two voice mails. One to tell me not to clean cat boxes because there was some kind of special bacteria in cat poo that could hurt the baby and one to tell me that she was buying me a box of raspberry leaf tea that one of her friends swore by when she was pregnant.

I was really beginning to regret telling her. Maybe she would calm down a little bit over the next few weeks although calming down was not exactly my mother's specialty.

I headed home after the evening classes were finished, ready to put the day behind me. Ted was planning on meeting me at my place.

When I walked in, he was in the kitchen and the apartment smelled really good.

"Sit down," he said, gesturing at the breakfast bar.

I sat.

"So what's the plan?" he asked, setting a plate down in front of me.

I sniffed at it. It smelled good. I looked up at him. "Have you known how to do this all along?"

"You mean cook?"

"Yes, I mean cook."

He shrugged. "Simple stuff, but yeah. I had to be able to feed myself. No one else was going to do it."

"So how come I didn't know this? Why have we been living on take-out food and grilled cheese sandwiches?" I demanded.

"I thought you liked it that way." He sat down next to me with his own plate and dug in.

I took a bite. It tasted as good as it smelled. He was right, though. I sort of liked the take-out-food thing. It was one of the many things that separated me and my way of life from my parents and their way of life. No dinner every night at 6:30 P.M. No dishes to squabble over. "So what's different now?"

He stopped chewing for a second and glanced pointedly down at my stomach. Then he went back to eating.

It would normally thrill me to not have to talk everything to death. I wasn't great at expressing my feelings or sharing. I blame it on years of keeping a lot of my life secret. It was easier to keep everything to myself, rather than picking and choosing what I could say and what I couldn't. I wanted a little more right now, though. I set my fork down. Reluctantly, mind you. Still, I set it down. "That's it. I am the vessel carrying your seed and suddenly I deserve fresh asparagus?"

"No. But you wanted a salad the other night and I thought maybe you wanted to start eating healthy because of, you know, the baby." He set his fork down now, too. "Are you trying to start a fight?"

Was I? I looked down at my plate. It still smelled really good and it wouldn't taste anywhere near as good cold. I picked my fork back up. "No," I said and took another bite. "If I was starting a fight, we would already be yelling."

"True that," he said and snorted.

I glared, but I didn't stop eating.

"So what's the plan for tomorrow?" He started eating again, too.

"I'm going to talk to someone who might have some information about anything happening in the woods up there. Then I'm going to check out Inge's sons. Meredith thinks they might be the creatures that bit Michael Hollinger. And then I have to work a shift at the hospital." I took another bite. "Do you know how to make other things or is this your only dish?"

"You're going to what?" Oh, boy. The fork was back down at the side of the plate.

"Which part was confusing?"

"None of it. I'm hoping that I misheard. You're planning to go check out the creatures that possibly bit an armed police officer and caused him to go off his rocker by yourself? Did I hear that part correctly?" Wow. He looked really steamed.

"Yes. That is my plan. I'm not intending on riling them up and engaging them in a fight. I just want to get close enough to give them more of a sniff, you know? And maybe see what they're up to."

"If you're within sniffing distance, you're in biting distance."

"I'm pretty fast," I reminded him. "Even now."

"They're fast, too. Remember? Fast and unpredictable and violent and poisonous," he reminded me.

"So what do you want me to do, Ted? Nothing? Someone

up there has Paul. I think these boys might be involved somehow."

He rubbed his hand over his face. "I'm worried about Paul, too, but I'm more worried about you and about . . ." His words drifted off.

"About the baby?"

He nodded.

"Say it. Baby. Baby, baby, baby. *B. A. B. Y.*"

"Melina, cut it out."

"If you want me to stop, say it. You've gone all weird with this. I don't get what you want or what you're thinking or what you want to do."

"I'm working on it."

"Yeah. I'm working, too, and tomorrow my work is taking me to try to find Paul."

MY MOTHER CALLED ME THREE TIMES AND TEXTED ME four before I went to bed that night. I was to make sure to get a lot of rest. I should consider drinking more milk. Did I want to move home? Had I given any thought to what kind of stroller I might like? Was Ted there? Would I like my father to talk to Ted?

I turned off the phone. I had two more texts waiting from her when I turned it back on the next morning. I didn't read them. I couldn't. If the idea of being pregnant was overwhelming to me, it was because I'd forgotten how overwhelming my mother could be, given half a chance.

What had I been thinking telling her about this? I sighed. I knew the answer to that one. I was feeling alone. Who do we all turn to when we feel alone and like nobody has our back? Mom. That's who. Even me. Even if I'd spent a lot of my life turning to my surrogate mom, Mae. I wondered if Mom had already been over to Grandma Rosie's. Probably.

Ted hadn't even tried to get me out of bed to go running with him at oh dark thirty. I supposed I should be grateful for that, but instead it felt like one more wall between us. I got into the shower by myself.

I didn't like it. He was still acting weird. That was totally my wheelhouse and I wanted him out of it. He gave me a kiss on the cheek good-bye and headed off to work and I got in the Buick to see if I could find some more information about Paul. I realized Ted was right. Maybe I shouldn't throw myself in the path of Inge's sons until I knew more about what I was dealing with.

I pulled up at the address that had been written on the back of the bark that Jenny had given Willow. It wasn't nearly as remote as Paul's cabin, but it wasn't exactly urban either. There were neighbors, but they were only visible from certain places and they definitely couldn't hear you scream, if you were so inclined.

I parked the Buick to one side of the driveway and walked up to the door and knocked. I could hear the sound of music inside. That was a good sign. I was hopeful that someone would be home. I was doubly hopeful that it would be either Jenny or Willow. Explaining myself to a strange dryad was pretty unappealing.

I held my breath as the doorknob turned and let it out in a rush when Jenny answered. She cocked her head to one side and gave me a funny look. "Do you have something for me?"

I shook my head. "I have a favor to ask."

Her eyebrows shot up. "Hold on a sec. Let me get my smokes. We can talk out here."

She came back out a second later, a cigarette dangling between her lips and a lighter in her hand.

"Seriously?" I asked.

"Why not? I'm not going to get lung cancer from them and they're handy if I decide to start forest fires."

Now my eyebrows climbed.

Jenny punched me in the shoulder and laughed. "You are so gullible! How long have you been doing this?"

I sighed and sat down downwind of her as she lit up. "Maybe too long at this point."

She rolled her eyes. "You're just a baby. So what's the favor?"

"I'm looking for information. A friend of mine is missing. I think someone's holding him somewhere. I'm trying to figure out where. It's got to be some place fairly remote."

"What kind of friend?" Jenny arched one eyebrow at me.

"The kind that howls at the full moon."

Now both brows went up. "Someone's holding a werewolf hostage?"

"I think so."

"They're not so easy to contain," she observed, taking a long, deep drag of her cigarette and, thankfully, blowing the smoke in the opposite direction.

I refrained from pulling my shirt up over my mouth. It was tempting, though. My senses are always extraordinarily sharp and pregnancy was making them even more so. The smell of the cigarette smoke was literally nauseating. "I'm aware. That's why I thought even if the place was really remote, it might have made enough impact that you or your, uh, sisters might have noticed it."

She thought for a minute or two and blew a few smoke

rings. "Have you talked to the Pack? They'd be the ones who'd know how to subdue one of their own."

I nodded.

"Why aren't they looking for him?"

I leaned forward, bracing my elbows on my knees. "They don't seem to have the same sense of urgency about it as I do."

She gave me a curious glance, but then shrugged as if she wasn't interested enough to delve into it more. Or maybe she was just respecting my privacy. Either way, I was happy not to explain it again. "Do you have any idea who is keeping him? It might help."

"I do. Her name is Inge. She's got a yarn shop."

Jenny's head shot up. "Norwegian? Frigga-worshipper?"

"That's her." I sat up, too. "You know her?"

"I more know of her. I try to stay away. Talk about a little black cloud in a dress."

"Tell me about it. She about knocked me over with a grief bomb the first time I saw her, and she didn't even know who I was."

Jenny nodded her head a few times. "She wouldn't either. She doesn't have enough of the blood to make her sensitive to someone like you. Or me, for that matter."

"Enough of what blood?" I asked. I was getting somewhere. I could tell.

"Frigga's blood. Duh." Jenny took one last drag of her cigarette and then ground it out in the dirt. I was relieved that she picked the butt up. A smoking dryad was hard enough to take, but a smoking littering dryad would be too much even for me, and my expectations of the supernatural realm were very low.

"You're telling me that Inge is a descendant of Frigga?" Great. Just freaking fantastic. Not only were there gods involved, I was messing around with their progeny.

"And Odin's. She's like a twenty-times great-granddaughter. That's why the blood is so weak in her. It's weaker than the dryad blood in Willow."

"How's Willow doing, by the way?" I should have asked sooner. I felt a little bad about that.

"Great. She should be back in a little bit. Maybe you'll see her before you leave."

"I'd like that. Now about Inge. If the blood is that weak in her, how do you know that she's got any at all?" I'd encountered a few people who had traces of all kinds of stuff in them. It was hard to detect even two or three generations down. Granted, blood of a god was stronger than say, blood of a pixie, but dilute it enough and there was no way for me to tell. Inge's intense melancholy kept me from checking her out thoroughly the few times I'd been around her, so I hadn't sensed it at all.

Jenny twisted her long blonde hair up behind her in a messy bun that looked like something from a fashion magazine. Some women had a knack. "You know about her kid, right? The one that died."

"In the car accident with her husband," I said. "Yeah. I know."

"Tragic, right? Totally devastating."

I agreed. Who wouldn't?

"So Inge kept going to the spot where the accident happened, up on State Route 89. She'd go there after the two older boys went to school and she'd sit there and cry. It was awful." Jenny made a face. "I mean, I couldn't blame her, but it's not something you want to hear day in and day out, and that kind of grief echoes through the woods around here like you would not believe."

I did believe. I knew how it echoed through me anytime I was near her, and she was trying to hold it in then.

"So one day, I guess it was all too much for her and she decided she was going to end it all."

"Commit suicide?"

Jenny nodded. "Yep. She had a gun. She had a note. She was going to shuffle off this mortal coil."

"What about the other children? The other two boys?"

"I'm not sure. I guess there are relatives she thought would take them and she thought that living with her in this state would be worse for them than not having her at all."

I recoiled, physically from recoiled Jenny. My hand went protectively to my ever-so-slight bump that was forming right below my belly button. I couldn't imagine it. I hadn't even met this little person yet and the idea of leaving him or her without a parent in a world this crazy and unpredictable made me shudder.

Jenny looked down at my stomach and then back up at me. "Are you . . . ?"

So much for keeping my own counsel. "Yeah. Is it starting to show?"

"Only when you stare at it like it's sending you messages." She smirked.

It sort of was. I looked back at Jenny.

"Seriously? Messages?" She leaned back and stared at me openly now.

"Sort of." I took a chance. "Have you ever heard of anything like that before?"

She crinkled her brow. "Yeah. I have. It's not, like, talking to you, is it? Because I've found that that doesn't come to much good."

"Not talking. There's been some zapping, though."

She snorted. "Nice. Already kicking butt and taking names while in the womb." She reached over and patted my stomach. "Nice work, little one."

There was a flutter of response. Jenny felt it, too. I saw her eyes widen.

"See?" I said.

"I do. You want to know the rest of the Inge story, though?"

I blew out a breath. "I do. What stopped her?"

"Frigga stopped her."

That surprised me. A lot. The days of gods and goddesses meddling in the lives of mere mortals tended to be things of the past. "Wow. How'd that happen?" Not just any goddess either. Frigga, wife of Odin. That was some pretty big goddess cheese.

"I guess Frigga had heard her in the woods and been moved by her grief. It is her blood, after all. Plus, Frigga lost a son, too. She knows how much that hurts," Jenny pointed out.

I was a little rusty on my Norse mythology. "Which son did she lose?"

"Baldur. Loki killed him with a mistletoe arrow and it was, in a way, Frigga's fault. She didn't get a promise from the mistletoe not to harm Baldur and she told Loki about it, too." Jenny shook her head.

It was coming back to me. Frigga saw that in the future Baldur would be killed so she tried to change his fate. She ran around getting promises from everything not to harm him, but somehow missed the mistletoe. Loki, the sneaky bastard, made a dart of it and tricked someone else yet into using it to kill Baldur. Seriously, why did they keep that Loki guy around? He caused nothing but trouble. "So Frigga stopped Inge. How?"

"It was pretty cool. There was this huge crack of thunder and then she was there in the woods. She took the gun from

Inge and gathered her up in her arms and just held her for a while."

"Then what?"

Jenny shrugged. "What do you mean? That was it. Inge didn't off herself."

I'd worked as a clerk in the emergency department long enough to know that if someone was serious about killing herself, stopping her one time was not going to do the trick. We've had more than our share of frequent flyers in the self-harming department and I'm pretty sure that's true of every emergency room in the country. Stopping someone once would be like buying a hamburger for someone who is starving. You gotta show up with another hamburger tomorrow, too. "How did you hear about all this?"

Jenny waved a long, narrow hand in the air vaguely. "Word gets around."

I heard the sound of voices come from behind the house.

Jenny's face lit up. "That'll be Willow and the others. You can say hello."

Jenny ducked into the cabin and came out a few minutes later followed by a radiant Willow. Seriously radiant. It was as if there was an actual light inside her that was beaming out at me. "Melina," she cried and ran over and hugged me.

"Hey, Willow," I said, my arms reaching up to pat her on the back. That was the right way to do that, wasn't it? The pat thing?

"Jenny says you're expecting." She held me out at arm's length. "Let me see. Oh, you're not showing at all."

"I'm sure that'll change soon." I wasn't completely looking forward to that part. I'd become pretty accustomed to my own personal center of gravity. I wasn't excited about it shifting.

"You'll have to come back and see us again when it does. I can't wait to see you all fat and swollen." She giggled.

"You look pretty amazing," I said, changing the subject.

"It's a reflection of how I feel. I can't even begin to tell you what this has been like. I feel more at home in my own skin than I have ever felt in my life. Ever. It's fantastic. I'm so grateful to you for helping Jenny get that message to me."

"It's my job, Willow. It's no big deal."

She hugged me again. "I know better. I know you checked on me. That's not your job. That's kindness and I appreciate it. If you ever need a favor that I can do, I hope you'll ask."

I assured her I would. I have to admit, I don't mind having a few chits owed to me out there. It tends to work in my favor. I said good-bye and left, chewing over what Jenny had told me about Inge.

An actual descendant of the Norse gods, living in our midst and running a yarn shop of all things. Although I suppose for a daughter of Frigga, weaver of clouds, that was only appropriate. Maybe that was where Inge got her facility with yarn. Some skills gets passed down.

Frigga had to have done something besides stop Inge from killing herself, but what? I knew what I would have asked for in Inge's place. I would want some assurance I would never have to feel like that again. I would want protection for my two remaining children and I'd want it as fast as I could get it.

I HEADED BACK TO SACRAMENTO TO WORK MY SHIFT AT the hospital. It was a surprisingly quiet night. I even managed to take a little nap in one of the waiting rooms halfway through the night. I could use a few more like this one.

After my shift, I made my way up to where my car was

parked, as always, on the top of the garage, open to the sky. My heart fell a little when I saw a box sitting on the hood of the Buick.

It had an address and a time written on it. I sighed. Generally, no one gave me a specific time that something had to be delivered. This was new and, honestly, kind of irritating. I mean, it was bad enough that I had to take time out of my schedule to deliver whatever was in that little box, but to be told exactly when I had to be there was particularly irksome. Good thing that whoever wanted it delivered had picked a time that I didn't have to be at the dojo or the hospital.

I squinted at the address. It rang a bell, but I couldn't remember why. I supposed it didn't matter anyway. It's not like I wasn't going to deliver it.

I pulled out my cell phone and texted Ted: "Have delivery 2 make. Home by 8."

I got in the car and started the engine. My phone dinged. Ted had answered: "Gr8. C u l8r." I checked my watch. I should just go make the delivery. At the most, I'd be five minutes early. Surely whatever goblin or ghoul required their package to be delivered at a specific time wouldn't be upset with me being early.

I needn't have worried. Traffic snarled up on I-5 the second I merged onto it. There are worse roads to be on than I-5. You could be stuck on the causeway between Davis and Sacramento. You could be crawling up Highway 50 to Lake Tahoe on the Friday afternoon of a three-day weekend. That's really about it, though. Five can totally suck.

I finally exited off onto Sutterville Road and headed east. I'm not entirely unfamiliar with this neighborhood. A lot of denizens of the dark choose to live in kind of questionable areas, and this one definitely fit that definition. It's not like I had a choice or like I hadn't had to go to worse places.

I mean, it was still California. The grass in the yards was still green and the streets were wide and clean, but there was no escaping the difference between this 'hood and the one where I grew up in the Pocket. For one thing, there weren't any gang tags sprayed on the walls in the Pocket.

I checked the address again. I had to be getting close. I started feeling an extra layer of unease. I knew why the street was extra familiar. I was getting close to the park where I'd first seen the *kiang shi*, the Chinese vampires that had been unleashed on a Latino gang in an effort to start a gang war in Sacramento.

They'd darn near succeeded, too.

The *kiang shi* were no longer a threat, though. They hadn't been for a while. Their arrival in Sacramento had turned my life upside down and given it a good hard teeth-rattling shake. In fact, without the *kiang shi*, I wouldn't be contemplating unwed motherhood now. Stupid Chinese vampires.

I checked the numbers on the businesses I was driving past. I should be at the address in a block or two. What or who on earth could have wanted me to make a delivery down here and why why why did it have to be at precisely 7:30 A.M.?

Okay. Here it was. Good bats in the belfry. It was a 7-Eleven. I pulled into a parking place. At least I could get a cold bottle of water while I waited. I got out of the car and noticed a trail of red rose petals leading around the side of the store. Did I smell cookies, too?

A trail of bloodred flower petals almost certainly had to be a message to me. It was weird, though. I wasn't getting a tingle. I had gotten a weird stomach flip-flop, but maybe that was the baby. I hadn't exactly been experiencing the rock-solid digestion I was used to having. Was I delivering this completely unmagical package to an unmagical being? It would be way too much to bear if I suddenly had to start making deliveries to 'Danes as well as 'Canes. Way too much. If I had a union rep, I would be on the phone to him or her right this very second and I would be making a complaint.

I didn't have a union rep, though, so instead I trudged around the corner on the trail of rose petals.

Ted was standing by the pay phone.

"What are you doing here?" I asked, looking around. Something was waiting here for me to make a delivery and it had wanted it right now. It wouldn't be good for Ted to get in the way.

"I'm here to take the box you're carrying," he said. I looked him up and down and noticed he was standing in a puddle of rose petals.

"The delivery is for you?" I stared more. Was this some kind of shapeshifter taking the form of my boyfriend? No way. I would totally have been getting some kind of tingle. Instead I was getting the distinct smell of vanilla that always seemed to surround Ted.

"Yes." He smiled. He reached out his hand. "Could I have the box?"

I handed it over. "What's going on?"

He held up one finger and unwrapped the box. Inside was another box. A little velvety box. The kind of little velvety box that jewelers give you a ring in. He dropped down to one knee. "Melina Markowitz, you have driven me crazier than any person has ever dared and that is saying something. You have challenged me. You have thwarted me. You have made me want to tear my hair out. I have never been happier than I am with you. Will you marry me?"

I stared at him. "Now? Now you're proposing?"

He stared back at me. "What's wrong with now?"

I stared at him. "Now? Now you finally do this?"

He blinked a few times. "It takes a little while to get a ring, Melina. I wanted to do it right."

"So all this time that you've been giving me the cold shoulder and shutting me out while I felt more alone than I've ever felt in my life, you were planning this?"

"I wasn't shutting you out. I was trying to keep a secret. You're hard to keep secrets from. Maybe because you keep so many of your own." His eyes were starting to narrow, but he was still down there on one knee.

"You're doing this here? Why here?" I gestured to the dirty parking lot and the gang tags on the walls of the 7-Eleven. It wasn't exactly romantic.

"It was the first place I ever saw you. You made your anonymous call to 911 from this pay phone." He was still on his knee.

"You were looking at me on a surveillance tape. Creepy, much?" I asked.

"Are you seriously calling me creepy? You were calling 911 to report that Chinese vampires were ripping apart gang members like one of your mother's briskets."

He had a point. He also still had a ring in a pretty velvet box that he was holding out to me while he stayed on one knee asking me to marry him. "Are you doing this just because I've got your bun in my oven?" I asked.

"It certainly prompted me to consider the question, but my answer would always be the same. I want to spend the rest of my life with you. Please say you'll marry me."

"How many kids do you want?" We'd never discussed these things and I felt we should before we made this kind of decision.

His brow furrowed. "I don't know. Maybe two. Three

seems like a bad idea. We'd be outnumbered. One feels a little tenuous."

That seemed reasonable. "Where would we live?"

"Melina, can we discuss this after you say yes? Something's digging into my knee and it's really starting to hurt."

"What makes you think that I'll say yes?" That was some nerve.

He stood up then. He closed the distance between us with one step, pulled me to him and kissed me very thoroughly. "You'll say yes because you love me as much as I love you and you know it's what you want to say. Now stop fighting it and say you'll be my wife."

"Show me the ring again."

He sighed, but he showed it to me. The diamond was pretty small. Like pinpoint small. Still, it was a diamond. "Fine. I'll do it." I reached for the box.

He lifted his arm, holding it just out of my reach. "You'll do what?"

"Marry you. Be your wife. Spend the rest of my life by your side. Bear your child. Okay?"

"Yes," he said. "Very okay."

He handed me the box. "Come on," he said. "Let's go home and call your mother before she sics Grandma Rosie on me."

I SPENT A GOOD PORTION OF THE DRIVE BACK TO MY apartment admiring the pretty. I liked the way the sun sparkled off the little diamond. It was probably a lucky thing I didn't plow into a parked car.

After we went in and called my mother with the news about our engagement and spent half an hour on the phone telling her that we hadn't made any specific plans yet, over and over and over, it was time to get back down to business, though.

"I think I've got this figured out," I told Ted.

"You want to fill me in?" he asked as he made an omelet. An omelet, I tell you! I couldn't believe my eyes.

"Let's say that Inge wants to make her sons into Ulfhednar so they can't be harmed," I posited, while trying to see exactly what Ted was putting in my omelet.

"I'm willing to stipulate to that." He popped two pieces of bread in the toaster.

"But the Norse blood is even weaker in them than it is in her. They can't become Ulfhednar all on their own. They need some kind of special help to make them more wolflike." Definitely cheese. Maybe some onion. Maybe red pepper. I swallowed hard.

"You think they're using something of Paul's to make them more wolflike so they can become these warriors that are impervious to wood and steel?" He set the butter and a jar of apricot jam on the counter in front of me.

"I do. Look at what happened to Michael Hollinger. They bit him and maybe exchanged some blood or some saliva or something and it infected him. Maybe Inge is deliberately infecting her kids with something from Paul. Maybe Frigga made her the silver net so she could catch Paul—or any of the werewolves—and use them as an unwilling donor."

He looked over at me. "That's not a bad hypothesis, but you realize that would mean that she would have to know that Paul was a werewolf."

I gnawed on the side of my thumb. "I know."

"Do you think she could have figured that out?" He slid the omelet out of the pan and onto a plate and set the plate in front of me. Then he started making his own omelet. "Eat. Don't let it get cold."

He didn't have to tell me twice. "I do. Chuck's been saying that people have been getting suspicious of him. Maybe she's one of those people. Plus, there's the whole Kevin thing."

He looked over at me from the stove. "What Kevin thing?"

"He's got a total crush on her. Maybe he let something slip. Maybe they're spending some time together and she figured it out."

"Do you think he told her deliberately?"

I shook my head. "No. He's a prickly SOB, but I felt like he was telling me the truth the other day when I followed him to his class. He didn't want anything bad to happen to Paul."

"So what do we do with this theory?" he asked.

"We go talk to Chuck," I said. "Wanna come with?"

He slid his own omelet onto his plate and sat down next to me. Mine was gone along with the two pieces of toast he'd given me. "I thought you'd never ask."

14

IT TOOK A WHILE TO GET CHUCK OUT OF THE HOUSE SO I could tell him my theory, but once we did it didn't take long for me to lay it out for him up at the overlook where I'd talked to him when I first started looking for Paul. It took even less time for him to see how very possible it was.

"Ulfhednar?" he repeated.

I nodded. "I think so. It makes sense."

He shot me a look. "How could that possibly make sense?"

I knew what he was saying, but I had no time to appreciate his sarcasm. "Look. The Ulfhednar are particularly associated with Odin. Inge is somehow tangled up with Frigga. Need I remind you that those two are married?"

"No. Thank you. I do have a basic understanding of Norse mythology."

I went on. "While the berserkers that were associated with Thor took on the characteristics of bears, the Ulfhednar took on the characteristics of wolves. Sort of man/wolf hybrids."

"Sort of like werewolves," Chuck said, his voice thoughtful.

"Yeah. Kind of like werewolves, but not exactly," I agreed.

"And you think Kevin is somehow involved?"

I hesitated. "I don't know. I know there's something between him and Inge. I don't know if she figured it out from proximity or he said something that made her suspicious or what. I do think he knows more than he's letting on. After all, he's the one who should have told you about Hollinger and McMannis weeks ago."

"So you think he withheld that information from me?" Chuck's voice was calm and even, but his fists were clenching and unclenching.

"I don't know, Chuck. You'll have to ask him."

"Let's do that then."

We trooped back down the hill. Chuck sent Sam to get Kevin and we spent a very uncomfortable half hour waiting for him as Chuck's anger grew visibly.

By the time Kevin arrived, Chuck was pacing while Ted and I tried to stay very still and quiet in our chairs. Every once in a while he'd pause as if something had suddenly occurred to him, then he'd continue pacing.

Kevin walked in with Sam behind him. Chuck stopped pacing, took one look at Kevin, pulled his arm back and socked Kevin in the chin with a blow that would have sent me flying into the next room. It only knocked Kevin to the floor.

"What the hell?" He stared up from the floor, rubbing his jaw.

Chuck put his boot on Kevin's chest and pushed him down. "Did you tell Inge what we are?"

"No! I would never have done that. She knew already. She'd guessed," he protested, cowering now.

"But you confirmed it for her." Chuck backed away. "You pathetic idiot. You're sleeping with her, aren't you? Four hundred years old and still being led around by your dick." He shook his head.

Ted looked at me, forehead lined with confusion. "I don't get it. If she had Kevin in her bed, why did she need to kidnap Paul?"

I turned back to Kevin. "Out of curiosity, if Inge had started asking for blood donations from you, would you have given them to her?"

He shook his head. "No."

"So you knew what she was doing? You knew she was turning those boys into warriors when there was no one to fight? Couldn't you see it would all end in disaster?" Chuck shut his eyes and shook his head.

"I didn't know. I suspected. I thought she'd get past it. We'd get Paul back. He'll survive this. He's tough." Kevin scrambled to his knees.

I turned back to Ted. "See? She knew she wouldn't get a willing donor. She had to wait until she could take someone. This was never about Pack politics. It was never about getting Paul out of the way. He was just in the wrong place at the wrong time."

Ted let out a low whistle. "Talk about bad luck."

"I think it's time for that luck to turn," I said. "I think I know where she's keeping him."

Chuck stared at me. "You are full of surprises today, Melina. Where?"

I twisted my hands together in front of me. "Where were you before you moved here, Chuck?"

"About ten miles southeast of here, near Jackson. Why?" He was answering me, but he was still looking at Kevin.

"Did you have basically the same setup there as you do here?" I asked.

Now he glanced over at me. "What do you mean?"

"I mean like the place where you held Michael Hollinger. Did you have something like that at your old place?"

"Of course. It's important to be able to contain a wolf that is out of control." The look he gave to Kevin was quite meaningful.

"Is it still standing?" I asked.

"As far as I know." He stared at me. "You think that's where Paul is?"

"It's the only thing that makes sense to me. Where else do you think you'd be able to contain a werewolf?"

He stood up. "What are we waiting for, then?"

WE MADE THE RIDE TO JACKSON IN GRIM SILENCE, EACH of us with our own private thoughts. Mine ran very dark. Were we too late? What kind of shape would Paul be in? What kind of protections would Inge have?

Chuck glanced over at me. "There's a back way in," he said, simply, knowing I would understand.

A lot of 'Canes built their places with escape in mind. One never knew when the villagers might actually show up with pitchforks and torches. Or some modern day equivalent of the same. Any way you sliced it, it was best to have a Plan B at the ready.

"What kind of back way?" I asked. Some were more accessible than others.

"A tunnel," he said simply.

I sighed. "So it's underground."

"Well, that's generally where most folk keep their tunnels, Melina," he said mildly.

As much as I appreciated the inappropriate humor, I still wasn't happy. I don't like underground places. They're usually dirty and there are often insects involved. I'm not going to squeal and run if a spider runs across my hand while I'm crawling through a dank hole in the ground, but it doesn't mean I like it. "Fine. How long a tunnel?"

He shrugged. "Long enough."

"I'm trying to figure out how far I'm going to have to crawl," I prompted.

Everyone in the car got very quiet. "You're not crawling anywhere, Melina," Chuck said, his voice still mild.

"Then how am I supposed to help get Paul out of there? Am I supposed to be the distraction at the front entrance, then?"

Ted leaned forward from the backseat and said, "You're waiting in the car."

My mouth dropped open. I have played all kinds of roles in all kinds of situations. It's part and parcel of the part-and-parcel-carrying business. But I have never been relegated to the role of the person who waits in the car. "I am not."

"Yes, you are." Chuck glanced back at Ted. I didn't care for the way they were exchanging glances, as if this had already been discussed between them. When had they done that? During one of the six thousand times I'd had to pee before we left? "You can't risk getting bitten."

"Who here can?" I demanded. Everyone was putting themselves at risk here. It wouldn't be just me. We were all putting it on the line for Paul, just like he'd always put it on the line for us.

"Most of us," Chuck said, glancing over at me. "Look. We know what happens if a human gets bitten. We watched it with Hollinger. The effects of werewolf blood or saliva wear off eventually. It won't be pretty, but we know how to deal with it."

I started to respond, but he held up his hand.

"We haven't seen what happens when a werewolf gets bitten by a Ulfhednar, but it can't be worse than being bitten by another werewolf and frankly that happens all the damn time. There's way too much roughhousing in the Pack some-times. It's like dealing with an entire herd of teenage boys." Again, he held up his hand before I could say anything.

"What we don't know is what this virus would do to an unborn child. We're not risking it. There's no reason to. Please don't argue with me, Melina. You know what I'm saying is true. You know it's right. For once, don't be contrary just for the sake of being oppositional."

I started to open my mouth again, but this time, I shut it myself. He was right. There was no way around it. It wasn't a risk worth taking. I slumped back in my seat.

Ted put his hand on my shoulder, but wisely didn't say anything. We rode the rest of the way in silence.

Chuck pulled the wagon up to a place that really didn't look like anything but the rest of the woods around it. There wasn't a clearing or a special stump or a ribbon tied around a tree. "Here?" I asked.

"About a half a mile in."

Ted got out of the car and stretched. "How can you tell?"

Chuck waved his hand. "You get to know a place when you live there for a few decades. Trust me on that."

Ted shook his head. "I'll have to. I don't think I've ever lived in one town for more than three years."

Chuck shuddered.

Within the next five minutes two more carloads of were-wolves in human form, Sam among them, arrived. More than a few snarled at me, earning them some low growls from Chuck. I guess being right about something didn't make you popular. Shame, that. Sam avoided my eyes and kept a healthy distance between us. I wasn't sure if it was anger or a cover. I didn't care. I was getting what I wanted. We were rescuing Paul.

"We'll walk in. We'd cover ground faster as wolves, but the tunnel will be easier to navigate in human form and I don't want any of us weakened by changing in and out too fast." A change could take a lot out of a werewolf. He was right. They were going to be a far superior force, but there was no reason to take any chances.

"I'll be here," I said as they started to march in, Ted among them. "I've got Sudoku on my phone. Don't worry about me."

No one laughed. I checked the time as they walked in. Four twenty-five. I'd give them one full hour before I came after them.

I did not do a Sudoku. I couldn't focus on the little numbers. I couldn't stay inside the car. I paced for a little while, but there really wasn't a lot of space to do it. Finally, I found a rock to sit on and sat and listened. At the very least, I would hear them coming. It was the best I could do.

There wasn't anything. Well, that wasn't entirely true. There were insects and birds and some squirrels, but they were just insects and birds and squirrels. They weren't even Arcane insects, birds or squirrels.

I put my hand on my stomach and felt my little peapod swimming lazy circles inside me and I let my heart ache for a moment for Inge. She had done this three times, but had only two sons left. No wonder she was willing to go to any length to protect her children. Her pain must have been unimaginable.

That's where I was when the two giant crows swooped over my head in the direction that Ted and Chuck and the rest of them had gone. Crap. Huginn and Muninn. I was pretty sure that meant Inge had reinforcements on the way. I texted Ted's cell phone to warn them and heard it buzz inside the car. Damn it. I tried Chuck's and heard it in the car, too. They must have all left their phones here.

If I wanted to warn them or help them in any way, I was going to have to find them. I stood and headed into the woods.

IT WASN'T TOO DIFFICULT TO TRACK WHERE THE WOLVES and Ted had gone through the woods. That large a group leaves a fairly large collective footprint. What I didn't want to do was go in the same way they had, though. If Huginn and Muninn had already alerted Inge and brought in the cavalry, I needed to find the front entrance and surprise them there. The only problem was, I wasn't sure where that was. I figured I would see where Ted and Chuck had gone and find my way around to the front entrance from there.

I don't exactly move on feathered feet, but I can be pretty quiet when I need to be. I slipped along disturbing as little as I could without giving up speed. I could not—would not—be too late.

Meanwhile, I listened. I was perhaps a quarter mile in when I started to hear the commotion. The snarling of wolves. The beating of hooves. I heard a hoarse scream and found myself repeating "Please don't let it be Ted" over and over again. I know it was selfish, but I've never pretended to be anything else.

I slowed as I got closer so I could get a look at what was going on. I hardly needed to worry about staying behind the trees. No one would have noticed me unless I sprang into the middle of the melee.

Ted was at the back of the pack and I let out a sigh of relief, although he was far from out of danger. At least he wasn't up front where a ridiculously tall woman with blonde hair dressed in gray was warding off wolves with a staff. It had to be Syn, another one of Frigga's handmaidens. She was charged with protecting thresholds. In the middle of everything, Gna, yet another handmaiden, rode a huge horse with nine hooves, striking out and leaving wolves wounded. Still, it was clear which way the tide was turning. There were simply too many wolves, no matter how many hooves that damn horse had. What was wrong with a basic four anyways?

I took one last look at Ted, sent a prayer for his protection up to I don't know who and started making my way around what was left of the structure.

I heard something, something big and moving fast in the woods. It was more than one. I reached my senses out toward the ones moving toward me and instantly recoiled. Not wolves. Not Paul. Ulfhednar. Inge was headed this way with her two sons. They were not alone either.

I cast around looking for a good vantage point. Clambering up a tree was an option. I climb well, even now with things starting to feel a little out of kilter, I was sure I could scamper up the big pine tree to my right. Then again, I was guessing Inge's sons could, too, and it was altogether too easy to run out of up. Then where would I be? At the top of the tree, either trying to fight or having to jump. Not good.

They were getting closer, covering ground quickly and not caring how many branches they broke on their way. They weren't worried about leaving a trail and being followed, that was for sure.

I scanned the area once more. I could get on top of one of the nearby rocks. I like high ground when I'm fighting, but it felt too exposed. I could be too easily surrounded and too easily knocked off balance these days. I know I'd only gained a pound or two and the shift in my center of gravity wasn't huge, but while I don't like to toot my own horn too much, I am a finely honed fighting machine. Those differences would have an impact and I wouldn't know how to adjust until I was already in the middle of the fight and that might be too late.

Speaking of too late, they were nearly here. I cracked my neck, bounced on my knees a few times and turned to face where I was pretty sure they would emerge from the trees.

That's precisely what they did about three minutes later.

Inge skidded to a stop in front of me. "You," she said, her intonation making it very clear what she thought about me.

"Hey, Inge, I'm sort of surprised to see you here, too. I think my friends were planning on meeting you inside." I kept my tone pleasant, but my knees loose.

"Your friends are easily distracted," she said, giving me a tight smile. Erik and Sven moved to either side of their mother. It softened me for a second. They were good boys. They wanted to protect her. They were also, at the moment, sort of monstrous.

"Generally, not really, once they're on the hunt." It was hard to shake a werewolf loose once he was on to you.

She snorted. "Werewolves. Drip a little blood around and they go kind of crazy, don't they? Especially if it's werewolf blood."

I cringed. "Paul's blood?" I asked, unable to stop myself. I shouldn't show weakness, and the tenderness I felt for Paul was definitely a weakness right now, but there it was. Stupid pregnancy hormones. Putting my heart on my sleeve.

She cocked her head to one side. "That would be the werewolf whose blood I have the easiest access to at the moment. Yes."

"So he's still alive?" I asked, relief flooding through me

at the idea. There wasn't much he wouldn't be able to heal from. As long as he wasn't actually dead, he would be okay.

She shrugged. I couldn't tell if that meant it didn't matter to her or if she wasn't sure. "I'm going to need you to get out of our way, Melina."

I shook my head and swallowed hard. "I don't think I can do that, Inge. I think we need to stay right here until my friends find us."

She laughed. Not one of those crazy maniac laughs either. More like the way my mother would laugh when I asked her if I could do something like go to a concert in San Francisco and drive myself, as if what I'd said was actually funny. "Sorry, dear, but you need to get out of the way before you get hurt."

I shook my head again. "No can do, Inge. You and your boys are going to have to go through me to get out of here." I swallowed hard and hoped they couldn't smell the fear. I did not want to fight those two boys.

Even a truly excellent fighter—and I am damn good, mind you—rarely gets out of a tough fight without the other guy getting in a few licks. In fact, letting the opponent think he's scored on you a bit is a great tactic. It makes him let his guard down. I've used it dozens of time. People underestimating me is one of the things that have kept me alive and well for this long.

This time, though, a scratch or a bite from Inge's Tweedle-Wolf and Tweedle-Wolfier could give me a lot more than a gash that might take some time to heal. This time it could turn me into a raving lunatic for a few weeks and no one knew what it could do to the little peanut swimming bliss-fully in its ignorance inside me.

I was still going to have to try, or at least to stall them until Ted and Chuck and the rest of them got through and rescued Paul. I strained my ears to see if I could hear anything and got nothing more than battle noises, but I couldn't tell what was happening. I couldn't afford to be distracted now either. I was going to have to focus on the fight in front of me and not on the rescue that might be coming through the woods soon.

"That would be a shame, dear. I'm sure you don't mean that." Inge smiled at me. "Kevin tells me that you're pregnant."

"Yep. Got a bun in the oven," I said, watching her sons. Generally, I like to keep a watch on my opponent's eyes during a fight. This was a little trickier when there were two sets. One was definitely the bigger of the two and looked older. Did that make him the leader? If so, I could just watch his eyes. It is amazing what most people telegraph with their line of sight before they take a swing.

On the other hand, just bigger and older didn't necessarily make you the leader in a fight. Sven was wiry and I bet he could use that to his advantage.

"Then I think you should back away slowly and let us through. You wouldn't want to do anything to harm the baby, would you?" Her voice had more than a touch of steel to it now.

I gave her a touch of steel right back. "No. I wouldn't. I wouldn't want to let you go either. I wouldn't wish your kind of trouble on anybody else's child."

"What kind of mother would risk her own child in a fight like this one?" Inge shook her head.

"You are. You're risking both your boys," I pointed out.

She laughed again. "Have you seen my boys fight? You'll be in ribbons in a matter of minutes."

I laughed, too. "You haven't seen me fight yet."

"Au contraire. I saw you finish off Gefion's cattle."

I shrugged. "Wasn't nothing, ma'am."

"No. It wasn't. You'll need a lot more skill than that to beat my boys back." She took a step toward me and both boys followed her lead.

I realized then that it was her eyes that needed following. I wasn't sure how she was communicating with her sons, but she was and she was definitely in charge. I focused back in on her. I bounced a little on the balls of my feet, keeping my knees loose. They were fast. I knew that. I'd have to be ready. I didn't like how they were closing the gap between us either. The shorter the span separating us, the less time I would have to react. I've got great reflexes, but it was two against one. "That's close enough, guys. Why don't you wait right where you are for now?" I tried to sound cheery. It's not my natural state, so it was a stretch.

"Why don't you make us?" Inge said, letting the two boys step forward without her.

"Fine." I lifted up my fingers and sent a zap at both of them. I hit each of them squarely in the chest. I would have patted myself on the back for my good aim, but was afraid my smoking fingers would singe me.

Erik blinked and took another step forward. Sven didn't even register the shock. Now I remembered Michael Hollinger saying he had hit them with his Taser and it hadn't slowed them down at all. Great. My one big new weapon was useless and the boys were still advancing.

"Run, Melina," Inge said, her voice soothing. "Save yourself and save your baby."

"I can't, Inge." The truth is that I often couldn't run. In that fight/flight instinct war that wages within most of us, fight pretty much always wins for me.

"Of course, you can. You can do it for the baby. There's so much we can't do for ourselves, that we can do for the baby, isn't there?" She smiled so sweetly and looked from one boy to the other. I had no doubt in my mind that she would do anything for her children. Anything.

"You couldn't do anything for one of your babies, though,

could you?" I asked. I know it was a low blow, but I would use whatever was in my arsenal.

Her eyes flashed, and for a second, I felt her tidal wave of grief encroach on my consciousness. I shut it out relentlessly. "What do you know about that?" Her tone was flat.

"I know you let your other son get in the car with the man you knew was an alcoholic. I know he died because of that." I watched her sway as my words hit her harder than any punches I could have thrown.

Then her chin lifted. "Then you understand why I have to protect Erik and Sven at all costs. I can't face that again. Jonas's death nearly killed me."

"Because you were his mother and you didn't protect him? You didn't do your number one job on this planet. You didn't keep your child safe." Again she swayed a little and Erik and Sven swayed for a second, too. Their mind connection must be a powerful one. On the other hand, I'm pretty sure if I didn't have my defenses up, the magnitude of her grief would have made me sway on my feet, too.

"I will never make that kind of mistake again," she said.

"But you have already," I pointed out. "You're experimenting on them. Injecting them with werewolf blood. You've been making them half-crazy."

"Half-crazy, but all the way invulnerable. You can't harm them with wood or steel. I'll admit, it took some trial and error to find the right dose, but they're good now."

"Yeah. They look great." I hoped she got the sarcasm in my tone. I zapped them again, just for good measure, even though I knew it wouldn't make a damn bit of a difference. I considered zapping Inge herself. She hadn't injected herself with werewolf blood. She wasn't an invulnerable Ulfhednar. I was pretty sure a good zap to the chest would be like hitting a healthy person with a defibrillator. In other words, it wouldn't be pretty. I also didn't know what would happen with Sven and Erik if their mother wasn't calling the shots. She well could be a restraining influence on them.

"Stop it, Melina. You're only annoying them." She was starting to sound tired.

"Annoying is one of my best skills." It was, too. Sometimes I could simply irritate someone into accepting a delivery from me. Perseverance was an awesome skill for a Messenger and another one I could thank Mae for.

"Please, Melina, don't make us hurt you," she said, her voice very soft now.

That's when I saw it, the chink in her armor. She didn't want to hurt me. She didn't want to hurt my baby. "I don't think you will," I said. "I don't think you would hurt me or my baby. I don't think you could bear to put another mother through what you've been through."

Inge took a small step back. Erik and Sven instinctively fell back with her. There it was. "You know I can literally feel some of your pain, don't you?" I asked. "It's unbelievable. I don't know how you get out of bed each day."

Her chin came up. "I get out of bed for Sven and Erik. They need me. I have to protect them."

"But you know you can't. Isn't that part of it? The big bad world is out there just waiting for them. I'm waiting for them." I took a step toward her.

Her eyes narrowed. I'd gone too far. "Go ahead, boys. Get rid of her."

And that was the moment that Chuck and three of his wolves came dashing out of the woods. The boys were pinned within seconds. Ulfhednar, especially faux-Ulfhednar, were no match for real werewolves and especially not for what looked like pissed-off werewolves. Chuck stood between the two prone boys, each with a wolf pinning him down with a huge paw on his throat, and howled three long howls.

I took care of Inge. As I secured her wrists behind her with zip ties, I whispered in her ear, "Don't ever threaten my baby or my friends again. Understand?"

It was another fifteen minutes before Ted and the rest of the wolves emerged from the woods carrying Paul on a makeshift stretcher. Or should I say what was left of Paul.

I shuddered when I saw him. He was terribly thin and his bare chest was covered with burn scars in crisscrossing patterns. There wasn't an inch on his arms that wasn't covered with needle tracks. I rushed to his side. "Are you okay?" I whispered.

"Better now," he whispered back through parched lips.

I looked over at one of the wolves carrying the stretcher. "Wouldn't he heal better in wolf form? Shouldn't he change?"

He shook his head. "He doesn't have the strength for that now. Maybe in a day or two. Right now, if he tried to change it would probably kill him."

I felt tears forming in my eyes. I'd never seen my friend so broken and weak. "I'm so sorry. I'm so sorry we took so long."

"S'okay," he croaked out between parched lips. "You came."

I couldn't say anything for a moment and I couldn't stop my tears from slipping out of my eyes and splashing onto his bare chest.

"Meredith?" he whispered.

"Waiting. So worried. I thought she was going to rip the entire forest apart."

He smiled.

"Thank you."

"For what? Almost not getting here in time?"

"Having my back."

I HADN'T BEEN AWARE OF WHAT GOOD COOKS WEREWOLVES could be. It didn't really strike me as a werewolfy skill. I mean, they liked to eat their meat while it was essentially still breathing. Apparently that was only in wolf form, though.

Sam set a bowl of stew down in front of me. The scent rising off of it, rich and savory and full of complicated spices, made my mouth water.

"We have really acute taste buds when we're in human form," he explained. "We taste more subtleties than a lot of folks."

I had pretty damn sensitive taste buds myself, but it had never translated into any kind of skill in the kitchen. I would have told him that, but I was too busy shoveling stew into my mouth. Who knew they'd have such a light hand with biscuits as well?

"Eating for two, eh?" he said with a laugh, sitting down on the other side of Ted.

"Cardamom?" Ted asked Sam, who nodded.

Chuck walked in, back in human form and hair still wet from a shower. I set my spoon down. "So?"

"So, he'll heal. We're keeping him upstairs right now. The w . . . I mean, Meredith is with him now. She's putting some kind of goo on all those needle tracks." He sat down. Sam got up and got another bowl of stew that he set down in front of Chuck. Chuck nodded his thanks.

"What about Sven and Erik?" I asked.

Chuck took his time chewing the bite of stew he'd taken. "They're down in the cells. It won't be pretty to have that blood wear off."

"And Inge?" Ted asked.

"She's down there with them, too. Won't leave. Won't speak either." Chuck accepted a biscuit from Sam, who then also passed the butter. I could see how it would get to be old to be low in the hierarchy of the Pack.

"Any sign of . . . anyone else?" I asked. I didn't want to speak their names. Using a god's name wasn't the same as calling one to you, but I don't like to take chances with these things.

Chuck shook his head. "Nope. We found the rest of that silver net while we were at the old place. You should take a look at it. It's . . . different."

He finished his bowl of stew and stood, leaving his crumpled napkin beside the bowl. Ted and I stood and followed him out of the room. Sam stayed behind to clear the table.

We followed Chuck through the house to a corner room. Laid out on a sheet on the table was the rest of the silver net. I almost gasped. It was gorgeous. I reached forward to touch it and Chuck flinched.

"It won't hurt me," I told him. At least, I didn't think it would. I had gotten a nasty shock from it the first time I touched the shred of it I'd found up at the cabin, but it was newer then. I got almost no tingle from this net at all, even though it was huge.

On the other hand, it would burn the crap out of Chuck.

"How did you get it here without scorching yourself?" I asked.

Chuck nodded at Ted. "He gathered it up in that sheet for us."

Ted made a little bow. "At your service."

I ran my hand over it. "It has almost no power left in it."

"I had the same feeling," Chuck said, sitting down across

the room from it all the same. "Have you seen something like that before?"

Generally, objects of power were not made to be one-use disposable kinds of items. They were meant to last. It takes a lot of energy to make something like a silver net that can catch a werewolf. You'd want it to hold its mojo for some time. "No. Most magic doesn't come with planned obsolescence."

"That's what I thought. They didn't want her to use this more than once. That's what I'm thinking."

"It would still hurt like hell if someone threw it over you," I pointed out.

"True." Chuck smoothed his beard. "Someone as powerful as Paul, for instance, still might be able to fight free of it."

"So . . . is Paul's blood more potent than a weaker werewolf's blood?" I asked, sitting down on the floor and leaning back against the wall. I was exhausted and I hadn't even done any fighting.

"I doubt it."

"Then I don't get it."

"Me either. I'm just pointing it out."

"Maybe it means they're done meddling, though. That would be good news."

Chuck nodded again. "I don't like messing with other people's gods. No good ever comes of it."

"So here's something that's still bothering me," I said. "How did Inge know when and where to snag Paul? That cabin isn't easy to find. I doubt I could find it and I'm a much better tracker than she is, I guarantee it."

"I'm sure you are." Chuck smiled. "I have no idea. Maybe she followed him."

"Can you imagine Paul letting someone, a 'Dane for Pete's sake, follow him to his special cabin? I don't care if she is a descendant of Frigga. She's still a 'Dane, and you know it."

Chuck shook his head. "Now that you mention it, no."

"Did you ask her?" I pressed.

Chuck laughed. "I don't think you understand the state she's in. She's not exactly willing to have a chatty conversation with us at the moment."

I settled back in my spot on the floor. "What about Paul? Has he said anything?"

Chuck shook his head. "Why does it matter anyway? He's here. He's safe. The matter's closed."

Clearly Chuck wasn't accustomed to sneaky thinking. It said something nice about him that he wasn't, but at the moment, I was more concerned with Paul's safety while he was still weak and vulnerable. On the other hand, little pitchers might have big ears, but big werewolves have huge ones. I didn't feel like hauling Chuck out of the house so I went and got a notepad and wrote down:

If someone told Inge where and when to capture Paul, that someone is probably a member of the Pack. That member is still here. That means Paul is still not safe.

He read the note and took the pen from me:

If someone betrayed us and Paul knew who it was, he would have told me by now. He's not that weak.

Ted whipped a notepad out of his pocket, you've gotta love a cop, and jotted down:

You're assuming that Paul knows. Maybe he doesn't.

Bless his pea-picking heart.

Chuck wrote:

*If he doesn't know, then he wouldn't be in danger,
would he?*

My turn again:

*Not necessarily. If I had betrayed the Pack, I would be
worried that Paul would remember some little detail
that would give me away. I wouldn't want him around
talking. I wouldn't want Inge or her boys around and
talking either. How are you going to feel if someone
kills one of them while they're in your custody?*

Chuck actually went a little pale.

Who? Who do you think it is?

I scribbled back:

*I wish I knew, Chuck. You know I suspected Kevin, but
I think we know the extent of his part in this. He went
only so far.*

Chuck replied:

Then how do we keep them safe?

Ted chimed in—in writing—again.

*I think you're going to have to let some non-Pack
beings do your guard duty. You've got me and Melina
and Meredith already.*

Chuck shook his head.

That's not enough to guard all of them 24/7 for however long it will take.

I answered:

I doubt it will take that long. Whoever it is will have to act quickly. What about Alex Bledsoe?

Chuck sputtered and scribbled:

You want me to allow a vampire here to stand guard in the middle of my own Pack? You think he's better equipped than one of my wolves?

I answered:

Yep. I do. He'd lay down his un-life for Paul. I'm sure of it.

I was, too. It wasn't the most typical friendship, but it was a true one.

Chuck was already shaking his head.

I can see explaining your presence as well as Ted's and Meredith's. You're already here, for one. How do I explain Alex being here without alerting the traitor that we're onto him? Don't even think about suggesting we sneak him in. There's not a wolf in this pack that wouldn't sniff him out from a solid mile away.

I was aware of that. I was equally aware that, in general, werewolves and vampires didn't tolerate each other very well.

*We could say he's here as my doctor. That he needed
to come and check me out because of the baby.*

I saw absolutely no reason not to use my condition for
any purpose that I wanted. There couldn't possibly be a
karmic payback for that, right?

The Pack won't like it. It'll raise everyone's hackles.

And I care about that why?

I waited a few seconds and then added:

*Do you have a better suggestion? Honestly, the more
you trust one of these guys, the less good idea it is to
put him or her on guard duty. If something happens,
one of your Pack takes the blame. Is that what you
want?*

Chuck rubbed his hand over his face.

*No. What I want is for this not to be happening, but
that doesn't appear to be an option. Make the call.*

"It's the right choice, Chuck. You won't regret it," I said
out loud.

"I already do."

Ted gave me a nod and headed out of the house to make
the call to Alex.

15

EVEN WITH TINTED WINDOWS ON HIS CAR, ALEX COULDN'T travel until after sundown. As a result it was hours before he arrived at Chuck's. He parked the Porsche in a very conspicuous spot, practically in the center of the cleared area that served as Chuck's driveway. I wondered if he thought one of the werewolves would key it just to rile him. Or claw it, I suppose.

I watched from the window as he got out, walked to the passenger side and helped Norah out of the car.

Damn. I hadn't counted on that. We hadn't been talking much, hardly at all since I kicked the door off the chain. I wasn't sure who was feeling more pissy, her or me. I met them at the door anyway.

"Thanks for coming," I said.

"It's no problem," Alex said, walking inside. Norah hung back behind him. He turned. "Are you coming in?"

She nodded and stepped through the door, too, her eyes big and round. "How many of them live here?" she whispered.

"I have no idea and there's no point in whispering. They'll be able to hear that just fine." I motioned for them to follow me inside. "Do you want to see Paul first?"

"Please," Alex said. Norah nodded, her lips pressed in a thin line. I wondered what she was afraid she'd say.

We went up the stairs to the room where Paul and Meredith were. Paul was asleep on the bed. The bruises on his arms were already starting to heal, but the burns across his chest remained angry and red. Meredith stood from the chair in the corner where she was sitting and threw her arms around Alex. "Thank you for coming."

He patted her back, looking a little awkward at the gratitude and the affection. I didn't blame him. It would have caught me off guard from Meredith, too.

Alex sat down on the bed next to Paul. Norah hovered by the door, shifting from one foot to the other. Was she that nervous or did she have to pee?

Paul stirred and opened his eyes. "Really? They send a bloodsucker to heal me? They must really want me out of the way."

"Oh, be quiet, puppy. Let me see what's been done to you." Alex took Paul's arm and examined the bruises and tracks. "Well, I think you can kiss your career as a junkie good-bye. Whoever did this scarred up your veins but good, my friend."

Paul sighed. "What will I ever tell my mother? She had such high hopes for me, too."

I felt the tight spot in my chest loosen a little. If the two of them were willing to poke at each other like that, things were going to be okay. Then I reconsidered. They'd probably talk to each other like that if they were standing side by side on the gallows about to get their necks stretched.

Alex had moved to examine the burns on Paul's chest.

They glistened with the ointment that Meredith had applied. Paul flinched a bit as Alex's hands stretched the skin.

"Your hands are cold," Paul complained.

"Pretty much always," Alex agreed. "Silver, I take it?"

Paul nodded. "Burns like a son of a bitch."

"You won't heal so fast from these," Alex observed. Not only did silver burn the crap out of werewolves, its effects lingered. A cut made from a silver knife would take significantly longer to heal than one made with any other kind of knife and would be much more prone to infection. On top of that, what we saw on the surface might only be the tip of the iceberg. Silver damage can burn deep under the skin of a werewolf, with tissue damage spreading beneath the skin unseen. The burns on Paul's chest would have to be watched and tended in a way that no other wounds he had would. Alex turned to Meredith. "What have you put on them?"

"Mainly cantharis. I didn't want to get too fancy." She moved the chair closer and took Paul's hand. He glanced back at her, but didn't say anything.

Alex nodded. "Sometimes simplest is best. We need to watch for infection, too."

Meredith blew out a breath. "I'll let you know if it looks like something's cooking in there."

"Good." Alex turned to me. "Your turn."

I held up my hands in protest. The checking out Melina because of the baby had only been a cover story. "I feel fine."

"Super. Is there some place with a little privacy or do you want to do it right here?" He smiled. Damn it. He was enjoying this.

I cocked my head to the right where there was an unoccupied room. "Fine. Let's go."

Ted followed us.

"Do I have to put on a paper gown?" I asked.

"Only if it turns you on," Alex answered, shutting the door behind us. "Sit down."

I rolled my eyes, but did. He set his hand lightly on my back and stood very still. I realized he could probably hear my heartbeat, my respirations and the baby's heartbeat without any fancy equipment like a stethoscope.

"Good," he finally said. "Everything sounds strong. Your heart rate is a little low even for you. Ditto on your blood pressure. Any dizzy spells?"

"Not lately," I said, which made Ted shoot me a look.

"There were dizzy spells?" he asked.

"A few. No biggie."

"How's the morning sickness?" Alex asked.

I thought about it. "Better, actually."

"Also good. Anything else you want to report? Anything unusual?"

"I think I can control the zapping better. I know when it's starting and I'm getting pretty good aim." This was why I couldn't go see an ordinary ob-gyn. How the hell would I explain that?

"You're going to have a hell of a time if the baby comes out able to do that," Alex observed. "I can't imagine anything more dangerous than a toddler that can electrocute her playmates."

I put my hand on my stomach. "Her? Do you know? Is it a girl?"

He laughed. "No. I was speaking metaphorically. You're going to have to wait and find out like everybody else unless you want me to sneak you an ultrasound in the hospital."

"I'll think about it."

Ted had stayed silent until now. "I think that's a good idea. And maybe one of those amnio tests, too."

"What's up, Boy Scout?" Alex asked turning to him.

"Nothing." He sat down next to me on the bed and put his hand on my back. "I just want Melina and the baby to get all the care they're supposed to get."

"Fair enough. I'll make sure."

Ted stood up and shook his hand. "Thank you."

Boys are so weird.

WE SET UP A SCHEDULE, SCRATCHING NOTES TO EACH other in a spiral notebook Norah had in her backpack. We'd each rotate through where Inge and her boys were being kept and upstairs with Paul in what we hoped would look like a fairly nonchalant rotation. I had my doubts we would be fooling anyone. On the other hand, whoever had set this all in motion had a fair amount of chutzpah. He or she still might think outsmarting us was possible.

We finished up our notes and Norah tore off half a piece of paper, scribbled something on it and handed it to me.

I took it from her.

We need to talk.

I took the pen from her and scribbled underneath it.

So talk.

Outside. Please? was her response.

I shrugged and headed for the door with her following. "We'll be back in a few minutes," I said over my shoulder to the others.

I led Norah out the back and into the clearing where Chuck and I had spoken about Michael Hollinger. I sat down on the same stump I had before. "What?"

She twisted her toe in the pine needles that covered the ground. "I'm sorry."

I raised one brow. "What for?" She wasn't getting off that easy.

"For not being, you know, more supportive." She still wasn't meeting my eyes.

"Whatever," I said and stood, starting back to the house.

"Wait," she called after me.

I turned. "What?"

"That's it? Whatever? That's all I get?" Her hands were on her hips.

"What did you want?" I asked.

"To talk?"

"Isn't that what we just did?" She'd said something. I'd said something back. I was pretty sure that was talking. Personally, I felt it was vastly overrated.

She made a face at me. "Don't be such a boy. Sit back down."

I returned, but I dragged my feet. I may be cheap, but I am not easy.

She twisted her hands. "I could have been a better friend when you told me you were pregnant," she finally said.

"Yes. You could have been," I said. Nothing she said was going to change that. I didn't really see the point of discussing it further. She'd said she was sorry. I'd said okay. It was time to move on.

"I should have been a better friend," she amended.

I shrugged and opened my mouth to say something snarky, then thought better of it. How many times had I lied to Nora? How many times had I put her in danger just by living with her? How upside down had I turned her life? "You've got like seven more months to be a better friend now."

She flung herself at me. "I'm so sorry, Melina. It wasn't nice. I was . . . I was jealous, I think."

I peeled her arms off my neck. "Really? You'd always dreamed of having an unplanned pregnancy when you weren't married?"

She made a face. "Not when you put it like that."

"I can totally understand. It's super-glamorous. When I barfed in the bushes in front of Ted? I don't think he's ever found me more alluring. And let me tell you about my swollen feet."

"Stop it," she said, giving me a little shove. "You're just trying to make me feel better."

I laughed. "Have we met?"

She laughed, too. "As a matter of fact, yes. I don't know what I was thinking."

"Come on. Let's go back in. We have work to do." I stood up and took her hand this time as I walked back toward the house. I took a few more steps before it hit me. I hadn't seen any crows in a while. Had Muninn and Huginn given up their watch on me? Or had they been called off?

I turned slowly around to see if I could spot or sense anything, but got nothing but a whole lot of werewolf for my trouble.

"What?" Norah asked.

"No crows," I said.

"Is that good?"

"Maybe." What I hoped was that it meant that Inge was truly on her own. Perhaps Frigga and Odin had lost interest in our little drama. It would be like them. Fickle creatures gods. I wouldn't trust them as far as I could throw them.

I wondered how far Inge had trusted them.

I HAD ASKED TO TAKE FIRST WATCH OF ERIK AND SVEN. For one thing, I wanted a better look at Chuck's facilities. A second advantage would be being away from everyone for a few minutes. As much as I loved not being lonely, I still needed a little solo time on a regular basis, a few minutes here and there where someone wasn't asking me a question or telling me about something. Believe me, no one down in the depths under Chuck's house wanted to get chatty with me.

Inge hissed at me for a second when I first walked in and then settled down in her cell, lying on the metal cot and facing the wall. What Chuck had set up in the basement was, for all intents and purposes, a jail cell. Actually, three of them.

They looked exactly like the holding cells you always see on television shows when people get arrested. There was a metal toilet and a metal sink sticking out of the wall and a metal cot, with a mattress on it, also attached to a wall. That was pretty much it.

Oh, the bars were coated with silver. That was different. Not that it made all that much difference for Inge. I wasn't sure if it made any difference for Erik or Sven. With the injection of werewolf blood, did they take on the vulnerabilities of a werewolf as well as a werewolf's strength? I knew they definitely were affected by the full moon. That was totally werewolfy. I figured I might as well ask. The worst that could happen would be that they ignored me.

"Hey," I said, trying to sound conversational. "Do you burn when you touch these bars?"

Erik walked up to within a few inches of the bars and raised his arms. Stripes were seared across them at the exact width of the bars on the cells. "Does that answer your question?" he asked.

"Pretty much," I answered.

He bared his teeth and growled at me.

"Don't talk to her." Inge had gotten off her cot and walked to the bars of her cell. "She's not our friend," she told her son.

"I think I figured that out, Mom," he said sounding like

a total teenager. No wonder they'd been so hard to control. Teenage rebellion crossed with werewolf blood injections? How volatile could Inge have made these boys? I shook my head. She'd done it for the best of reasons and with the purest of motives. She'd wanted to protect them. She'd wanted to make sure her children were safe. She'd managed to do it in a way that was completely wrong for so many people and for so many reasons.

I turned to her. "So how did you get Frigga to weave you that silver net?" I asked.

"She didn't." Inge went back to her cot.

"Oh, come on. She had to have at least helped. No way you could have done that on your own. You don't have enough of the blood in you to make an object of power like that." I walked over to her cell and leaned against the wall next to it.

Inge stiffened. Something about saying she didn't have enough of the blood in her had bothered her.

"Did she spin the silver and then you wove it?" I pressed.

She turned away from me, but I knew somehow I'd hit a nerve. But which one? "What did Frigga get from it anyway?" One thing I knew about most gods and goddesses was that they didn't do anything for free. There was always something in it for them.

"She got us," Sven said from his cell, glaring at me, eyes glittering behind his silver bars.

"I told you to hush," Inge said.

Sven retreated away from the bars again, but didn't stop staring at me, his eyes glowing red in the dim light.

A few cogs clicked into place. I turned to Sven. "Frigga wanted Ulfhednar again, but not only was your mother's blood too diluted to have much power, yours was even more diluted, wasn't it?"

No one answered me. They didn't have to. "She made

the net for you to capture a werewolf so you could try to strengthen their blood. In return, they owed her their lives." I shook my head. What had gone wrong, then? Why wasn't Frigga here protecting her new warriors now?

"But they were too volatile, weren't they? The more werewolf blood you gave them, the less you could control them." I was starting to get it. "She cut you loose, didn't she? That's why you were running away from the battle. You couldn't count on her protection anymore, could you?"

That was why Huginn and Muninn had disappeared. She didn't care what I did because she was abandoning her little project and Inge with it. I heard a small sob coming from Inge's cell and realized how on the mark I'd been.

"Frigga's not the only one to abandon you, either, is she?" I sank down on the ground so I was closer to eye level with the cot. "Someone in this Pack was working with you, too. Not just Kevin. In fact, Kevin wasn't really working with you at all, was he? You used him." I shook my head. He hadn't been that hard to manipulate either. "Who else was helping you, Inge? Who told you where you could find Paul and when he would be vulnerable and alone?"

There was still no answer from the cell, just the quiet sobbing of a mother whose heart had broken into too many pieces.

As it turned out, she didn't need to answer. The night split with the sound of a horrible roar of pain. It was coming from the direction of Paul's room. I left the basement cells at a dead run.

I COULD SMELL THE BURNING FLESH FROM THE FIRST floor. The thought of it gagged me, but I couldn't let it stop me. If someone had attacked Paul again, I wasn't sure he would survive. His body had taken too much of a beating to heal itself as it should. Why wasn't Alex or Ted making whoever it was stop? The screaming was terrible. It didn't even sound like Paul.

I took the stairs three at a time, trying hard not to think about what would happen if I tripped and fell and landed on my stomach. I rounded the corner to see why it didn't sound like Paul screaming.

It was because it wasn't him. Norah and Alex had Sam pinned beneath the silver net that had been used to kidnap Paul.

"What are you doing?" I asked. "You're burning him!" I tried to grab the edges of the net and pull it off of Sam. I couldn't bear to see his young open face twisted in agony like that.

"Careful, Melina. I don't want to let him up until he drops the knife," Alex shouted to me over Sam's roars of pain.

That's when I saw what he had in his hand. The knife was wicked and long with a vicious curve to its blade. It shone in the light.

"Unless I miss my guess, the blade is pure silver," Alex said, giving the net a shake. "Drop it!" he commanded.

"NO!" Sam shouted and then screamed again as the silver came into contact with new areas on his body.

I walked across the net and stepped on Sam's wrist. His fingers opened and the blade dropped from them. Without taking my boot off his arm, I reached through the net and plucked the blade out. "Let him up," I said. "Now."

I turned. By now, there were at least ten of Chuck's were-wolves gathered around us. I held the blade in front of me and stared at each one in turn. "Don't even think about it," I said.

Then I sank down onto the floor next to Sam. "This is some kind of mistake, right? There's an explanation."

He stared up at me and under the pain, I saw an expression on his face I'd never seen before. It looked an awful lot like hate. Then he spat at me.

I wiped the spittle off the side of my face. "I trusted you. I thought you were helping me. I thought you were helping Paul."

Sam laughed. Or I think it was a laugh. It came out more like a rasp. "I know. That's what made it so effective. You made it easy for me to keep track of you."

My shoulders slumped forward. Suddenly I was terribly tired. "Why?"

He shook his head. "I can't believe you even have to ask. Look at where I am in this Pack. They have me working in the kitchen. I cook. I clean. I might as well be a chambermaid. I'm a werewolf, goddamn it."

"You did it because you didn't like your chore list? Why didn't you just ask Chuck for something else to do?"

Chuck stepped forward from the crowd. "It doesn't work that way, Melina. You earn your way up in the Pack. Sam had a long way to go to earn his way up."

"I'm young. I'm strong. But there were so many to fight and challenge between me and the top. With Paul gone, the infighting would start. They'd take each other out and get out of my way." Sam curled onto his side, wincing.

"How did you know about Inge?" I was still confused. It still didn't make sense to me.

"How could anyone not know about Inge?" He tried to laugh again, but it sounded even worse. "She broadcasts her emotions around like a TV station. You'd have to be blind, deaf and dumb to miss it."

"But the part with Frigga? How did you know about that?"

"That? That was just dumb luck. I was there in the woods

that night. I saw her. I saw her try to kill herself and saw
Frigga stop her. I knew those sons of hers could never be
Ulfhednar without some assistance. They're just kids.
There's nothing that special about them."

"Did you know what they were doing to Paul this whole
time?" I finally asked. That was the part of it that horrified
me the most. Maybe it shouldn't have been. Maybe I should
have been more horrified by the fact that he was so willing
to manipulate all these beings around him that had pledged
to always have his back. Maybe I should have been more
horrified at the way he manipulated a woman's grief over a
dead child. I wasn't, though.

He shrugged. "Pretty much. What did it matter, anyway,
though? No one even thought he was missing until you came
along. Everyone thought he was off on some personal retreat
or something. He would have been dead before anyone realized anything was really wrong if you hadn't stuck in your
nose in where it didn't belong."

I stood and looked at the Pack. "You can take him," I
said. I let the knife dangle from my hand at my side. I didn't
let go of it, though.

I WENT BACK DOWN INTO THE BASEMENT, TO THE CELLS,
taking one step at a time and not rushing. It was quiet. I
thought maybe all three of them might be asleep. I didn't care.

"They just caught Sam trying to finish off Paul," I said.

Inge stiffened on her cot.

"Yep. It's all over now. That's the last of your allies,
isn't it?"

She didn't say anything. I don't know what I expected
her to say anyway. I just thought she should know. I stood
and headed back to the stairs, then I heard a groan.

I turned. Erik's face contorted and he doubled over. I rushed to his cell. "What the hell?"

"Erik!" Inge screamed.

"Chuck, something's wrong!" I yelled, hoping that everything I thought I knew about werewolf hearing was correct and that he would be able to hear me no matter where he was in the house.

Erik's brother curled into fetal position on his cot and let out a groan, then began to shake.

"Chuck, now!" I yelled, not sure what to do.

Inge had thrown herself against the bars that separated her from her sons. "What is it? What's wrong?" She thrust her arms through the bars and Erik lunged at her. She barely retreated in time to avoid being slashed with the claws that had suddenly grown out of Erik's fingertips.

I turned to run up the stairs and get help, but Chuck was already running down them. "What?" he demanded.

I pointed to the boys' cell. He turned and his shoulders dropped. "Oh, that's where we are. You might want to leave, Melina."

"Excuse me?" I asked, staring at him. "You're saying this is an expected phase?"

"Well, it's what happened with Hollinger," he said, leaning back against the wall.

"Do something," Inge yelled at him. "They're in agony."

"Sure are," Chuck observed, not moving and not raising his voice.

I stared at him, too. "You're really not going to do anything?"

"What would you have me do?" he asked, his tone calm and conversational as Sven now exploded out of fetal position, flipped onto his back and arched up as if he was having a seizure.

"I don't know. Drug them. Tie them down. Something." I was actually totally voting for drugging them.

He shook his head. "The toxins have to work their way out of their systems. I don't know what would happen if we drugged them, and frankly I have no idea what we could drug them with. Have you ever seen a drug have much effect on a werewolf?"

"Is this what Michael Hollinger went through?" I asked, wincing away from the cell again.

"Yep."

"Help them," Inge demanded. "Make this stop."

"Sorry, Inge. I can't do that."

"Can't you see they're in agony? What are you doing to them?"

"I didn't do anything to them," Chuck said, his tone still even, but I could hear the anger beneath it. "You did it. You kidnapped one of my pack, held him hostage, tortured him and injected his blood into your sons. You're not going to get a lot of sympathy from me."

Inge backed away into her cell. "I never meant for this to happen. I just wanted them to be safe. I couldn't bear to see them hurt."

Erik let out another terrible howl and then collapsed to the floor shaking and sweating.

"Good job with that," I said.

"You don't know!" She whirled toward me and screamed. "You don't know what it's like. You don't know what kind of pain it causes to see one of your babies hurt."

I stared at her. Through all this, I'd felt so much compassion for Inge. I knew how protective I already felt of this little being I had inside me and could only imagine how much fiercer that feeling would be once it was a baby I could see and hold. It wasn't until this moment that I realized that the only thing that Inge cared about was her pain. It was all about how bad she felt when one of her children was hurt. "You are a terrible mother," I said.

"What?" she shrieked. "Look at how far I went to protect them. How dare you say that!"

I shook my head. "This wasn't about protecting them. You made them take terrible risks." I pointed to the cell where her sons writhed on the floor and, oh ick, frothed at the mouth. "You didn't do it for them either. You did it for yourself. How selfish can you be?"

She gasped and clutched her hand to her heart. "Everything I've done has always been for them."

I shook my head. "I don't think so. A good mother would never have even contemplated killing herself rather than raising her children. You would have orphaned both those boys if Frigga hadn't stopped you."

Her hands went to her mouth. There wasn't much she could say to that. We all knew it was true.

"You turned them into monsters with no self-control just to keep yourself from feeling any more pain," I continued. "A real mother would endure anything to keep her children safe."

"Shut up!" she screamed. "You don't know anything about it. You're not even a mother yet."

There it was. That little flutter kick right below my belly button. Bitch was lucky my little peanut didn't want to zap her. "You're right. I'm not a mother yet, but I have a mother and a damn good one at that." The truth of that resonated through me. I'd been so worried about whether or not I could handle motherhood. Of course, I could. I had the best role model on the planet.

Well, maybe not the planet. Still, she was a damn fine mother and I knew she would never ever have injected me with werewolf blood to spare herself pain.

16

I PUT ON ONE OF THE SMOCK TOPS WITH THE GIANT BUTT
bows that my mother had bought me and looked at myself
in the mirror. I didn't need to switch to maternity clothes
yet, but I knew it would please her to see me in the shirt
she'd bought for me.

Ted came up behind me and slipped his arms around me.
"That's so . . . cute."

"I know. It's awful, isn't it?"

"Not at all. It's just not your usual style."

That was true. For one thing, it wasn't black. For another,
it had a giant butt bow. I am not a giant-butt-bow kind of
girl.

"Let's go," I said. "We might as well get it over with."

He glanced at his watch. "We have a few minutes since
we're not picking up your grandmother."

I had mixed feelings about that. I liked picking up
Grandma Rosie. On the other hand, I liked that Patrick was

having to do a few things now. Apparently being the vessel that contains your parents' future grandchild gets you out of tons of stuff. I wondered if I was even going to have to help set the table tonight.

"Is Norah ready?" I asked.

"And waiting."

"Let's be early. It'll freak my mother out."

"Now that's my girl," Ted said, smiling.

I was glad we were able to smile again. It had taken a few days. Paul was healing well, although the silver burns looked like they might leave permanent scars. Chuck was closing down his contracting business and moving the Pack. Paul was not going with him. I can't imagine how wrenching a decision that must have been for him. I also can't imagine how it must have felt to realize that if it had been left to the Pack that I had pledged myself to, I'd still be in a cell being used like a soft-drink dispenser to turn two ordinary boys into something very nasty. I don't think Chuck felt very good about that either.

The other wolf not planning on moving with the Pack was Kevin. He'd been the werewolf equivalent of excommunicated. He'd also claimed Inge as his mate so that she and her boys would be under his protection. Otherwise I'm pretty sure that Chuck would have killed all three of them.

Which brings us to Sam. Long-legged, earnest, sweet-appearing Sam. If there was one thing that broke my heart about this whole situation it was Sam. I don't know how I could have been so wrong about him. Chuck wouldn't talk to me about what had happened to Sam. He said it was Pack business and not for me to concern myself with. Paul said the same thing.

We were pulling up at my parents' house no more than

twenty minutes later. "This feels weird without your grand-mother," Norah complained from the backseat.

"I know. Maybe we can take that back from Patrick, but let's make sure he has to take out the garbage or something else we don't want to do instead," I said.

I barely got my car door open and my father was there helping me out of the car. He kissed both my cheeks. "You look beautiful, Melina. You're glowing."

I wasn't sure about the glowing thing, although I apparently did it in the womb. I did feel a lot better than I had for the last few weeks. Maybe it was having Paul back where he belonged or getting past the first rough few weeks or Mom's raspberry tea. I wasn't sure. I was just glad to feel better. "Thanks, Dad. You're looking good, too."

He hugged me and laughed. "Come in. Your mother made flank steak."

I knew. I'd chosen. I decided not to flaunt it. I got to pick two times in a row. Getting my way was reward enough. We were also having cheesy potatoes and buttered carrots. It wasn't a meal that was good for the cholesterol, but it was good for my heart in a whole different way.

An hour later, I sat and watched my family as they argued and laughed too loud and got into each other's business. I watched as my grandmother totally set my mother's teeth on edge. I also watched as my mother made sure my grand-mother had everything she needed in reach without ever asking for any of it.

I reached for the glass of sparkling cider that my mother had purchased just for me and the diamond in my engage-ment ring winked in the candlelight. Ted was deep in a discussion with my father about Peyton Manning's move to the Broncos. My father threw his head back and laughed at something Ted had said and I felt that weird melty feeling in my chest I got nearly every time I looked at Ted.

He'd been right, though. He had disappointed me. I suppose it was my own fault. My expectations were awfully high. But it also opened my eyes. I was so glad to have him here by my side. I had never known anyone like him. The fact that he loved me still seemed like some kind of miracle.

If he hadn't proved himself to be the man I thought he was, though, I still would have been okay. I looked around at my mother and my grandmother and my aunt. They would have been here for me. My mother knew more about me now than she had since I was three, and her support was unwavering. Grandma Rosie hadn't batted an eye about my pregnancy before I'd even known what I was going to do. And Aunt Kitty? She'd already purchased two receiving blankets and a set of footed pajamas, and I wasn't even out of my first trimester yet.

I'd been spending a lot of time wondering about what kind of mother I was going to be. I still didn't know. I did know, however, that no matter what, I'd know what good mothering looked like.

My mother hadn't been able to protect me. Despite her best efforts, I'd died for a few minutes and come back irrevocably changed. Inge hadn't been able to protect her child either. There were probably going to be times I wouldn't be able to protect my baby. I was going to do my damnedest, though. That was for sure.